THINK BEFORE YOU SPEAK

The Bartender Babe Chronicles
Book Two

D. A. Bale

Think Before You Speak is a work of fiction. Characters, names, places, incidents, and organizations are a product of the author's imagination or are used fictitiously. Any resemblance to actual persons living or dead, business establishments, events, or locales is entirely coincidental.

Think Before You Speak
D. A. Bale
Copyright © 2022 D. A. Bale
Published by D. A. Bale

Cover design by GetCovers.com

All rights reserved. No part of this document or the related files may be reproduced or transmitted in any form, by any means (electronic, photocopying, or otherwise) without the prior written permission of the author.

ISBN: 1534600612
ISBN-13:   978-1534600614

ALSO BY D. A. BALE

<u>The Bartender Babe Chronicles</u>
Look Before You Jump
Think Before You Speak
Knock Before You Enter
Die Before You Wake
Aim Before You Shoot
Shoot Before You Blink

<u>The Deepest Darkness Series</u>
Running into the Darkness
Piercing the Darkness
Rising from the Darkness

The Study
a novelette

DEDICATION

To my nephew, Wes

Because you're the world's greatest Dallas Cowboys fanatic, even though I still root for the 49ers to whoop their tush every year. I hope you share the same warm memories of that Christmas I sang to you my personal rendition of *Cowboys Roasting on an Open Fire* set to the tune of *Chestnuts Roasting on an Open Fire*. It continues to make me feel all toasty inside, even though the revised wording is long out-of-date.

ACKNOWLEDGMENTS

As always, a great big thanks goes to the members of my critique group – thank you so much, Brainstormers, for your insight on that first draft. I wrote this one way too fast to not have a plethora of mistakes for you to wade through.

Deb and Sandra, my devoted beta readers for this series, your constant encouragement on what you love about Vicki kept me going on that final draft. This one required so much rewrite, I wasn't sure at times if I was going to keep story continuity straight.

Geraldine, Glenn, and Dayna, thank you for helping me muddle through some of the details about the history and structure of the Alamo. My anality was on display with all of my itty, bitty, detailed questions. You were all so blessedly patient.

The world's biggest Dallas Cowboys fan – Wes, you helped me 'see' the new Cowboys Stadium and hear the crowd from a real, live spectator's perspective. Without your excitement and appreciation of all things silver and blue, I doubt if I'd have included the scene I wrote near the end of this novel. Instead, you gave it the life it needed.

CHAPTER ONE

Temptation has a name.

His name is Zeke Taylor.

And if circumstances didn't change pronto, I'd either succumb to the temptation to tango between the sheets or end up committing something akin to a felony to avoid that thar Texas Ranger.

No matter what I did to resolve the tension between us, I'd end up in a position potentially rivaling the epic breakup breakdown of two and a half years ago.

In other words, I was screwed.

I stared into my strawberry sweet tea, wishing for something stronger with lunch. Something more in the range of the Long Island variety.

"Victoria? Victoria!"

Mom's voice finally seeped into my gray matter. "Huh?"

Pursed lips greeted me across the linen covered table of my mom's favorite Dallas restaurant. The server interrupted, setting Wedgewood china bowls on the ruby-red chargers before placing a matching tureen on the table.

The aroma of lobster bisque made me think of colder

water where the succulent critters originated. More comfortable temps brought to mind the approaching football opener. Which assured me *slightly* cooler weather loomed on the horizon.

Bring it on, God, 'cause I was done with August's hellish heat.

After the waiter ladled a miniscule portion of bisque in each bowl, Mom waved him away with a flick of her wrist.

"Have you even heard a word I've said since we arrived?" she asked.

"Sure," I responded too cheerfully over the stringy strains.

"Then what have I been talking about for the last ten minutes?"

"Um…a sale at Macy's? No wait, Neiman Marcus."

Mom just shook her head.

You know the one. Full of disappointment for being unable to accept lost causes. It's a reaction I get a lot these days.

From more than just her.

"There's been another delay with your apartment."

"Again?" I whined like a three-year-old.

"And Reginald said it may be a few weeks more before you can move back in," she finished.

I plunked the spoon into the bowl and sank my face into my hands with a groan. This was so *not* what I needed to hear right now.

Buckle up and get ready for the recap, folks.

Five weeks ago my mom and her interior designer corralled, confiscated and basically took over my apartment after an uninvited co-worker decided to alter the décor from Mid-Eighties Motif to Early American Landfill.

You know. Trash the place.

The guy pretty much released a nuclear bomb in my apartment and left me with little but the clothes on my back.

If Bud had done anything during his rampage to hurt my sweet baby kitty, my former co-worker would've ended up with more than a bullet through his brain, I can tell you that.

But I digress.

The apartment reordering left Slinky and me temporarily homeless. If not for the good graces of the aforementioned Ranger Taylor, my tabby and I might've spent those weeks sleeping in my Corvette.

My car was definitely a sweet ride, but cramped quarters were not made for cozy canoodling.

'Course all this mess happened while I was between boyfriends. Er, uh fellow nighttime excursion enthusiasts.

Alright fine, I'll call a spade a spade – hook-ups!

'Cause I don't do the boyfriend thing no more.

However, the current sleeping arrangement of me on the living room couch while Zeke slept with only the thin wall of his bedroom to separate us was doing more than trying the soul of this bartending babe.

It also made it a hell of a lot more difficult to honor my summer pledge to lay off the getting laid.

Which had me almost on my knees before my mother in the very pubic – I mean, public – restaurant setting. Not a very lady-like thing for a once proud and pampered twenty-six year-old debutante.

Plus, I didn't want to risk scuffing up my new tiffany-box-blue pumps on the travertine tile floor.

Hello, priorities people!

"Please, Mom. I've gotta get out of Zeke's apartment before *I'm* the one who ends up in jail for murder."

Mom dabbed the linen napkin on her rose-tinted lips

before replacing it in her lap and straightening her shoulders like a good former Miss Texas.

"That's not funny, Victoria."

"Who said anything about being funny?"

That got me the stare.

You know this one too. It's something mothers perfect before squeezing their young from the womb.

I'm ninety-nine point nine percent certain those hours expectant moms spend in front of the mirror aren't merely for judging her expanding girth.

She's practicing.

Those hormones are doing more than merely changing her physical appearance. They're restructuring her brain chemistry. Bequeathing her with that sixth sense.

Creating eyes in the back of her head.

'Cause this here crumb cruncher never stood a chance getting away with crap from the moment I was born. Though that might've had more to do with the fact that I had not only a mom watching over my every move, but the equivalent of a full-time nanny nagging me too.

Which was another reason I needed to get back to living on my own. Nannies weren't supposed to make you weak in the knees.

"You just helped clear Robert Vernet of the murder of his wife, at great bodily trauma to yourself I might add, not to mention the emotional trauma to your mother." She sniffed with more than a touch of theater, then fanned her face with the napkin in true southern style. "It's in poor taste to joke about such things."

"Who's joking?" I remembered every last bump, bruise, and bashing like it was yesterday.

'Specially the part where Bud tried to toss me off my apartment building rooftop like a ragdoll.

"Is Zeke no longer being hospitable, Victoria? I'd be glad to call his mother."

"I don't need you to call Mrs. Taylor, Mom. I just need to return to my own space. Rediscover my Zen, 'cause his couch is killing my back."

Mom's brilliant green eyes widened. "Are you telling me that man has left you sleeping on his *sofa* all this time?"

"Would you rather I slept with him in his bed again?"

That earned us furtive glances from nearby tables.

"I meant, why has he not given you the bedroom and taken the sofa for himself? That would be the safest and most gentlemanly thing to do."

"Zeke is a Texas *Ranger*," I emphasized for her benefit. "They haze the gentleman right out of 'em during initiation week."

"Well, you could stay with your father and me, you know. There's plenty of room at the estate."

"Yeah, that'd work real well, Mom." Sarcasm dripped from my words.

Or maybe that was sweat.

"I must say, though, I'm glad to know you've learned to restrain your..." Mom paused to fan herself again with the napkin, casting stealthy glances at nearby diners before whispering. "...urges."

Bisque threatened to shoot down the wrong pipe as I struggled to restrain my laughter.

My mom tries so hard to modify her language to avoid anything that sounds overtly sexual.

In Mrs. Audra Bohanan's vocabulary a woman isn't pregnant, she's *with child*. A married couple doesn't have sex, they have *relations*.

If it wasn't for the fact that little ol' me existed, I'd swear my mom was still as pure as the Virgin Mary.

Now me?

It's a well-known fact I'm more the Mary Magdalene type. There's even a police report from the summer of my fifteenth year to back up my claim to non-virginal fame.

That was when the aforementioned Bobby Vernet and I got caught with our pants down. Or more like tossed into the nearby pasture. All while doing the deed in the bed of his brand-spanking new Ford F-150.

Did I also mention he's the only son of Mom and Dad's church pastor?

With that wedge of misunderstanding between us, bridging the ever-expanding gap between my mom and me presented a constant challenge.

Our Tuesday lunches and shopping excursions were about the only solution we'd come up with to stay connected since I'd moved on from the family confines. My escape to freedom was a matter of self-preservation.

And my only saving grace where my dad was concerned.

The truck bed debacle cost the sperm donor upward of ten million dollars toward the building of the new Celebration Victory Church, a building dedicated to the spreading of Dennis and Mary Jo's version of the gospel.

The kind that involved more fleecing of the flock than shepherding, I might add.

The *donation* to the building fund was my dad's way of offering penance for bringing me into the world. Like father like daughter, I guess.

At least in one way.

I'd discovered the photographic evidence long ago to prove it. And it'd take a whole hell of a lot more than ten million to absolve dear ol' dad of all those sinful multitudes.

But I digress.

I took a long drink to stem the blazing heat beams inching closer from the glassed-in reflection. Or maybe it was to delay the uncomfortable conversational turn.

Funny how the idea of having a conversation with my mother about *urges* devolved into a struggle for me this time.

Guess I'd learned avoidance from the best.

"I've turned over a new fig leaf," I finally responded. "Figured it was a good time to practice the art of self-control when it comes to my *urges*."

Mom delicately cleared her throat. "I'm glad to hear it."

I didn't mention the fact that it had become more necessity at this stage.

Ever since the uncomfortable closeness experienced at the governor's dinner a few weeks ago, I'd not only slammed the brakes on budding intimacy but had shoved the transmission into reverse at a hundred miles per hour, leaving skid marks on a potential relational restoration that only a street racer would love.

Nowadays Zeke and I were doing everything we could to avoid one another. Not hard at present, with Zeke on some big case and keeping odd hours.

Since I started working nights as a bartender, I've become a late sleeper. The job with the Texas Rangers made Zeke an early riser.

And yeah, I meant that to sound dirty.

I quickly quashed *that* mental picture – exactly like I'd been doing for the past five weeks.

"I just need to return to my own place, Mom. What all is Reggie still waiting for? Kitchen cabinets? Countertops? A new commode?"

"Actually, the holdup is delivery of the bedroom furniture," she offered with another napkin wave like a white flag. "Some sort of strike at the manufacturing facility."

But I wasn't ready to surrender. "Do I have a couch though?"

"Yes, but…"

"I'll take it."

"You can't sleep on the floor, Victoria."

"But you said I have a new couch. On site and ready for sleeping, right?"

"A sofa isn't for sleeping, dear."

"Hello? I've slept on one for the last five weeks. The only difference now is that I'd be on my *own* furniture. In my *own* apartment. Breathing my *own* air."

For emphasis, I took a deep breath and let it out with an exaggerated sigh that again garnered more than my fair share of outright stares this time.

Mom took the hint. Or took pity on me. I'd take whatever leverage our little bit of drama provided.

She slid the phone from her purse and placed the call to the interior designer. "Reginald dear? Do we have any update on Victoria's bedroom furniture?"

A pause. "Mm-hmm."

Another pause. "I see. Can we get that over there today?"

A final pause, then Mom cast a smile my way. "Oh, you're always so thoughtful, Reginald. Let us finish up our luncheon, then we'll meet you over there in an hour or two. *Ciao.*"

My heartbeat ticked up a notch. "It's in?"

"Not the furniture, unfortunately, but the mattress and box springs will be delivered to your apartment this afternoon. Do you think you could live with that in the interim?"

"Does a cat hack up hairballs?"

Mom wrinkled her nose. "Really, Victoria."

CHAPTER TWO

Is it cowardly to pack up and leave a Good Samaritan's place without telling him?

I just don't handle emotional exchanges very well.

Not that Zeke's emotional, mind you. It's more that over the last month and a half, he's vacillated between showing interest in getting back together and keeping his distance. He had to be about as tired of my presence as my spine was of sleeping on his sofa.

Plus, it was hard – er, difficult thinking about him in the other room. On the other side of that thin apartment wall.

Wondering what he was doing. Remembering our past involvement. Imagining all those times of his mouth on mine. Hands exploring parts unseen.

Whew, did the temperature spike all of a sudden?

In other words, Ranger Zeke had cured me of such intimacies. With him at least. The falling out hit me right between the shoulder blades almost as much now as when I caught him over two years ago with arms wrapped around my long-time mortal enemy.

My last boyfriend quickly became my last *ex*-boyfriend. We hadn't spoken again until June when I'd asked for his help to clear Bobby of murder charges.

Since then I'd come to a realization.

I sure knew how to hold a grudge.

After that convoluted comprehension wormed its way into my conscience, years of Sunday School lessons finally paid off.

It was time to forgive Zeke for the past, forget about it, and move on.

The forgiveness part wasn't all that hard.

I think.

And I'd had no trouble moving on with other guys.

Obviously.

Forgetting about the betrayal, however, took on a degree of difficulty that would make an Olympic diver think twice before attempting.

That said, I was making progress.

Sorta.

Maybe I'd better just grab the cat and go. No preambles. No awkward moments.

Simply leave a check on the way out the door so he couldn't balk again at trying to pay my share during the overlong stay.

His key I'd figure out how to return to him later.

The only things I had to pack up from Zeke's Country Hoedown this time were Slinky's food and toy emporium, then the new wardrobe Mom had purchased for me with the black AmEx.

Simple, right? You'd think.

It wasn't until I finished gathering my things from the closet that I realized the magnitude of all she'd bought me the last five weeks. The teeny trunk of my Vette and the passenger's seat were bursting by the time I tucked Slinky into his crate, took one final turn about the apartment, then locked up and left.

A resurgent memory of the last time I'd pulled out of this parking lot ached behind my ribs.

Heartburn. Too much seafood at lunch.

Yeah, let's go with that.

But the heartburn turned into nervous excitement as I neared my building near Dallas's Historic West End. Excitement about going home. Nervous to see what Reggie and Mom had concocted in my absence.

Since Mom footed the bill for the forced remodel, I'd known early on that I'd have absolutely zero say in the final outcome.

Talk about heartburn.

See, she has very traditional tastes, whereas I like eclectic and a bit industrial.

Mom was a silk, lace, and florals kind of woman. Bright and cheerful. Delicate and feminine.

I was all about solids. Metal studs. Darker, more ominous motifs. And leather.

You know, something with attitude and a bit more bite.

With Reggie at the helm, my anxiety was somewhat assuaged. He'd never let me down before and was sure to find ways to keep the decor true to the Vicki standards. The designer knew me better than any other man.

No, not in that way. The guy was about as flaming as a man could get.

Between Easter and Christmas decorations – not to mention the home overhaul every few years – he'd been a fixture around the Bohanan estate since I last toddled out of a diaper. If anyone knew what I'd like, better than I did myself in fact, it'd be Reggie.

"Well, Slink," I said after pulling into my garage unit. "We're home again."

My tabby just looked at me with those bright green eyes. Then returned to licking his butt.

So gross.

I grabbed the critter crate and lugged my cat into the building, leaving mounds of clothes and shoeboxes behind for toting in later.

As I trudged upstairs to the fourth floor, the welcoming scents of musty warehouse and good ol' southern fried chicken were joined by a sawdust and paint chaser.

The brand new front door greeted me with a fresh stain of walnut. The thick and heavy wood sent my bare knuckles barking with a single rap.

What the hell was this thing made of? Hedge? Reinforced steel? Hedge-covered reinforced steel?

For a second I wondered if anyone on the other side could even hear the deep-throated *whack* until the slide, thunk, and click preceded the opening creak like in a bad horror movie.

"*Mein liebchen!*" the interior designer cried, throwing dark chocolate arms around me before shoving the door aside for me to enter. "Come. Come. See vat Reginald accomplished in Victoria's absence, yes?"

First I had to tear my eyes away from the glaring suit jacket. Bright purple, green, red, and black swirled in a dizzying array across the designer's torso, topped by an old-fashioned cravat resting under his chin and jutting out like a pincushion on steroids.

The black cigarette pants, while easier on the eyes than the color kaleidoscope up top, were not made for middle-aged men. Every bulge, crease, and crevice were outlined in vivid relief.

A shudder rippled right through me.

One thing you could always say about Reggie Brown, I

mean Reginald von Braun? You'd never forget him once you met him.

Maybe that was the genius part behind his marketing madness.

The guy was a lot of things – or *wore* a lot of things – but brilliant designer topped the list, evidenced by the fact that every notable family home in the Dallas metro area sported a one-of-a-kind Reginald von Braun design.

Just don't judge him by the fake accent and the loud clothes.

Mom came strolling from the bedroom with a worried smile on her face, tucking a stray hair strand into her coif.

"Well? What do you think, dear?"

What did I think? Hard to say.

The only thing I recognized was the bank of tall windows off the dining area. Reginald had listened and kept the window seat area just for Slinky, where my critter liked to bask in the sunlight.

But what really caught my eye next was the industrial brick wall dividing the living area from the bedroom.

"This is beautiful." I touched the reddish stones and fresh mortar. "How did you get it to match the brick between the windows so perfectly?"

Reggie pursed his lips. "Ah, but Reginald can work miracles, no?"

"It must've taken an act of God to get removing this wall past the landlord."

"No, no," Reggie said, waving his arms. "Zee brick was already zere. It only took removing zat disgusting sheetrock and zee plaster to uncover her radiance."

"Well, I love it." I planted a kiss on Reggie's stubbly cheek before checking out the kitchen. "And this kitchen...wow."

Cabinet style had a more traditional feel – definitely Mom's doing. Stainless steel counters topped gunmetal gray lower cabinets while a polished cement counter covered the island with swirls of rich color reflected by pendant lights.

Industrial motif heaven. Score one for Vicki.

The new furniture was pretty traditional too but in a color palette of charcoal leather, muted tangerine, and aqua striped tones. No florals, thank God.

This I could definitely live with. Once again, Reggie had saved my carcass.

My usually unperturbed and composed mother wrung her hands. "What do you think, Victoria?"

In an unusual move on my part, I embraced my mother and pecked her on the cheek. "It's perfect. Thank you, Mom."

Irish eyes widened then crinkled in a smile as she held me at arm's length. "Oh, I'm so relieved. I wasn't sure about some of the fabric choices, but Reginald assured me this was what you'd like."

I looked at Reggie. "Even after all these years, you haven't forgotten my tastes."

"Reginald von Braun never forgets." The hip jutted out while his hand waved around as if holding a cigarillo out of boredom. "He always knows vat the ladies vant," he said with a brow wiggle.

I laughed and pecked him again on the cheek. The nice thing with having a gay friend was that they loved hugs and kisses from just about everyone.

Plus, you didn't have to worry about them feeling you up like a testosterone-fueled teenager.

The only thing butch about Reggie was the familiar TAG Heuer blue-faced watch. More a pronouncement of status than fashion when you compared it to everything else he wore.

A quick peek into the virtually empty bedroom revealed pearl gray paint saturating the walls and a king-sized mattress and box springs dressed with assorted pillows, sheets and a blanket neatly folded at the foot.

Once in the bedframe, I'd be climbing Mount Everest every night just to go to bed. That might make things interesting. Very interesting indeed.

All commercials stated that a solid mattress was the key to a good night's sleep. I looked forward to testing that theory tonight. Alone.

Girl Scout's honor.

Sunlight slanted across the window seat where my contented kitty lounged.

After Mom and Reggie left I changed into something more comfortable, put up my hair, and brought in all my crap from the car. It was fun puttering around my brand new old space, familiarizing myself with the surroundings and making little adjustments to furniture placement.

I'd just finished moving the desk when someone's knuckles sank into the door with a dull thud. Opening the heavy wooden door was like swinging open a vault at Fort Knox.

I really needed to ask Reggie what it was made from.

But that idea ejected from my gray matter when Zeke glared down from beneath the black Stetson topping his six-foot-five frame.

"Wanna tell me what this is?" He held up the check I'd left on his kitchen counter.

"Um…payment for services rendered?"

And no, that wasn't meant to sound dirty.

An eyebrow arched before he ripped the check into confetti. "I never asked you for anything, Vic. Thought I was helping out a friend."

"And while I appreciate that, I figured it was best to keep things on an equitable basis. You know, no expectations?"

His cheek muscles twinged. "When were you going to tell me you were moving out?"

"Today?" I squeaked.

Tired eyes darkened before he looked away. It took all of two footfalls for him to walk through the doorway and take in every inch of the remodel.

"I like what you've done with the place. It fits you...mostly."

"Mom paid, so I can't complain. Reggie looked out for me though." I took a deep breath then released it on a sigh. "I'm just glad to be home."

That got me a grunt. "Looks like someone else is glad too."

Slinky had left his sunbeam filled nest to curl around Zeke's ankles with a purr as loud as a motorboat.

I looked down with a scowl. "Traitor."

Zeke chuckled then bent to scratch my traitorous tabby behind the ears.

"Oh, you forgot this at my place."

He flung a fluffy gray mouse toy across the room, sending Slinky skittering after it. It looked like the one Zeke had bought for him during our refugee status days. It had surprised me to see the Ranger had a thoughtful side when it came to critters.

Until I realized he was buttering up my kitty in an effort to try and get into my pants. Or up my skirt. Didn't work then and it sure wasn't gonna work this time.

I think.

"Let me get your key."

I dug through my purse before extracting and holding it out to my former landlord. Er, the Good Samaritan.

Friend was a word I still hesitated to use where Zeke was concerned. Reminded me a little too much of the *boy*friend variety.

He held his hand open so I could drop the key into his palm, almost as if he were as afraid of touching me as I was of him.

But that didn't stop the musky scent of the great outdoors from overtaking *eau de new construction*. It touched me all the way. Down. There.

My thighs clenched.

Having Zeke in my apartment, standing so close I could feel the warmth radiating off of him, proved too much for my present euphoria. My heart pounded as dark eyes trailed from my hand to my lips. Breath stilled when his gaze met mine.

My nether regions jumpstarted after weeks of forced hibernation.

That promise I'd made to go to bed alone tonight swept away like the deck chairs off the Titanic. I suddenly wanted Zeke to take me in his arms and do unspeakable things to me.

All night long, y'all.

Instead he slipped the key in his pocket, planted a kiss on my forehead, then turned and walked right out my door in two strides.

Right outta my life.

After staring at the closed door for a few, I looked down at Slinky. "Looks like it's just you and me again, pardner."

My traitorous tabby just cocked his head and stared at

me before spitting out the toy and then settling again in the window seat to lick himself.

My eye roll of disgust landed on the top of the new stainless fridge. The *empty* top of the new stainless fridge.

Too bad Mom was a teetotaler and hadn't replenished my liquor stash. I could really use a shot of Jack about now.

Or three fingers of scotch.

A Long Island iced tea anyone?

I knew the best place in town to get a drink or two. Probably wouldn't cost me a thing either.

Can you say Grady's?

I sure can. Could.

Oh hell, just get in the car.

CHAPTER THREE

The bar tends to be slow and quieter early in the evenings.

'Cept for wet t-shirt nights.

And when I'm tending bar. 'Cause I have a tendency to bring a little bit more fun to the fiasco.

Rochelle was a different matter. That cherubic chic was a classy cowgirl.

My co-worker had seen a lot in her thirty-some years. Had the little boys and the single parent moniker to prove it.

She never talked about how her ex ran off and left her with nothing, and we all knew better than to ask. As a frequent sufferer of foot-in-mouth disease, I'd made that mistake only once.

Boots were never intended for mouths or asses, folks.

Trust me.

Schedules at work had gone a little screwy since our former co-worker got caught in a drug ring and murder moment. When he'd tried to launch me off my rooftop for a brief flight sans wings, my boss sent Bud down under for an eternity of keeping the likes of Joseph Stalin and Adolf Hitler company.

This employee shortage was a boon for Rochelle by opening up another bartender position. Higher wages, better tips, and more hours than the server position allowed Rochelle the opportunity to start saving up so she could eventually move her little family out of her mother's place.

Over the last few weeks, I'd guided and grilled her on mixing drinks. Taught her the fine art about reading people and entertaining customers to earn better tips.

She was a natural in the making drinks category. Mimicking my daring form of entertainment?

Maybe that's a category best left to my arena of expertise.

Rochelle perked right up when I lassoed myself to a barstool.

"Hey, Vicki. What're you doin' here on your night off?"

"I've officially moved back into my apartment."

"Congratulations." Rochelle beamed as she swiped a spot in front of me. "Guess that's cause for celebration."

"More or less. But since I've yet to restock the fridge, I ain't got no booze at home for celebrating."

"Bummer." She filled mugs from the tap before setting them on a tray. "Sounds like a good time for a tea from Long Island."

"No truer words were ever spoken."

"Coming right up," she quipped, sliding the beer tray up onto the bar.

As Rochelle set to work on my drink, warm lips landed briefly on the back of my neck.

A husky voice followed. "Ya didn't just do a good job trainin' our girl, Vic. You did a *very* good job trainin' her."

I turned around to a languid milk chocolate gaze and a smile tilting one edge of my boss's mustache.

"Hey, Grady."

The tepid interaction was about par for the last few weeks. Our waltz of Grady advancing and me retreating had formed a skid mark bigger than the ones my Vette left in a sudden start or stop.

Maybe it had something to do with him firing the kill shot through Bud's brain that night. Or something to do with the newfound discovery my boss was actually an undercover ATF agent and clandestinely worked with Ranger Taylor on occasion.

It couldn't be that Grady was concerned I'd spill his secrets in a drunken melee.

Could it?

Don't answer that.

As Rochelle set the full-to-the-brim glass before me, a wave of Grady's hand comped my consumption and sent Rochelle to wait on a couple at the end of the bar about one step shy of needing a room. The way that couple was going at it, they were on the verge of violating two commandments, three Texas statutes, and four of Newton's laws.

I focused in on my drink with a cough. No matter how hard I tried to escape it, that nagging nookie temptation was everywhere.

"This sure is a new look for you," Grady said, taking in my sweat-streaked tee, comfy shorts, and droopy ponytail. "Dusty chic?"

"More like grimy girl," I returned.

That got me a chuckle. "So how's the new old place?" the boss man asked, sliding in next to me.

I finished a desperate pull on my straw with a sigh of liquid satisfaction at the buzz already building in my brain. Yes, I'd taught Rochelle the mixing drinks part of the job *really* well.

Boy howdy. "I take it you've already talked with Zeke?"

"Yep."

"And you know he's ticked at me?"

"I think it's more you scared him by leavin' his place without informin' him," Grady asserted.

That rankled my catnip just a bit. "Is this what I have to look forward to now? The two of you whispering behind my back and sharing my every move with one another?"

"You've nothin' to worry about, Vic. Zeke was concerned about what might've happened to you, is all."

Happened to me, shnappened to me. The guy could've picked up the phone and called. Or texted.

But no. The ratfink Ranger had to go and get Grady involved like a trail boss circling the wagons before a raid.

Men.

"Just because you two work together on occasion doesn't mean my day-to-day affairs are fodder for gossip."

"Affairs?" The rise of his mustache signaled more than understanding of my alcohol-induced accidental double-entendre.

"You know what I mean." I punched his thigh. "I got more'n enough of Gossipers 'R Us from the pious parishioners growing up. I don't need it from you two."

"You have my word it won't continue," Grady pledged, jostling the laden beer tray. "Enjoy your drink then go home and get a good night's sleep. I need you in full Vicki mode for the start of the alcohol X-games tomorrow night."

"Yes sir, mister boss man, sir." I saluted before taking a huge slurp of my drink in preparation.

Where'd he get such an idea as the alcohol X-games anyway? I was still trying to wrap my head around an ATF agent running a bar as part of his cover.

Suppose it made some sort of sense, being close enough to hear all about the *action*, so to speak.

In more ways than one.

I laughed out loud at the dirty thoughts roaming through my gray matter then stared into my glass. My *empty* glass.

What all had Rochelle put in there anyway?

Said barmaid wormed her way over, and together we watched the boss's retreating backside. A sigh escaped from one of us – okay, both – as he bent over to hand out beer to a table of college-aged females, offering a bird's-eye view of his jean-clad butt to more than just them.

"Mmm," my co-worker murmured. "Would you look at that?"

"Boy howdy."

"Reminds me of a little somethin' I marinated and threw on the grill for dinner last Sunday."

"I see that," I said with a tilt of my head, handing over my glass. "But those gals are too young for his brand of sausage."

"A woman of any age would have to be dead not to pay attention to a man with an ass that fine."

Ice clinked somewhere in my periphery as I took in the scenery up ahead. I think I purred.

Rochelle paused after she dumped another Long Island iced tea on the bar in front of me. "Well?"

"Well what?"

"Are things finally back to normal between you guys?"

Normal?

Apparently I sucked at subtlety.

As Grady finished flirting with the fishes and moved on to another table, I realized nothing had yet been resolved between us about the secrets revealed the night Grady wrote Bud's name on a bullet.

I also hadn't considered how my discomfort had affected the rest of the staff either.

"Yup, right as rain," I lied.

Don't judge.

"It's about time." She vigorously toweled a glass until I thought it'd shatter before she set it down. "You two have had everyone around here on edge for so long now, I didn't think things would ever return to normal."

"What *is* normal these days?" I philosophized.

She leaned across the bar. "So was he that *good* or that *bad*?"

I took a long pull through the straw before coming up for air. "With what?"

"You know." She gestured suggestively with both hands.

"Rochelle!"

"Well?" A devious grin spread across her face like liquid butter.

"Is that what everyone around here thinks?"

"It's kinda obvious *something* happened between you two."

My turn to lean forward and whisper. "There never has been, nor will there ever be, any tangoing between the sheets where Grady and me are concerned."

Chestnut brows pinched. "But I assumed, with the way you two act around each other and the sexually charged atmosphere…"

"It's just a game. A ruse. Something we do for fun."

"I know some other ways you could have even more fun."

"Yeah, me too," I responded, tossing a last glance over my shoulder as Grady meandered toward his office. "But it's never wise to mix business with pleasure."

No matter how sorely I was tempted.

"Smart girl," Rochelle said, then sighed. "Sleeping with

co-workers only complicates things."

"Here-here," I said, raising my glass.

Rochelle's stare trailed away to over my head. "But a customer? Now that's an opportunity."

I twirled the barstool around to lock with familiar ice-blue eyes closing in on me. Mussed dark hair hung over his forehead, and the impeccably tailored cobalt-blue shirt hugged him in all the right – yet oh-so-wrong – places before opening to reveal the plunge of tanned pecs I knew well.

And not just from his photos in magazines.

I swallowed the knot in my throat as my heartrate ticked my temperature toward volcanic.

"Welcome home, Nick."

CHAPTER FOUR

So much for promises to lay off the...

Aw, forget it.

I awoke late the following morning in a tangle of sheets, accompanied by a stitch in my side, a slight hangover, and an intermittent pulse beating against my cheek.

Thump-thump. Thump. Thump-thump.

The first thing I noticed when I opened my eyes was Slinky's butt, his tail languidly flipping and flopping across my face like a rolling and thunderous timpani instead of the usual crashing cymbals.

When I went to remove him, the floor was much closer in the daylight than when I'd gone to sleep last night.

Oh. Right. Almost forgot.

After nearly two months of inactivity, my sexual energy was a coiled spring released like a bullet on a hair trigger.

Just call me the Energizer Bunny. I'd kept going and going until the new mattress slid right off the box springs.

After the second time, we'd decided it was safest to leave it where it'd ended up.

As I flopped out of bed, I rediscovered a thing or two about muscle memory. First, it's pretty quick to dissipate when said muscles are left to atrophy for more than a week or two. Second, they're pretty quick to let you know they're out of shape once you use them again.

It took a bit more than a little effort to get my carcass moving toward the kitchen, but I finally dug out my robe and headed for a caffeinated fill-up.

Another good thing about Mom? She refuses to buy me liquor, but she definitely doesn't skimp on those necessary Bohanan staples. Like coffee. And Oreos.

Not two cans, but two *cases* of Colombian roast took up the floor space in my tiny new pantry. Smack dab next to those were a whole box filled with packages of chocolaty goodness. Breakfast coming up.

Hey, if donuts were considered breakfast, cookies weren't that much more of a stretch, right?

As the fragrant, steamy aroma wafted from the percolating pot and cookie crumbs gathered at the corners of my mouth, I bowed my head against the cool stainless steel countertop and gave thanks for my thoughtful mother.

God bless her.

Guilt followed soon after the first gulps awakened my brain enough to engage. But not because of my Oreo feast.

In my apartment less than twenty-four hours and already I'd returned to my Mary Magdalene ways. For weeks I'd struggled against those pesky urges and succeeded while under Zeke's roof.

My own roof?

Yeah, I'd had about as much self-control as a certain police detective in a pastry shop when Nick showed up last night. He'd been away all that time too – somewhere in Europe, I think – with no word on when to expect his return.

Not like we were boyfriend and girlfriend or anything. Hell, I'd been a free agent the entire time.

So what was the real reason I hadn't taken advantage of the opportunities when Zeke had presented them?

Danger! Danger! Rocks ahead!

Avoidance tendencies kicked in right as Nick's warm body pressed up from behind and pushed me against the counter, wrapping me in his arms and enveloping me with his sexy scent.

"Mornin' luv. Sleep well after powerin' down?"

From what I felt, it wouldn't take much to get him powered up again.

Who was I kidding? With the Aussie accent that curled my toes, it wouldn't take much to get *me* going again.

I greeted him with a kiss of *eau de coffee breath* and a hint of an Oreo chaser before tearing myself away.

"Uh, yeah. You?"

"Like a rock."

My hand shook a bit while pouring him a cup – and it wasn't from too much caffeine.

"Sorry again about the whole bed situation."

"No worries," Nick said, hip checking me. "I 'ave slept in worse situations."

I'll bet.

Coffee only sloshed a little as I thrust the mug between us. "A lot happened around here while you were gone."

"So I see," he said, taking the cup and strolling about the apartment in all his naked glory.

Don't you just love the European mindset about nudity? They're so uninhibited and unashamed of wearing nothing but their birthday suit, while this here red-blooded American filly clung to her robe like Batman to his cape.

Nick ambled about admiring my new furnishings and offering me a daylight view of all God had blessed him with.

Every tanned, toned, and tight inch. Every. Last. One.

'Scuse me while I mop up the drool from my new kitchen floor.

"This must 'a been what kept you busy while I was down unduh."

"Actually this was my mom's doing," I said. "And her interior designer. If Reggie hadn't kept Mom in check, you'd be looking at a whole lot of lace and a heaping bunch of florals instead of stripes, studs, and leather."

"Then what kept you from callin', luv?"

"Say what?" was all I could think to say to the sudden whiplash in the conversation.

He faced me with a furrow dipping beneath the mussed hair. "I's overseas for near two months. No message whatsoever from m' girl."

Okay, there was no *friend* attached to the *girl*. I could handle that.

"Goes both ways, Nick. If you'd wanted to converse, all you had to do was pick up your own phone."

And they say girls are needy. Sheesh.

"Shoot schedules and locations were in constant flux, luv. I could never properly calculate the time difference to know when t' call."

"You coulda let your fingers do the talking."

All that got me was a puzzled look.

I tapped my fingers in the air. "You know…text?"

Or take a remedial math class, but I kept that tidbit to myself. No need to be rude and disrespectful. At least not out loud

'Specially after all of the stunning things he'd done to me last night.

He caught me in his arms and lifted me up onto the kitchen island. The pout disappeared and a sexy smile replaced it.

"Let's celebrate m' homecoming then."

"Didn't we do that last night?"

I shivered as he nipped my ear and worked down my jaw.

"I 'ave got a brief shoot down in San Antonio early next week. How 'bout we drive down Sunday and spend some one-on-one together."

He was ready for a little one-on-one right now from what I could tell through my thin robe.

"I-I've got work on Wednesday night next week."

"Piece 'a cake. The shoot's scheduled Monday and Tuesday nights. After I'm done, we zip up the motorway in time for work. All's good then?"

Wait a minute? A road trip? With Nick?

Weren't we just arguing? Weren't we just thinking about no *friend* with the *boy*?

Oh, yeah. That was me.

My knees were knocking from the intimacy a trip together implied.

Or maybe it was because of overworked muscles from the night before.

Perhaps more from what his roaming hands were doing to my body as Nick stripped me of the robe and his mouth explored.

A combination of those three explanations?

Yeah. Let's go with that.

San Antonio, here we c-c-come!

CHAPTER FIVE

It bothered me how well Nick could manipulate me.

And yeah, that way too.

He'd discovered my weakness. How to get almost anything he wanted from me. With awesome sex he could steer me easier than a bit in a filly's maw.

So with that mental image, I had even more to chew on during the four hour drive south. A road trip. Together. Just me and Nick.

Ho boy.

That bespoke an intimacy I hadn't experienced since the epic blowup with Big Z. This train was barreling down the tracks toward the ravine so fast, I'd have to jump off soon before becoming a wreck on a wreck.

But as a captive audience, I had to at least try and make the best of the next few days. But in order to do that, I had to make it through the car ride first.

So what could we talk about? Did we even have anything in common?

Besides that.

Okay, talking about his car might work. The sweet Jaguar F-Type R Coupe cut down the interstate as smooth as an all-star running back through a defensive line. The thing had enough horsepower to challenge my Vette in a street race.

For a second anyway.

'Bout the only thing that could possibly make it better was if the Jag was a convertible. And black.

But I wasn't about to yield my good ol' American-born hot rod to some foreign piece of luxury without more information. Even if it was a gorgeous model that made me want to take it for a spin on my own.

The pearlescent charcoal gray didn't hurt its chances either. It'd look great as an accessory to the new paint on my apartment walls.

"So," I said, dipping my toes into the conversational waters. "What're the specs on your Jag?"

"Specs?" Nick questioned.

"Like the horsepower."

"Um...not sure."

"Torque?" I pressed.

"What's that?"

Yeah, this was going well. "I'm assuming it's a V-8?"

"Like the vegetable juice?"

The scenery of brown scrub fields and grazing cattle flashed by almost as fast as my life. How could a guy own a car worth nearly a hundred grand and know nothing about it? Every man I'd ever known could rattle off the specs of their vehicle down to the brand of spark plugs in the coil.

Hell, even I could tell you that much. Guys weren't the only sex to have a thing for their vehicles. Most of 'em got a hard on just thinking about them.

This was going to be the longest trip of my life.

"So what *can* you tell me about this car?" I tried again.

"Well...it's got leather seats," Nick offered with a patty-pat to the buttery soft interior.

"I see."

"And they're heated."

"Okay."

Heated seats weren't really a necessity in Texas. More like a novelty. 'Specially in August. But I was willing to give him that one since heated seats came standard in most high-end cars these days.

The continued car interrogation took up all of about – two minutes?!?

Lord help me.

How had I gotten myself wrangled into a road trip with Nick? What were we possibly going to talk about for the next three hours and fifty-eight minutes?

It came to me about then like a ten-pound sack of stupid dropped on my head. Nick and I had never really talked.

Most of our conversation up to that point had been more along the line of *hey, Vicki* or *hey, Nick* and *oh yeah, just like that* instead of chatter about banal and mundane things. He'd never even shared where exactly in Europe he'd disappeared to for the last couple of months.

That's a lot of geography to encompass in one statement, folks.

For the next couple of hours I whittled through every topic I could think of, watching the imaginary stick disappear as fast as my gray matter, until I finally got him talking about his modeling gigs.

Big mistake.

By the time we checked into our hotel along the San Antonio River Walk, I knew more about the vapid and shallow world of fashion than I'd ever conceived possible. I wasn't sure I'd ever be able to get my brain cells back after that.

Mom would love hanging out with Nick. 'Cept for the part about my uncontrollable urges when he came around.

Don't get me wrong. We all know by now I liked *wearing* fashionable clothes, shoes, and the assorted accessories. The weekly shopping excursions with Mom and her monthly credit card bill proved it.

I just didn't give a flying flip about what *this* designer said about *that* designer or the horrors experienced working with certain Hollywood celebrity types. But apparently that information is well-known among the fashion elite.

And Nick described every tiny tidbit of associated gossip.

In agonizing detail.

I swear, the Celebration Victory Church ladies would love to have Nick speak at their next Thursday luncheon. They'd gawk and fawn over him like preening peacocks about as much as they did Reggie.

But by the time we arrived in our room and the door clicked shut, thoughts of cars, clothes, and the church ladies who loved them went out the window. Nick proceeded to spend the next couple of hours showing me any number of reasons why neither of us fit in with the clerical crowd.

In delectably delicious detail this time.

By dinnertime, this philandering filly had worked up an appetite no mere hay and oats could satisfy.

While I showered and prepared to make myself presentable, Nick stepped downstairs to the weight room to get in an hour of iron pumping. Don't know why he felt the need for exercise after all we'd gotten.

The life of a male model, I suppose.

When he returned to the room, he leapt into the shower

before tossing on some clothes and sliding a bit of product into his hair. After five minutes of prep work, he still had to wait on me to dig heels out of my suitcase.

So. Not. Fair.

The sun hung on the horizon as we made our way down the river walk, casting a golden sheen across the top of the muddy water. It reminded me briefly about that trip to Venice Zeke and I had taken years ago.

Strolling arm in arm along ancient pathways. Riding in a gondola beneath the San Marcos Bridge.

The flung cigarette butt that nearly set my Vera Wang strapless dress on fire.

Then there was the scent of rotting fish embedded in every pore and fiber. Took me at least three washings to get the stench out on our return home.

Ah, the fragrant memories.

Even after dithering as long as possible, we were early for our dinner reservations. But the gracious host seated us within two minutes of our arrival.

After getting wine orders out of the way, I excused myself and escaped to the bathroom to wash my hands.

Hey, that's my excuse, and I'm sticking to it.

Besides, I practically needed another shower after the short stroll in the heat and humidity. The gauzy strapless had wilted and clung to my curves like melted wax.

One thing I was grateful for? That Nick hadn't made reservations for the riverside terrace.

Talk about melting.

I pressed a moist, cool towel to the back of my neck and sighed. Was this how I was going to spend the next couple of days? Hiding out in bathrooms? Seeking all manner of excuses to escape Nick's company?

He'd mentioned the photo shoots were going to take

place late in the evenings. If he was going to be gone all night, that meant he'd spend most of the day sleeping in.

A few hours of playtime in the afternoon. An early dinner together. Okay, yeah. I could do this.

Couldn't I?

I gave myself a good stare down in the mirror to find some cowardly lion courage. Then with shoulders back to accentuate my positives, I tossed open the ladies room door and strutted down the hall.

Then barreled smack dab into a brick wall wearing an impeccably tailored gray Armani suit.

"I'm so sorry," the deep voice rolled over me as he extended a hand to help me up from the floor. "Are you alright?"

The hand was baby soft without a callous in sight along his dark chocolate palm. A hand that had never know hard labor.

A hand topped by a wrist exhibiting a familiar blue-faced TAG Heuer watch.

As I stood, I stared up at a strange yet well-known face, completely incongruous to his usual appearance and within my present location.

"Reggie?"

CHAPTER SIX

"Vicki?"

The shortened name on the interior designer's tongue sounded stilted from the usual *mein liebchen* or *Victoria*. The man holding my hand showed no signs of the guy who sported loud clothes and an even louder mouth at times.

No too-tight cigarette pants. No frilly hot pink flamenco shirt or psychedelic kaleidoscope jackets. The dark gray Armani suit fit him like a tailor-made ensemble, topped off with a non-flashy, conservative white shirt and navy blue tie.

The usual wildly fluffed hair, speckled with generous hints of gray these days, was smoothed back to show off a strong forehead. A forehead made more distinguished by wire-rimmed glasses.

My usually flaming Reggie looked – for lack of a better word – manly. Masculine. Handsome in an older James Bond kind of way.

I shivered with the dichotomy. "What are you doing here?"

"Well I...uh...," Reggie stuttered in the deep voice before throwing open his arms and breaking into his usual squeal.

"Victoria, darling. How pleasant to zee you 'ere of all places."

I allowed him to quish me in his arms and plant a quick peck on either cheek before he drew back and stared at me with wide eyes brimming with discomfort.

And fear. He knew he'd been had before I even said anything.

"What's all this?" I asked, pointing out his appearance from top to tail.

"Oh, *mein liebchen*, you must know it eez necessary to one's health to flutter away once in awhile, no?"

"Get away? Yes. Do a one-eighty to your appearance and kick the accent before recovering it in the endzone? Not a chance." I crossed my arms. "Sounds to me like Reggie has some 'splaining to do."

"Now, now, now," he scolded, wagging a finger in my face. "Vat vould Victoria's mother say about how she speaks to her elders?"

"How about we call her right now and find out?" I said, whipping out my cell phone as if channeling said mother.

"Wait," Reggie said as he grasped my hands.

I arched a brow as my heels started tapping away on the tile like a ticked-off telegraph.

Decision made, he deflated with a sigh. "Alright fine." The accent disappeared again. "If I share, will you promise to keep what I say between us?"

"You know I will."

Not like I didn't already know about some of his real history. There were perks to having once dated a Texas Ranger.

Plus, I'd had my own suspicions from before the time I could say *photograph*.

"You could completely destroy my reputation, not to

mention my career if this gets out in our normal circles."

"Good thing I'm not normal," I quipped. Then noting his despair, I nodded. "Your secret's safe with me."

Reggie gave me the once over, apparently satisfied with my vow of silence. "Where are you staying?"

"The hotel just up the walk." I jabbed my thumb in the general direction.

"Can you meet me by the indoor pool around midnight?"

"How about eleven?" I countered.

My brain could use the extra time away from Nick. Now if only I could come up with a good excuse.

"I'll have to take my date home," Reggie said. At the unspoken question in my raised brows, he spilled. "We met online, okay?"

I put up my hands to stop him. "Say no more."

"How about you and I meet somewhere in the middle then…say eleven-thirty?"

"Deal."

Whatever Reggie had planned to do in the men's room was forgotten as he straightened his suit and strolled from the hallway.

I peeked around the corner to see him seated near the center of the restaurant, away from windows and prying eyes. The biggest shocker of the night?

His date was female.

After dragging out dinner as long as possible before returning to the hotel, Nick was none too happy with my excuse of not packing enough condoms and going out to buy more.

Hey, I had to come up with something believable in

order to sneak away to meet Reggie. I doubt if mentioning running into a friend from Dallas who needed to talk would've satisfied him either.

The man was a machine.

Still, I made my apologies, said I wouldn't be long, and told him to wait up until my return.

Probably not the best choice of words

'Specially when a wicked smile leaned into his lips. That was gonna cost me later.

But you'd get no complaints from me.

Reggie sat at a cast iron table near the pool when I entered the empty atrium. The bite of chlorine was strong enough to burn nostril hairs.

He wore the same strange attire – for him anyway – and sported the same good looks for a man approaching the far side of middle-age. My Nick-fogged brain kept attempting a reboot in order to smooth over the incongruity of Reggie's normalized appearance.

The contents of a glass from the hotel bar swirled before he took a sip then noticed my approach and held a second glass of wine out to me as I sat. I gladly took it and swallowed half the contents in one gulp.

"Was that your boyfriend?" Reggie benignly asked without the usual accent.

I think I actually growled. "Just a friend."

A lip purse full of doubt puckered my way. "Are the two of you staying in the same room?"

"Yeah."

"Sleeping in the same bed?"

I crossed my arms. "Maybe."

That earned me a short snort of amusement before Reggie went all serious. "I'll bet you have a few questions for me."

I nodded. "A few more than I used to have, that's for sure."

A sheepish frown marred his sculpted face.

A guy his age should have a healthy dose of wrinkles already, which made me wonder if he'd resorted to Botox before posing for a profile. From what Rochelle had shared about her experience with the online dating world, lying about one's age was pretty much a given.

"Are you mad at me?" he asked.

"Mad? Nah." I paused. "Confused? Maybe a bit."

"Where should I begin then?"

I drained the rest of the liquid courage from my glass with a satisfied smack. "How about I start?"

Concern and confusion swirled across the angular planes of Reggie's face. "Okay."

I took a deep breath before plunging ahead. "I know all about your juvie record."

Eyes bugged out in unexpected shock. "Say what?"

"And your real name," I continued. "I've known for a long time, Reggie Brown."

Fear twisted his features until he looked like I'd punched him in the gut. For a second I was afraid Reggie would keel over and I'd be forced to either perform CPR.

I was not about to be left to try and explain a rather awkward encounter to my mother. CPR would be easier.

"D-does your mother know?" Reggie stuttered.

"No, no. No worries from that corridor."

"Then how...?"

"I used to date a Texas Ranger. Matter of fact, we're still...friends."

I almost choked on that last word. Still wasn't sure what to call Zeke. Former lover? Recent landlord? My nemesis?

No. Lorraine Padget already owned that title.

"Go on," Reggie verbally nudged.

"Well see, I have this ability to read people. See past the BS," I explained.

"I'm well aware of your intelligence, though why you stay in a dead-end bartender position, I'll never…"

"*Anyway*," I interrupted before he started sounding like the sperm donor. "I've suspected since I was a kid that you were playing a role of some kind. And that the German accent was fake."

"How…?"

"But that wasn't until my teen years."

Reggie turned green and looked like he was gonna hurl.

Better hurry this along. "It wasn't until I mentioned it to my…Ranger that I found out about your past gang associations," I finished blurting out for all the world to hear.

Good thing the pool was closed at this hour.

In case you weren't yet aware, I have this disease. You might've heard of it. Foot-*in*-mouth?

Has nothing to do with cows, unless you too have developed a taste for the funk and flavor of toe jam mixed with shoe leather.

The sucked-in breath devolved into a welling tears that almost stopped me.

For a second anyway.

"But I've never told anyone," I assured. "Well, except for Zeke so he could look you up for me. But he wouldn't say anything either. I swear."

Reggie sucked in staccato breaths like an asthmatic about to pass out from lack of oxygen. "I thought I'd put all of that behind me…when I left Texas…for New York. Changed my name. My persona. It took years to…get that accent down…just right."

"No doubt," I said, rubbing his hand and willing him to take a deep breath before I went hunting for a paper bag.

Not sure how I'd locate one in today's recyclable world.

He took a moment to get himself under control. "When I returned, I'd left Reggie Brown behind and came back as Reginald von Braun, designer extraordinaire." Arms spread wide in exaggerated animation before drooping down the sides of the chair with a sigh. "No reputable family will allow juvenile delinquent *Reggie Brown* into their home if this gets out."

"You don't know that," I offered in a weak attempt to make him feel better.

"Oh, Victoria. You were lucky to grow up in that world. You've no idea how catty the wealthy can be to an outsider."

That's where Reggie was wrong. Being a part of *that world*, where wealth and power were mere façades to hide the rotting carcass hidden beneath the surface, brought only misery and despair.

I knew firsthand the cattiness of that crowd – and continued to enjoy the freedom of breaking away from it.

But every choice had a price, and the reaper had come to collect on Reggie's.

"Can I ask you a personal question?" I ventured.

"No, I'm not really gay either," Reggie whispered.

Whoa! Was not expecting that confession. "Really?"

"It was all part of the persona I built while in New York. The gay community there is vibrant and full of talented people in the world of design, and I saw it as a way to make a splash and rub shoulders with some of the best. But when you're only pretending..."

He rubbed a manicured hand across his cheek, which called into question how much pretending he was doing. "I've felt awful and disgusted with myself for years because

I used those friendships to further my own career."

"And you've only *pretended*? For thirty years?"

With mocha skin it's hard to distinguish a blush, but the pregnant pause about had me kicking myself for asking about what was clearly none of my business.

Damn my disease-ridden mouth.

"So was that woman you had dinner with tonight your girlfriend?"

"We met online a few weeks ago and have talked on the phone since." He shrugged. "With minimal contact in the San Antonio area, I thought it was a safer this way. Far enough away from my usual circle while still close enough to make any potential relationship work."

"Makes sense."

"Dressed like this, who would notice, much less recognize me?" Reggie asked. "What are the chances I'd run into you?"

"One in a million?" I squeaked.

Reggie cradled his head in his hands with a groan. "So now what do I do? Work is booming. I've got an interested buyer for the business. I'm all set to retire on top, and now this."

"Go on as before," I said, avoiding the retirement subject and contemplating life without my flamboyant friend. "I'll always keep your secret, Reggie."

"What about your Ranger friend then?"

"I can talk to him if you'd like."

He waved the offer away with a sharp flick of his wrist like the Reggie I knew and loved. "No need. If a Texas Ranger can't be trusted, we're all in trouble."

"Here, here." I raised my glass and licked the remaining drops. "I really need to get back to my room. When are you heading home?"

"Tuesday morning. The job awaits," he said in his usual dramatic fashion before wilting like a flower on the vine. "I really thought I'd left it all behind...until recently."

"You mean besides running into me tonight?"

"Well...yes." A tear snaked down his cheek and left a splotch on his lovely suit.

I reached across the table and grasped his baby soft hand. "There's something more you're not telling me. What is it?"

"Oh, Victoria. If only you were the one I had to worry about, this would all blow over like the latest political scandal."

"You're scaring me, Reggie. Who else knows?"

He shook his head. "I have no idea. But whoever it is they're...they're blackmailing me."

CHAPTER SEVEN

There's something about the Alamo that brings the fight out of any native Texan.

Morning, noon, or night, standing on the flagstones of the complex made you just want to call out that venerated, barnstorming battle cry – *Remember the Alamo!*

Maybe it was just me.

Or more that I wanted to string someone up for going after dear Reggie.

Nah. It probably stemmed from something more visceral.

Like jealousy.

Monday night I stood waiting inside the edge of a flashing photography perimeter set up around the Church, the most familiar and recognizable of the buildings in the Alamo complex. The massive photo lights were bright enough to sunburn the average person on this warm night, with flashes in such rapid succession as to induce seizures.

I got nauseous if I watched too long. Or maybe that was the alcohol.

After the latest dizzying session ended, colorful gel lights splashed over the limestone walls in a web of color as worker bees changed up the set for the next shoot segment.

Gawkers and passersby were in short supply this late in the evening, but that didn't stop the few strolling by from getting a birds-eye view of plenty of skin.

And I'd assumed modeling was all about the clothes.

My mistake.

When Nick came tromping from the makeup tent in boots and little more than a white speedo and Stetson, with a couple of six-shooters holstered low on his hips, I got to wondering exactly *what* he was supposed to be modeling.

After a skimpily attired female with a black hat nuzzled up to him wearing the feminine version of the boots Nick sported, I realized the footwear were the fashionable items up for bid in the next make-out – er, photography session.

The little green-eyed monster of jealousy clawed onto my back when the photographer had her climb up Nick like a pole. Then mount him like a stallion in the next shots.

The glass of wine I held emptied right quick. Before shards embedded permanently in my palm, I had to search out the service tables for another one.

Now I understood how models stayed so skinny. No food to speak of, but water and wine flowed in abundance. Considering the plentiful libations and church locale, I half expected to see Jesus himself to walk by any second.

Irritation heated my collar when another girl handed the female model a lasso and riding crop. If smoke signals started rising from my collar, we'd both be in trouble.

Instead I convinced the beverage attendant to hand over a bottle of whatever was handy. Champagne. Not my first choice in preparations from the vine, but it worked in a pinch.

So this was fashion modeling.

Looked more like one step shy of Porn Stars 'R Us.

Made me wonder if the Daughters of the Republic of Texas would classify this display as an offensive desecration of the historic site or if they'd line up to get their pictures taken with Nick.

Hmm. How much had I drank? I seemed to be channeling Mom and the pious purveyors tonight. Not a pleasant thought.

Time to get a grip.

This was Nick's job, and I had to deal with it instead of acting like a jealous, juiced-up female. A ball and chain. Like a...*girlfriend*?

Oh, hey-to-the-nay. I needed a distraction right quick.

"No, I'm here to see Victoria Bohanan."

Ask and you shall receive.

Reggie's pleasant tenor broke through the darkening haze, and I hustled my heated haunches over to the guarded check-in set up around the shootout.

"It's okay, guys. He's with me."

The two security guards gave me the onceover before one checked a clipboard. "Vicki, right? Says here you're a guest too."

"That's right." I hiccupped. "Of Nick's."

I pointed to the area of flashing lights where the female model had lassoed a stallion and was pawing at his pecs.

And I'd thought those were all mine.

"Guests can't have guests, ma'am."

"Just as well. Care for a walk, Reggie?" I asked, handing over the bottle to the clipboard-less guard. "I could use a little fresh air."

Arm draped through Reggie's, we strolled across the cobbled square toward the garden.

"You're late," I admonished. "If you'd waited any longer to arrive, you would've had to scrape a female off the limestone walls of that church."

Reggie chuckled, the bastard.

"Can I assume you mean that model over there and not you?"

"Hey, I'm not drunk." The sudden stumble betrayed my words.

"You sure about that?"

"It's these damn cobblestones," I complained. "They were not made for walkin' in heels."

"Of course not."

The world righted itself when I stopped leaning so heavily on Reggie's arm. Okay, maybe I was a little tipsy, but I wasn't yet slurring my words which meant I was on this side of full-blown inebriation.

I'm a good ol' Texas gal – a woman who could hold her own in a catfight *and* hold her liquor.

"So why are you so late?" I asked. "Afraid I'd outed you?"

"I outed myself, if you recall."

"Apples and oranges."

I puckered up and gave him my best raspberry, which ended up a little more slobbery and wet than I'd intended.

"I must admit though," Reggie began hesitantly. "I was feeling rather paranoid after our brief conversation last night."

I patted his arm. "How many times does a girl have to promise not to tell a soul?"

The dark stare penetrated mine as if he attempted to read my increasingly fuzzy mind. It took a few moments longer than usual before realization swept over me like a hail of bullets and cannon fire.

"Wait a sec." I stopped stumbling and faced him. "You don't think *I'm* the one blackmailing you, do you?"

"The thought did cross my mind throughout the long and labored night of tossing and turning," he admitted. Then he released a gut-wrenching sigh. "But the more I thought about it, the less I believed you capable of participating in such a twisted game, Victoria."

"Damn straight."

"Besides, you're more the type to storm into my shop and blurt out your findings in front of staff and customer alike."

A knowing grin stretched across his face and made me want to smack it right off him. But there was some truth to his statement. Tact and discretion were things my mother had tried to teach me.

And failed.

"I can vouch for Zeke too," I offered in reassurance as we took up our stroll again along the lighted path.

"Like I said last night, if we can't trust a Texas Ranger, then we're all in trouble."

I chuckled before sobering with a hiccup and a not-so-suppressed burp. Another reason I didn't care for champagne? Too many bubbles made for potential embarrassment.

Belching in public may work in certain European settings, but Americans tended to frown on the unladylike practice. It's one area in which my mom and I tend to agree.

"So this blackmail," I began. "The letter arrived a few weeks ago?"

"Letters," Reggie clarified, drawing out the 's'.

"Can I see them?"

"They're not something I keep on my person. There's the possibility I'll lose them or forget to remove them from pockets before having Han take my laundry to the cleaners."

It definitely wouldn't help the situation if Reggie's

assistant got wind of scandal. The rest of the staff would hear about it within five minutes.

Han was a likeable guy, but he could sure talk the hooves off a horse when he got going.

"When we return to Dallas though, I'll want to look at them."

Reggie hung his head with a long, drawn-out and exaggerated sigh this time.

Divas.

"Hey," I said, "you've asked for my help. This is me helping."

"Alright. Just remember not to breathe a word of this in a text, email, or voicemail message."

"Paranoid are we?"

"Don't I have reason to be?"

"You got me there," I admitted. "So the focus of the letters is primarily on revealing your past?"

Reggie nodded.

"There's nothing in them about the present fact that you're..." I glanced around before leaning in closer to whisper. "...not really gay?"

This time Reggie shook his head. "Nothing in that regard."

"Does anyone know about your lady friend?"

"I haven't told a soul," he offered, signing a cross over his heart. "And all correspondence I do is from my home computer or phone."

"You still have a landline?" I asked incredulous.

"Just because something gets old doesn't mean it has lost its usefulness," Reggie quipped with a wave of his hand.

I wiggled my brows. "Are we talking about technology or the human condition here?"

"Don't get tawdry with your elders, young lady,"

Reggie said, channeling my mom. "But yes."

I wasn't even going to touch that answerless answer. "Have you revealed anything about your history to this new *friend* of yours?"

Reggie sobered in an instant. "No."

"So that makes it more likely the culprit is someone from your past," I mused as the path steered us toward the fountain.

Reggie stiffened beside me as another voice called out.

"Vicki!"

Nick's barely clad physique rushed around the corner of the limestone church and stopped when he saw Reggie and I together.

"What's all this then, luv?"

"Nick, I...um...this is my good friend Reg...Reginald von Braun," I stuttered.

Not sure why I felt like the kid caught with her hand in the cookie jar after the pawing and petting I'd witnessed in front of the camera earlier.

"Your interior designer?" Nick asked, giving Reggie the once over.

I mentally slapped my forehead. Shoulda given Reggie's real name instead of the one of his public persona. Well, I guess Reggie's real name now *was* Reginald after having it legally changed, but I still preferred his real, real name.

You know what I mean.

Reggie dropped my arm and fell right into character with a glance of his own up and down Nick's frame before ending with a purse of lips. "At your service, darling. Does Nick need a redesign too, or shall Reginald help vith something a little more personal, no?"

The come hither response didn't seem to faze Nick.

Guess he'd been hit on one too many times in the fashion industry for it to affect him anymore.

"I really like what you did with Vicki's place," Nick said. "My apartment could use your expertise."

Personally, I liked Nick's industrial loft style. But I wasn't about to deny a friend additional business.

'Specially when he could use the distraction.

Reggie drew out his card and fluttered it along Nick's pecs as he sidled in closer. "Just give Reginald a call vhen you return to town, yes? See vat ve can cook up in zee oven."

"I'll do that," Nick acknowledged, glancing at me with a grin.

"I'll be seeing you, *mein liebchen*. *Ciao*," Reggie called over his shoulder before sauntering off with a marked jiggle of hips.

"I think that was for your benefit," I said, pointing at Reggie's retreating butt.

"Hmm," Nick murmured, watching a little too long for my comfort. "What's he doing here?"

"Visiting a friend."

"Someone besides you?"

I patted smooth and freshly powdered pecs. "Jealousy doesn't become you, Nick."

"There's nothing there for me to be jealous of, luv," he said with a chuckle.

If he only knew.

CHAPTER EIGHT

I've heard it said a trip together is the best measurement of a relationship. This one sucked river water more than all the fish in San Antone's canal.

Nick slept very little on our trip. Which meant instead of him working most of the night and sleeping during the day while I traipsed about San Antonio, we'd spent almost every moment in each other's company for the past seventy-two hours.

That's three whole days, folks.

I was seriously working up an aneurysm.

While Nick was great in bed – I mean really, really great – little else positive could be said about his abilities.

Nocturnal or otherwise.

Conversation lacked in every way imaginable. If it didn't have anything to do with fashion, fashion designers, or amorous activities, Nick was like an airheaded walking stiff.

Pun intended.

No matter how good Nick was in the sack, it took more than sex to keep a relationship afloat.

Whoa! Did I just say that? Maybe I was finally growing

up after all.

Don't bet on it.

For the majority of the drive home, I'd drifted between sleep and feigning sleep to avoid listening to Nick flap his yap.

Before the Jag had come to a complete stop in front of my apartment building, I flicked open the passenger side door and grabbed my suitcase from the backseat in one smooth move. The transmission about ground into a loose collection of nuts and bolts in a rock polisher when Nick shoved the sleek vehicle into park while still rolling.

"Thanks, Nick. Had fun and all, but I've gotta get ready for work. Call me!"

Almost wished I hadn't added that last part. It was like throwing fuel onto a dying flame, his face lighting up from distraction to renewed hope in our undying love.

Just kill me now.

Probably not the best thought to have, considering I'd almost met that fate mere weeks ago. But if I didn't get away from the lovemaking machine pronto, I might be tempted to make that thought a reality.

Thus I raced up the stairs into the sanctuary of my place as fast as possible, slamming the door shut with a sigh, and scooping up Slinky for a welcome home snuggle.

Janine had left a note on the fridge, outlining in agonizing detail Slinky's care the last few days. The chart notated the time fed twice a day, the measurement and type of food provided – wet or dry – and a checkmark for scooping the litter once per day.

All this, in addition to how long she'd hung out playing with the critter and his apparent mood, as if she was some sort of feline whisperer.

See? This is why my best friend made such a great

doctoral candidate. She was anal and unashamed.

I plopped down on my sofa and stretched out with the cat on my chest. Then I typed a message to Janine, informing her I was home, before setting the alarm on my phone.

A couple hours before I had to make my way to the bar meant a thorough nap was on the menu before I made any rash decisions concerning Nick. Perhaps everything would work out in the long run once I gained a little restorative perspective.

Yeah, I didn't think so either.

So with that happy thought, I turned off the phone alarm and sat up, much to Slinky's frustration. How could I sleep with the chaotic thoughts rumbling through my head? Nick was a distraction I simply didn't need right now, especially with Reggie's blackmail problem churning in my gut.

The last time I'd helped a friend, it almost hadn't ended so well for little ol' me. Who did I think I was to be dipping my toe into another person's business? Wasn't like I was a private eye. Nancy Drew anyone?

Hmm. There was only one other person besides Zeke I could talk to without giving away my offensive playbook.

Not that I had much to go on yet anyway. The idea of finding a blackmailer was just way different than tracking down a murderer. But it'd be safer for my carcass in the long run, that's for sure.

Guess instead of a nap, it was time for Nancy Drew to go see Detective Dingbat.

Detective Horace Duncan and I have a love-hate relationship.

He loves to hate my interference when it comes to his investigations. I hate the love he shows my God-given assets.

Namely my boobs.

We'd had the distinct displeasure of working together after Bobby's wife's death.

Okay, *working together* wasn't quite an accurate depiction of what transpired. In actuality, he'd caught me sneaking around inside Bobby's house and threatened to arrest me. If it hadn't been for Zeke, I'd have served one to life for breaking and entering.

Okay, maybe that was a bit of an exaggeration. I'd had Bobby's permission to be there. Even knew where to find the spare key.

'Course I didn't realize being an active crime scene usurped homeowner consent. 'Specially when said homeowner was the prime suspect at the time.

The other reason I didn't trust Duncan was the teeny tiny fact he'd tried to lay blame on me for killing Bobby's wife. Something to do with phantom texts I hadn't sent. Then there was that pesky police report from our involvement when I was fifteen, which had made the dingbat detective think there was a plot afoot between old lovers.

Thank God Reggie's blackmail situation didn't involve a homicide. Therefore, asking Duncan a few simple questions couldn't be misconstrued as interference this time. Therefore, any threats to throw me in jail would be about as empty as a natural blond.

Oops. Apologies to my best friend.

Even for a supposedly busy homicide detective, I wasn't surprised to see Duncan firmly ensconced behind his desk when I stuck my mug into his sector, busily pecking away on his keyboard like a starving woodpecker.

Duncan's waxy dome gleamed with perspiration, even with the air conditioning blasting out blessed cool air. Maybe typing was his workout *du jour*.

I sauntered up in my daisy dukes and plopped onto the corner of his desk with my newest pair of Tony Lamas dangling in full view. The tapping stopped as Duncan checked out the latest morsel occupying his desk.

And I ain't talking donuts.

It's a firmly established fact that God made men visual creatures. I had no qualms about using my feminine wiles – or in this case, freshly shaven legs – to full advantage when the need called for it.

Regardless of how many showers I'd need after enduring Detective Dingbat's mental undressing.

His perusal finally made it up to my face. "If it ain't Nancy Drew. Don't tell me you've found another dead body."

"I've never *found* a dead body," I retorted. "I almost *became* one."

"Minor detail."

"Not to me."

"Which brings us to the question of why you're interrupting my busy afternoon and preventing me from going home before midnight."

I made a pointed effort of glancing around his desk at the various piles of paperwork, a few greasy sandwich wrappers and empty coffee cups thrown in for good measure. I half expected to see the corner of a pastry box sticking out from among the debris.

"Looks more like you're attempting to write the next bestselling crime thriller."

That got me an exasperated *humph*. "Not too far off.

With all the CYA necessary these days, more than half the job anymore is writing reports."

"That must suck."

"By the fathoms," he admitted, spinning his chair around to face me. "Which brings us back around to why you're here. Doing more *legwork* for the Ranger Corps?"

"Ha-ha, no," I quipped. "Blackmail."

"What'd Zeke do this time for you to threaten him with blackmail?"

"Nothing. I'm talking me."

A smart-alecky retort died on his lips. "Hold on a minute. Someone had the audacity to blackmail *you*?"

I snorted. "Like I have anything worth blackmailing for."

The grimy gaze took another whirl over me. "That's not what I hear."

My vision narrowed as I offered up my best evil eye, which probably came across more like trying to stifle a fart or something.

Sounded like the church crowd weren't the only ones who liked to gossip and rumor-monger when given the opportunity.

"For now, let's talk hypotheticals."

I had every intention of keeping my big mouth shut when it came to the specifics of Reggie's situation. I had a promise to keep, after all.

Duncan spun back around toward his computer. "Well *not* hypothetically speaking, this is homicide. If you want to talk to someone about blackmail, you'll need to start with the robbery unit."

"Don't you all go through the same stuff at the academy?"

"Yes, but..."

"Then you've gone through some basic training about blackmail, right?"

That earned me a grumble with a few choice words thrown in not fit for feminine ears.

I pressed my advantage. "Haven't you had some homicide cases that involved blackmail or extortion?"

"Look, Nancy Drew," Duncan said, whirling his chair around again. "I've got things to do, and they don't have anything to do with blackmail...yet."

"Just answer one question."

"No."

I recrossed my legs to better advantage. "Please?"

Duncan sucked in a breath before huffing out like a deflating balloon. "Okay, one."

I leaned forward, catching a brief glimpse of a familiar name on the detective's computer screen before he caught me and turned it away from my line of vision.

I filed it away for later. "Why would one person attempt to blackmail another?"

"Any number of reasons. Most common would be to cover up a sexual indiscretion, drug use, criminal business practices..."

"I'm talking the blackmail*er* not the blackmail*ee*," I clarified.

"That's easy," Duncan said without missing a beat. "Either the blackmailer is desperate for money or they want revenge."

That little tidbit gave me a more concrete place to start.

Now if the letters from Reggie's blackmailer offered a hint as to his or her reasoning, we'd be able to wrap this little speedbump up and put it in the rearview window before the weekend.

We could do that, right?

Nah, I didn't think so either.

Ever since Bud ate a bullet, it'd been just me and Grady on Wednesday nights.

Though last week had shown that our camaraderie contained flickering signs of life, it was doubtful things would ever be the same between us. After all, it wasn't every day you discovered your boss was an undercover Fed.

'Course my uncomfortableness might also have something to do with this thing called a guilty conscience for thinking Grady was a drug dealer and a killer. Just for a sec though.

Honest.

As I bent over to grab a couple of cold brews from the refrigerated case, I felt rather than heard his approach over the thrum of music. Thigh brushed my butt as I stood and looked into warm chocolate depths.

I popped off the bottle tops with a satisfying spit and hiss. The edge of Grady's mustache tilted as he took them from me.

"I'll deliver those," he said.

His husky voice rumbled through me and touched me all the way down to my…

Toes?

Odd. Grady's sexy voice used to touch me in a whole different area. Somewhere north of my knees and south of my waistline.

Maybe my trip with Nick had satiated me *too* much. And numbed my brain.

"The couple at that table over there," I offered.

As the boss sauntered away to deliver libations, a familiar group walked in and sat down along the bar.

I relaxed with a grin. "Hey, it's my favorite trio. Things One, Two, and Three."

Cornflower-blue eyes beneath flattened amber hair widened. "What happened to Radioman?"

"Oh sorry, Things One and Two and *Radioman*," I said with a wink.

"That's better," Radioman responded, offering up a wide smile that made my legs go all noodley as I slid a bottle of Sam Adams his way.

Satiated too much? Let me rethink that for a sec.

"Which Thing am I?" the dark-headed lawyer asked. "One or Two?"

Their balding banker buddy just snorted derisively and thumbed Radioman. "Why does he get a cool nickname while we're relegated to a stupid Dr. Seuss moniker?"

"Because." I bat my lashes. "Radioman comes to see me more often."

"Yeah?" Banker Boy challenged. "Well unlike him, we both have *real* jobs."

"I don't know what you're talking about," the lawyer challenged, taking the scotch straight from my hands and throwing it back like a shot, ice and all. "I get to spend my days arguing with people."

"And you like that shit?" Banker Boy asked.

"You forget, I come from Italian roots. Other people pay me to do what comes naturally." He held up the empty glass. "Can I get another one?"

"Italian, huh?" I asked intrigued, sliding the double Jack and Coke toward the banker before pouring another scotch for my lawyer pal.

"With a little Scots and Irish thrown in somewhere along the line. But until you come up with a cooler name than Thing One or Two, how about calling me Seth?"

"Nice to officially meet you, Seth." I grasped his outstretched hand, experiencing a tingle up my arm. "So how did you decide to become a lawyer?"

"A lawyer is like a Marine – the few, the proud."

"More like the blowhard, the cocky," Radioman offered with a grin. "The one who likes to hear himself talk and talk…"

"This coming from the guy who gets paid to blather on the radio," I interrupted with a thumb directed his way and received a sultry wink in return.

Definitely not satiated.

"Where do you get that lawyers are few?" Banker Boy asked. "Colleges are spitting out so many lawyers every year, I think the average in the United States is like one for every seven hundred people…men, women, *and* children included."

"That's a lot of blather," I said, joining them for a round with three fingers of Jack.

"That may be true," Seth acknowledged. "But ask yourself one question." Dark eyes narrowed. "How many of them are actually *practicing*?"

"Touché," I cried, clinking my shot glass against Seth's. "Our Italian friend just won another argument."

"Touché is French," the attorney corrected. "Not Italian."

"Work with me here. I'm rooting for your team."

The *practicing* attorney stood and took a bow to applause from more than his friends. Humor – and a bit of interest – gleamed in his eyes.

As the ruckus died down, I made my way down the bar to take care of other patrons while Banker Boy stepped away to take a phone call. Not sure he'd like it if I called him that aloud. The moniker for Radioman had come so effortlessly upon meeting the Three Musketeers.

The others were gonna require a bit more hitch in my gray matter's giddyup.

Not like I had any more room in there, what with worrying over Reggie. He'd had years to practice the role he played so effortlessly before the public, and neither the past nor the present-day façade changed the way I saw him.

Reggie would always be a good friend because he was a good man.

So why had someone resorted to blackmailing him?

The *why* was obvious.

If my experience of humanity's ability to hold a grudge was any indicator, then Reggie's juvie record getting out portended an approaching storm of devastating proportions. His lucrative design business would crash and burn faster than a pileup at NASCAR.

The *who* remained the biggest question.

It had to be someone with ties either to Reggie's past or someone who had access to those criminal records.

Zeke again came to mind, but I quickly discounted the notion. The Ranger might be a lying, cheating bastard when it came to fidelity among the female persuasion, but he took his work-related duties quite seriously. No way would he ever stoop so low as to sully the Ranger code.

And it wasn't like he needed the money. The family ranch kept the Taylors sitting pretty for the cowpoke clan. Zeke would probably inherit that sprawling spread someday.

So scratch one Zeke Taylor from the list of suspects.

That left the new girlfriend, a nosy client, or someone from Reggie's past who'd put two-and-two together and gotten my friend in their sights. I needed to touch base with Reggie to find out exactly *when* this had all started, *how* this had all started, and to get my hands on the blackmail notes.

One thing I'd learned when last helping out a friend? No one was safe from suspicion, which meant everyone was a suspect.

That included my folks.

With my dad behind mom's credit card bill, I could definitely see the sperm donor using blackmail as a tool to gain leverage over someone. After all, he'd proven long ago he had no qualms about seeing how low he could go.

And I had the photographic evidence dangling over his head to prove it.

Wait a sec. Did that make me a blackmailer too?

Don't answer that.

CHAPTER NINE

The hold Han had placed me on extended past five minutes, so I took another moment to refill my coffee cup.

Again.

Gray matter swirling over Reggie's predicament, I'd awakened much earlier than anticipated this morning.

Meaning someone was about to be served up on toast.

As a bartender, I'm late to bed and late to rise. If I see anything before ten o'clock in the morning, bitchy mode kicks into play. There've been many a man on the receiving end of my too-early-morning wrath.

Unfortunately for him, today's pâté preparation was gonna be Reggie's assistant.

When he finally found the time to return, I thought my eyeballs were gonna pop right out of my head from the pressure buildup.

"I'm sorry, Miss Bohanan," Han responded in his nasal tone. "But Reginald still isn't answering his phone."

"Well, when do you expect him to return from his appointment?" I huffed in my best debutante demonstration.

"Oh, you know Reginald. He returns when he's ready. Perhaps around lunchtime?"

"Doesn't he have other appointments today?"

"Yes, but he doesn't always return to the studio between them. Thursdays he's usually out making sure all projects are on track before the weekend," Han continued, his voice dropping to a whine. "Those visits don't include me."

Sucked to be him. But I didn't have time to find a violin and sympathize with the help.

I took a deep breath and tried again. "Can you at least leave a message for him and ask Reggie to call me ASAP?"

Something in my voice must've said *desperate*. Han's voice ticked up with a measure of concern – or was that excitement?

"Is there a problem with your remodel? Perhaps I could come by and consult with you."

"No, everything's fine with the remodel."

Then why was I calling? What excuse could I offer that wouldn't give anyone the impression I needed to talk to Reggie about anything other than business?

"Uh...it's just that I'd like to talk with him about...pillows," I faltered before jumping in with both feet. "Yes, I was thinking about adding a few more decorative pillows for when my bedroom furniture arrives."

Mom was a big fan of throw pillows as an easy fix to change up the seasonal décor throughout the mansion. Pillows on the sofa. Pillows on the chairs. In the window seat.

Mounds of puffy poofiness across the beds. Pillows billowing from every nook, cranny, and crevice. Pillows everywhere you looked.

I'd really come to hate pillows over the years.

Thank God Reggie had gone easy on them when redecorating my place. Thus far, I'd only counted two in the window seat and two on the couch, as long as you didn't count the two on my bed.

Those were for actual functional folicking and not mere festooning.

Han's voice fairly dripped with longing. "I tried to tell Reginald we were going too light on them around your apartment."

"It's just that…"

"I have all of the swatches here, so all you have to do is tell me which ones to order. Or did you want to add some additional colors? Patterns? Maybe some floral to offset the stripes."

Florals? Oh, the horror!

"Just have Reggie call me when he touches base," I instructed.

Disappointment echoed through the connection. "I will do so, Miss Bohanan."

I hung up as fast as I could then set a fresh pot of coffee brewing and jumped in the shower. I'd barely wrung the water from my long, ebony hair when a *thwunk* thudded through my apartment.

That new door was gonna destroy plenty of knuckles. Might need to check with Jimmy-the-Super about wiring up a doorbell or something.

A quick wrap-up then I dragged the digit damaging door open to a loud and boisterous greeting.

"*Mein liebchen!*" Reggie cried and barreled into me with a hug before pulling back and giving me the once over. "Victoria could turn a man with one glance in that outfit, no?"

"Cut the act, Reggie." I shut the door. "It doesn't work on me anymore, remember?"

He slid aside enough for me to take in skintight red leather pants and a matching bolero jacket.

"Blame it on the clothes," Reggie said in a deeper voice sans accent. "They help set the mood."

"And the scene," I replied, taking in the fluorescent orange and pink silk shirt cascading with ruffles. "Momma's gonna need sunglasses with you in that getup."

"The one nice thing about this persona," he said with a flounce. "Getting dressed in the mornings can be a real riot. The fashions are what I'll miss most when I retire."

His gaze fell to the notepad on the coffee table where I'd spent the better part of last night – more like early this morning – making notes.

A few moments was all he needed to plop on the couch and scan the list of potential suspects. "Your mother?"

I sat down beside him, grabbed the notepad and picked up a pen. "One thing I've learned the hard way is that anyone…even those closest to you…can be a suspect."

"Frankly, my dear, I'd sooner suspect you than your mother." With typical Reggie flourish, he snatched the pen from my fingers and summarily crossed off *Bohanan* from the list. "She is not capable of such deceitfulness."

"But you don't know my dad," I countered. "The *real* side of my dad. He'd skin you alive if it made him a buck or two."

"All highly successful businessmen have their dark side."

"Oh yeah, Yoda? For the sperm donor, it's not a side but a feature."

"Well, I won't have suspicion directed toward your family. It's ridiculous."

"Fine." I pinched the revolving pen and made a show of thoroughly scratching the family name from the list. "Happy?"

"Much."

I sure as hell wasn't ready to scratch the sperm donor from my mental list. As far as I was concerned, he'd take top honors in every category at the Evil Villain awards ceremonies.

The winner of *Best Dad* goes to Frank Bohanan in the categories of *How to Manipulate to Get Your Way*, *How to Torment Your Family*, *How to Blame Your Daughter for Everything Wrong in Your Life*, and my personal favorite *How to Use the Church to Discover Your Next Hook-up*.

Remember that photographic evidence I mentioned? The photos I'd discovered in the Galveston vacation home were safely tucked away in a place only Janine and I knew about.

Talk about your blackmail.

In my defense, I'd never once asked for money.

Unlike Reggie's predicament.

"Did you bring the letters?"

Reggie nodded and reached into The Bag.

You know how most businessmen carry briefcases? Well, interior designers carry enormous totes that yawn open for miles, revealing like a magician's hat color swatches, fabric sample rings, hardwood and tile flooring options, photos, sketchpads, folios and files.

The one time I'd suggested loading it all into a laptop to lug around easier, you'd think I'd suggested scrapping scripture or something.

The current favorite was a huge Prada tote that probably cost upward of eight-thousand dollars and looked like it could hold information on at least half the Dallas population. Even with all the crap in the way, Reggie was still able to reach right in and pull out two letters without having to dump and sort through the contents.

Can you say *organized*?

"Here," he said, handing over the letters. "And before you ask, no. I don't recognize the handwriting."

I gingerly held the envelopes. "Maybe we should wear gloves so we don't disturb the fingerprint evidence."

Zeke would give me a hearty handshake for thinking of that. Then he'd smack us upside the head for handling the paper first.

Reggie stared at me as if I'd sprouted antennae from my head and my skin had turned a vile shade of green.

"And *why* would we need to worry about fingerprints?"

"To help lead us to the culprit, silly."

"And *how* are we going to get fingerprints? We'd have to turn these over to the police, who would then open an investigation, about which the scandal would make headlines, which would bring about the ruin of my life...which is what the blackmailer is threatening to do anyway!"

"Gee," I muttered after that long soliloquy. "Why didn't I think of that?"

"Now who's silly?"

Made me want to slap myself right about then. Hanging out with Nick so much had definitely dulled my gray matter.

See ladies? This goes to show you that even good sex isn't enough to justify staying with someone who brings you down instead of up.

Mentally, that is.

I opened the earlier postmarked letter then the second and studied the calligraphy. Such handwriting style wasn't widely known these days but still taught in cotillion circles.

Both were the same heavyweight linen paper. Not cheap. Dallas postmark, so the culprit was someone local. Or at least someone who had access to the local postal service.

That didn't mean the San Antonio sweetheart was off the hook. Might simply be the blackmailer's clever ploy to focus more on the local populace to throw us off their trail.

The first letter referenced the demand for a hundred grand or they would release Reggie's juvie record to the media. The enclosed copies of the New York court documents showed the legal name change accompanied by the design school admissions forms, neatly tying the pieces of Reggie's past and present together.

After my experience obtaining copies of Amy Vernet's vital statistics records, that meant the blackmailer had to either work in that office or knew someone who did.

But then that threw a wrench into my supposition the culprit was local.

Perhaps they had friends in or near New York willing to help in this scheme.

Or knew someone in the legal profession who could work the system.

Then where did that leave me?

Yeah, I was gonna get a monster headache if I didn't rein the brain in. For now, I'd keep it simple and work from the local angle.

The second letter included reference to a post office box key and the location of said box for the cash delivery. The envelope had a faint outline puckering the corner, but no key.

"Okay," I said, after studying the letters and settling in for the long haul. "These appear to have been written by the same individual. First one postmarked four weeks ago. The second two weeks after. Do you have the post office box key this one mentions?"

"Yes," Reggie affirmed, producing the key from The

Bag. "I've spent the last few weeks going from bank branch to branch to withdraw the cash needed. They wouldn't let me do it in one lump sum without some document reporting the withdrawal to the Feds."

"The dreaded currency transaction report."

"You know about them?"

I nodded. "Anytime my dad dealt with a bunch of cash in hand, he'd spend the next week grousing and grumbling about how the government should keep their nose out of taxpayers business."

Reggie's eyes widened. "Do you think someone was blackmailing him?"

"Probably just the opposite."

Wisely, Reggie left that alone.

I pointed to the second letter. "It says here you were supposed to leave the cash in the box this past Tuesday by midnight. Did you already do that?"

"Yes, shortly after returning from San Antonio. Ever since I've watched the comings and goings to see if I recognize anyone. But I can't keep doing it. I still have a business to run…for now."

"No one you recognized then?"

Reggie shook his head. "Ridiculous to do that, considering most of my clients have staff who run their errands. But I did go inside this morning before coming over here and the bag of cash was still there."

"Whoever it is may wait awhile before collecting," I mused aloud. "Wait for the furor to die down."

"Or they know my car," Reggie supplied.

I picked up the notepad and scanned the list I'd started. "Okay, so who among your clientele have been unhappy with your work?"

Reggie waved his hand about and slipped back into the

accent. "Not a soul vould dare be displeased vith a Reginald von Braun design."

"Still, I'll need a client list."

"Proprietary information, darling."

"You want my help?"

He snorted, returning to full-on diva mode. "I'll get you a print-out. I can't have any of the staff discovering an email, and the list is too long to text."

"That's fine. What about the girlfriend in San Antonio?" I asked, returning to the local versus non-local conundrum like a hamster racing in the wheel to nowhere.

"We've only shared the most basic personal information when we started talking on the phone. That would've been about two weeks ago, *after* the letters arrived."

"Still..." I tapped the pen against my lips in thought. "The timing of your meeting with her is interesting. I need a name and any history you have on her."

"There goes my private life," Reggie muttered.

I ignored him. "Then last, what can you tell me about your gang years."

A definable shudder passed over him, sending silk ruffles rippling like a butterfly emerging from a cocoon.

"I'd not thought about it for so long...until all of this started."

"What was the name of the group?" I asked, ready to detail every painful memory like a court reporter during a trial.

I hoped Reggie realized I wasn't trying to be pushy or bitchy on purpose. If we didn't go through this exercise, he just might find himself sitting in a courtroom for real.

"You do realize this is a dangerous line of questioning."

"But it's gotta be done," I urged. "Name that gang."

"Will you promise to treat this as a path of last resort?"

he begged.

"As all the cop shows say, a good investigator goes where the evidence leads. Gang name, please."

He met my pointed stare before relenting. "The Switchblades."

I flipped through the notepad and wrote on a fresh page. "Do you remember the leader's name?"

"Yeah." Reggie's voice dulled. "Switch."

"Switch from the Switchblades?" I had to work hard to stifle a chuckle.

"It was a local group. He kinda started it."

"Did you ever know his real name?"

He scrunched his forehead in concentration. Lips pursed before the light of remembrance widened his eyes. "Tomas. Tomas Ricardo."

"Two first names?" I questioned. "Seems a bit odd. Are you sure that's his real name and not another cover?"

"Oh, yes. I remember stories about him being teased as a little kid. That's why he created the gang when he got older, to give himself a cool nickname."

I raised a brow.

"Well, it was cool back then."

This time I didn't bother trying to hide my laugh. "When would being called *Switch* ever be considered cool?"

"Because that was his signature. He always took a switchblade to his enemies."

"You mean to warn them off?"

"No." Reggie's tone sobered to a whisper, as if fearful of being overheard. "To gut them."

Oh, what fresh hell was this?

CHAPTER TEN

If there's one thing Mom and I agree on – besides the spending power of her credit card – it's that homemade chocolate chip cookies heals all woes.

Scraped knees in pre-school? Chocolate chip cookies.

Boy troubles in middle school? Chocolate chip cookies.

Rescuing my apartment from a tornadic terror? Fresh-from-the-oven cookies saved the day once again.

Outside the Oreo stash, I was pleased to discover tubes of cookie dough in my new freezer. Figuring out the new all-digital oven was the only thing standing in the way of chocolatey satisfaction with a milk mustache chaser.

I finally prevailed and dragged a full plate of not-too-scorched confections downstairs to apartment one-oh-two, the home of my would-be and wounded savior. Sanctuary to the only other person I knew with gang ties.

Jimmy-the-Super and I had an avoid-at-all-costs relationship, meaning I paid my rent on time and hightailed it out of there during the bi-annual bug hose down. Gave him no reason to bother me in the interim, mainly because he kinda creeped me out with all the scars and tattoos.

But after his attempt to keep my sorry carcass from

being thrown off the roof – and taking a bullet in the process – I realized Jimmy had a heroic streak. Therefore, he might also have a softer side I'd yet to see through the hulking three hundred pounds of bulk and muscle.

Plus, I was pretty sure there were some dead gang skeletons in his closet that might put me on the right path in my quest to help Reggie.

But when Jimmy opened his apartment door with his arm in a sling, that creepy skull tattoo on his bicep winked in the shadow and light between the thresholds and brought my prior fears to the forefront.

I smiled – or at least tried to – and held up the cookie plate to the brawny man.

"Welcome home?" I squeaked.

Eloquent I wasn't. At least not around Jimmy.

There was something about the tattoos and the jagged scars on his face that had me swigging a big shot of discomfort and a chaser of flat-out fright.

Or perhaps my unease stemmed from the fact that the guy always seemed too knowledgeable concerning my comings and goings. Still, he deserved thanks for coming to my aid that night.

Even though it didn't turn out so well for him.

Jimmy grunted like a good Texan. "Been home for a month, unlike you and that cat."

What'd I tell you?

"Call this a thanks offering then, for saving my life."

That got me a hard stare. "I was little more than a distraction for all of two seconds."

He had a point. "Well then here's to those few seconds of distraction that kept me from becoming a pavement pancake."

The skull tattoo winked as he opened the door wider.

"You wanna come in?"

I gulped. Cross the threshold into the unknown? Enter the lion's den? But if I was gonna be useful to Reggie, those gang-related questions begged to be asked.

I stepped inside.

The apartment was surprisingly clean for a man. I mean, for a currently one-armed man.

It was a mirror image of what mine used to be – you know, that whole eighties theme. Furniture was older, but in good condition with decent slipcovers. The electronics were state-of-the art.

A bank of small, dust-free monitors took up most of the space on the corner desk. So that's how he knew so much about my activities. Cameras scanned the parking lot and each floor's main hall, providing Jimmy with more than a bird's-eye view of everything in and outside the building.

I unwrapped the plastic wrap from the cookies and set the plate on his coffee table, while Jimmy opened the fridge and grabbed a jug.

"Milk?" he asked.

"Uh...sure," I hesitated, wracking my brain to come up with more than small talk – and failed. "I like your place. It reminds me of what mine used to look like BB."

"BB?"

"Before Bombing."

I think the bulldog-like growl was supposed to be a chuckle. "Believe it or not, your remodel kinda lit a fire under the new landlord. Sounds like the whole place is gonna undergo a refresher."

Two words in those sentences caught my attention: *new* landlord and *refresher*.

Both portended an increase in rent, something I could ill afford with all the time off I'd been forced to take while recovering from injuries. Nearly two months later, I was still in catch-up mode with some of the bills.

And no, I wasn't about to ask for anymore assistance from my mom.

"Sounds expensive," I said.

Jimmy shrugged and handed over a glass before snagging another and sitting on the sofa before the cookie offering. "It's overdue, and so far there's been no talk of rent increases."

"That's good to hear."

"They're gonna start on the couple of empty apartments first then others as tenants move out."

He popped a cookie in his mouth and then grimaced. Picking up another one, he flipped it over to study the *slightly* burned underside. Jimmy tossed me a smirk before shoving the cookie in his mouth then took a careful drink of milk to mask the flavor char

A gourmet chef I will never be.

I tentatively picked up a morsel and nibbled the extra-crispy edge. "What about your apartment? Are they going to renovate it while you live here?"

A little drool dribbled at the edge of his mouth, caught quickly with a napkin. "Nah. They'll move me over to the empty one across the hall after renovatin' it."

"Well that's good. It'd suck to work here and not get to enjoy at least one of the perks."

I took a sip of milk. Nice and cold, perfect with a good chocolate chip cookie. Too bad mine strayed a bit from the *good* category.

Okay fine, they strayed more than a bit.

I gestured at his sling. "How long are you going to have to wear that thing?"

"Until the doc clears me. The bone is pretty well healed

by now."

I almost spewed milk. "Bone? What bone?"

"Think I was wearin' this from a little gunshot wound?"

"Well I..."

"When that asshole shot me, the bullet bounced off my collarbone. Doc had to bolt the shattered ends together with titanium and what amounts to crazy glue."

"Ouch. No one told me that."

"Like I said, it's pretty well healed, but the doc won't release me for anythin' other than light duty for a few more weeks. Might even order me to some punk-ass physical therapy."

With that attitude, I already felt sorry for whoever got assigned to his therapy.

"Do you need some help around here until then?" I smiled. "It's not like I owe you my life or anything."

"No thanks."

He returned the smile – a little lopsided – which brought me around to the real reason for my visit.

Okay, okay, I had an ulterior motive with the cookie reception after all. Jimmy's civility only lulled me into seeing him as almost human.

"So what happened here?" I asked, pointing toward the corner of my mouth. "Was it a gang fight or something?"

The smile dissipated. "Where did you get the idea I was in a gang?"

"Oh," I stammered. "I-I just assumed with the tattoos and all..."

"Tattoos are from a stint in the Army. The scars are courtesy of shrapnel from an IED in Iraq." He dabbed at his mouth again. "The Bell's palsy? I guess you could say that's from God."

Warmth flooded my face. And trust me if you haven't

figured it out yet, I don't blush easily. Much.

But once again, that dreaded foot-in-mouth disease had reared its ugly – er – heel?

"Sorry. I just assumed. But you know what they say about assumptions," I said, descending into full-blown babble mode. "I mean, how many people can say they have Bell's palsy anyway? I didn't mean anything by the gang reference."

"That's why I couldn't get a good bead on that guy who manhandled you without endangerin' you too. In the military if you can't properly sight your weapon in a shootout, you're a greater liability than an asset. It's why I got a medical discharge after multiple episodes."

That was the longest speech I'd ever heard the super make. Normally it was a couple of words. Better yet, a grunt.

"Will it ever go away?"

Jimmy shook his head. "Looks like I'm one of the lucky four percent. At least it hasn't permanently affected my taste buds though."

When he shoved two cookies in this time, I had my doubts about that last statement. Guess Jimmy had adjusted to the flavor of chocolate chip charcoal.

"So why're you askin' about gangs?" he asked around the crumb cascade.

"Well, I'm looking for someone."

"Who?"

"Some old gang leader in the area. Someone who goes by the name of Switch."

Jimmy gave me the once over as if determining whether I was a worthy opponent.

Don't think I made the cut.

"Let me tell you somethin'." He set down the glass of

milk a little too hard. "The last thing a girl like you should be doin' is tryin' to get in touch with that man. Believe me...he's already a little touched...in the head."

The last point he emphasized with a finger to the temple like a gun. I really could've gone without the reminder of my rooftop dalliance with Bud.

And hey, I was a bonafide woman, not just some *girl*.

That kinda twisted my catnip all sorts of wrong, and for a second I forgot who I was talking to. That lulled with civility thing came right around and bit me in the butt.

"I need to find out some information..."

"Then find it another way," Jimmy bellowed, standing straight up off the couch and marching toward the door without consideration for his healing collarbone, my ears, or those of the other tenants in the building. "Don't even consider that direction. If somethin' happened to you, your..." Jimmy stopped and his lips thinned into a hard line.

"My what?" I asked intrigued, lurching to my feet and following him toward the door.

"Just take my advice. Avoid gettin' involved in some gang turf war. You might find yourself at the wrong end of a switchblade...or worse!"

He slammed the apartment door in my face with a rattle guaranteed to wake the neighbors from their siestas.

So much for trying to be nice to the guy. I brushed the newfound camaraderie with Jimmy aside and started up the stairwell. It took all of trudging up one floor before it hit me.

If Jimmy had no gang ties, how did he know Switch?

CHAPTER ELEVEN

The semi-final round of the alcohol X-games kept the bar hopping all night long.

With me slinging out drinks in such rapid succession, I had no time for even a sip to wet my whistler. Or to stew on the conversation with Jimmy.

While keeping beer and the shot-of-the-night prepped and ready for Grady to hand out to game participants, I also had to serve observers sitting at the bar. We were in danger of draining every keg and bottle within a five-mile radius.

And keeping all the neighbors awake. The decibels increased throughout each heat until the roof threatened to tear right off like a direct hit from an EF-2 tornado.

When one of the final two contestants drunkenly stumbled out of his lane to fall headlong into a thirty-two triple D, we may've even registered somewhere on the Richter scale.

By closing time, I was ready to make an appointment to see an otolaryngologist. See, there's a reason why they go by the more simple term of ear, nose, and throat doctor. At this rate, I'd need hearing aids well before my thirtieth birthday.

Since Rochelle was now familiar with the rigors

associated with tending bar, I welcomed her assistance with clean-up and had her heading home within the closing hour. A final alcohol tally, and I carted the till to the boss.

Grady didn't even glance away from the bank of security monitors until I chucked the cash drawer on his desk with a clatter.

"Did good tonight," I said. "But we've got an emergency on our hands."

"Late for a date with the pretty boy?" Grady asked.

"No."

"Out of clean panties?"

"Grady!"

"Then what kind of emergency?" he asked, rewinding a post-closing view of patrons congregating in the parking lot.

I handed over the bottle count tally. "The tap is just about tapped out and spitting foam. And if we don't get a few more friends like Jack Daniels and Jim Beam in here pronto, there'll be a lot of crying going on tomorrow night."

"Can I assume the cryin' will be led by yours truly?"

"Are you kidding? I didn't have time to drink tonight."

Grady stopped what he was doing and turned the chair toward me with a squeak. I wanted to smack the mustache tilt right off his face.

And I don't mean with my mouth either, folks.

I think.

"Sit down, Vic."

Have you ever had a boss tell you to take a seat? From what I've heard, it rarely portended anything good. It put you on the defensive quicker than a possession change in the final seconds before halftime.

"Don't you dare fire me, Grady," came spurting from my diseased mouth before I could think straight. "I'll...I'll...sic my mother on you."

That sent the boss into a chortling belly laugh. "Why on earth would I fire ya?"

"Well, for one because you're afraid I'll spill the beans on your *other* job."

That shut him up right quick – for a second or two. "If you can avoid sharin' my secret when you're drunk, ya sure as hell can hold onto it when you're sober."

"Unless I wanted to blackmail you," I quipped, thinking again of Reggie's need for secrecy with his past.

Grady shook his head. "Ya ain't the type."

Unless it pertained to the sperm donor, but I wasn't about to open that bottle and pass it around the barrel. I kept those pictures safely tucked away less purely for insurance purposes.

"So then why've you been acting all weird around me these last few weeks?"

The squeaky chair released a full-on screech like an opening door in a horror movie when Grady slowly leaned back. "I'm not the one who's been actin' weird, Vic."

"Then what do you call all the tiptoeing around you've been doing lately? Avoiding flirting all the time or coming behind the bar with me? You've been staying cooped up in here so much too, and it's not just me who's noticed."

"Again, I ain't the one who's been tiptoein' or avoidin'," Grady declared. "And what I've been cooped up in here doing so much has to do with that *other* job, which is why I asked you to sit so I could pick your brain and get some insight."

The rebuttal ready to spew from my lips dissipated like the crowd after a missed last-minute two-point conversion.

"You're on a case involving the bar?" I asked.

"I'm always on a case. This one may or may not involve this guy."

Grady had stopped the surveillance frame on a grainy image of a couple of guys talking in the parking lot. I leaned in closer to get a better look at the group.

"Do ya recognize anyone?" Grady asked.

"I'm not sure, but that one there looks like…is it?" I focused on the thinning top of the head and the stiff bearing lodged in a suit. "I think it might be Banker Boy."

"Banker Boy?"

I shrugged. "Some of the regulars earn pet names."

Grady smirked. "I'd hate to think what pet name you've cooked up for me."

"You're not a customer."

"I'm your boss."

"Exactly. You have a title."

"Which is?"

"What else? The Boss."

"Catchy."

"I try."

That earned me a smirk before Grady got down to ATF business again. "What can you tell me about this Banker Boy?"

"Not much," I admitted.

"Impressions?"

"Of the Three Musketeers, he's the least likeable, though that may have more to do with the fact he's stingy with tips."

"What about his two friends?"

"They're good guys. The dark-headed one is a lawyer, and the other…"

"Yeah, we all know what you think of Radioman," Grady acknowledged with a grin.

I punched his arm and got another laugh for my trouble. "Don't know why I keep working for you."

"Hey, just a minute ago you were worried about gettin' fired."

"Well, we both know that won't happen anytime soon," I muttered, taking another hard look at the stilled screen image of Banker Boy.

The three guys surrounding him looked rough. Not the usual suspects he came in with.

Trust me, if Radioman had been within a hundred yards of the bar, my nether regions would've set off like a cell phone on vibrate.

I asked the question building in my brain. "Is this footage from tonight?"

"Yep."

"I don't remember seeing him here."

"Me neither, which is why this parkin' lot interaction caught my eye."

"It was rather busy, so it's possible we just missed him."

"Hmm," he murmured, sliding the till into the safe before resetting the cameras, then grabbing his Stetson and escorting me out of the office to set the alarms.

As we walked across the empty lot to our vehicles, Grady offered up a pat on the back just above my haunches. "You did good tonight, Vic."

"Are you talking with the clients or surveillance?" I asked, enjoying a little too much the warmth of his hand on my hip.

"Uh-huh."

Guess that was all the information he was willing to offer. For once in my life, I didn't push the issue.

We stopped off at my Vette, and Grady leaned on the hood while I fumbled for the keys.

"When Banker Boy comes in next," I started, "do you want me to do a little fishing?"

"No fishin', Vic. Just keep your eyes and ears open. This might be a situation where a couple of low-lifes were harassin' an innocent bystander."

I stopped fumbling in my purse for a half sec. "You don't really expect me to believe that, do you?"

"We're only blocks from the edge of gang territory, so anything's possible."

No mustache tilt. No slow, easy smile. The milk chocolate gaze hardened into obsidian disks. My boss let down the good-ol'-boy routine and revealed his undercover persona. It was a little frightening.

And kinda hot.

"Let me help, boss," I pleaded. "With a little alcohol, I can get any man to talk. A lot of alcohol, and I can tell you what his momma called him before he got out of diapers."

"I realize you're no wilting flower, and you've got good instincts. That's why I asked for your impression of this guy. But leave this alone and let the professionals handle the bad guys, sweetheart."

With that, he pushed away from the Vette and climbed into his black Dodge Ram, shining the bright lights atop the roll bar until I climbed into my car with first degree burns.

And not just on my skin.

First Jimmy had rained on my parade by telling me to avoid a gang leader who had to be about as old as dirt by now. Then Grady dressed me down for offering to get information from a patron who frequented the bar.

Pretty crappy of him, if you asked me. Wasn't like the boss hadn't asked for my *impressions* or anything.

I peeled out of the parking lot with the truck not far behind and made to head toward home.

After offering up a southern salute out my driver's side window, I turned onto the next street while Grady's Ram thundered through the light with a honk of acknowledgement. I waited for a couple of beats at the following stoplight before shooting a U.

When told to stay out of other people's business – or away from a crime and gang ridden area – most smart and intelligent individuals would do just that.

Perhaps I was buoyed by a sense of invincibility after escaping only slightly scathed the last time I'd helped out a friend. Maybe it was an unrequited death wish I carried.

The truth? I have a bit of a stubborn streak.

Well, and Grady had pissed me off.

The low-lifes of Dallas tended to congregate not too far from my home and work near the Historic West End. In the eighties, the area was reclaimed and revitalized into a hopping hangout for the yuppie crowd. Over time though, the pond scum gradually crept in unnoticed until a turf war broke out and drove more than a few businesses away.

Nowadays you could walk up one side of the street and be as safe from trampling as a daisy in the sun. But if you crossed to the other side, you were kinda on your own.

I only hoped I kept close enough to the edge of the dark side as I slowly drove down the one-way street. Streetlamps on this side of the road flickered yellow with a mere heartbeat of life.

This late at night – or early in the morning, take your pick – I prayed the area was like the majority of Dallas. After the bars closed and the drunks made their way home, things tended to quiet down pretty quick. Folks had to sleep sometime.

The thought stopped me short.

What did I hope to accomplish by cruising along a known gang hangout in the middle of the night? If I expected everyone to be asleep, then what, if any, information did I hope to discover about this Switch guy and if he knew about Reggie's current predicament?

Yeah, I'd obviously not had enough to drink at work.

Or maybe that stubbornness had gotten in the way of rational thought. It wasn't the first time. If history bore out, it wouldn't be the last time either. The old gray matter grew a little fuzzy on the reasons behind my reckoning.

Chain link fences surrounded most of the brick and stone structures, providing little protection with all of the yawning gashes big enough to drive a Smart car through.

Just as I was about to discard this doomed idea and turn around, a rumpled and dilapidated kid, no older than six and barely out of diapers, ran through my high beams and snuck through one of the fence openings.

I quickly parked along the street opposite a ramshackle automotive garage to catch my breath and killed the headlights. What the hell was I worried about, when a little kid ran full-bore *into* gang territory?

I throttled down and exited with my flashlight while locking down the Vette nice and tight. I may be dumb, but I'm not stupid.

Hey, I heard that!

The clatter of a broken bottle 'bout had me piddling in my panties. What if someone chased after the kid? I listened for the scuff and scuttle of racing feet.

Nothing.

I stepped to the alley and peeked around the cut chain link separating the buildings. A shine of the flashlight revealed the glimmer of glass, oily puddles, and scattered cigarette butts.

No movement. No nearby sounds. The kid must have found a hiding place or was long gone.

I sighed in relief and turned toward my car. My

flashlight beam highlighted the posse surrounding the Vette and glinted off their weapons.

If I didn't know any better, I'd swear those were switchblades.

CHAPTER TWELVE

The ragtag horde inched forward like a pack of wolves on the prowl.

I took a hesitant step backward into an oil-sheened puddle. So much for my new sandals.

Young pups glared from ravaged faces. I doubted any knew of the original leader of their pack, but that didn't stop me from asking the idiot question of the day.

"Is Switch around?"

Like a carefully choreographed scene from a bad horror flick, blades clicked open with a flash of metal.

Before I could gulp or squeak, the growl of engines and peel of tires echoed from the garage. Headlights blinded as trucks barreled to the scene of my crime of stupidity.

I wanted to drop to the pavement, curl into a ball, and kiss my ass goodbye when I realized I was the line of demarcation between rival gangs in a turf skirmish. I was about to become someone's bitch.

Or worse.

I firmly believed in God in those seconds. I was willing to walk on coals. Kneel and cross myself. Dance in the aisles holding snakes. Chatter in an indistinguishable tongue. I'd do pretty much anything but drink poison to cover all denominational bases in order to secure my rapidly approaching eternal reward.

Hell – I mean heck – I'd even confess to everyone within hearing range to the time I blamed Lorraine Padget for putting liquid laundry soap in the church baptistery, effectively shutting down any and all baptismal activities for a month.

Heat swarmed my legs as engine warmth revealed how close the trucks had pulled in behind me. The metallic click and clatter of chambering rounds resounded too close for my bodily comfort.

So I did what any good ol' Texas gal who'd recently visited the Alamo would do. I held my ground against unbeatable odds.

Or perhaps it was more fear had frozen my feet where I stood.

Come on, folks. Let's not quibble over minor details when I was about to become Swiss cheese on someone's sandwich.

A voice from behind yelled through an intercom. "Disperse or we'll open fire!"

Disperse? What gang leader used a word like *disperse*? Did their order include me? I'd be glad to disperse. That is, if I was capable of shuffling over to my Vette.

Until my next thought 'bout had me piddling in my panties.

What if instead of a simple gang at my rear I'd become fodder for a group who kidnapped hapless and helpless females to sell into prostitution rings? What if instead of stewing about black*mail*, I was about to be sold into the black *market* and pawned off on some ancient, wealthy sheik to spend the rest of my life doing the Timbuk two-step?

Okay, okay. So I'm neither hapless nor helpless. Most of the time.

Present circumstances excluded.

Grumbles rumbled through the guys in front of me, and a smattering of anger reflected across the headlighted faces, accompanied by a sprinkling of fright on others. Those *others*? Looked like they were only a few years out of diapers.

And like me, might need another one real soon.

"You have ten seconds," the voice hollered again.

Those holding the switchblades didn't stick around for a fight with the rival gang about to take me prisoner.

The rival gang who had a loudspeaker system mounted on one of their vehicles.

A loudspeaker system with a slightly warbled yet – now that I thought of it – somewhat familiar voice.

The drawn-out creak of an opening door finally had me turning around to face my fears head on. As he stepped to the side of the headlight glare and my eyes adjusted, I realized I'd truly stepped knee deep into the crapper.

I was about to be someone's bitch alright.

Jaws clenched in anger as he ripped the riot gear helmet from his head. Daggers practically shot from his eyes and skewered me to the spot.

If I could've thought of anymore clichéd sayings, I'm sure they would've fit the look on Zeke's face.

His voice hissed through clenched teeth. "You'd better have a good explanation for what you're doing here, Vic."

Explanation? Yes.

How good it was would be something Zeke and I would debate until the second coming.

"Are you out of your mind?" Zeke yelled, leaping from his truck after we'd pulled our vehicles into the parking lot of my apartment building. "What the hell were you doing in that part of town?"

Instead of answering, I drove the Vette past his Kevlar-clad form and into the garage space before slamming down the door with a metallic rattle. When I turned around, his glare practically stabbed my carcass to the side of the garage.

Nothing he did would intimidate me after the scare I'd already had that night.

I think.

With a flick of my ponytail, I strode past and marched across the lot. His much longer stride made it easy for him to keep up.

"You grew up in your little ivory tower," Zeke fumed and fussed. "You can't fathom a time when your knight-in-shining-armor won't show up to rescue your sorry ass."

"You used to think my ass was less than sorry, if I remember correctly," I snarked, lengthening my stride until I was in danger of either breaking into a sprint or snapping my sandal straps. "And when did you start claiming knighthood status?"

"Someone's gotta do it, sweetheart."

The second sweetheart of the night. Zeke must've already gabbed to Grady.

"Check your armor at the door then, because from this angle there's no shine and plenty of chinks out of it."

"And whose fault is that?"

I slowed and tossed him a glare of my own. "And speaking of ivory towers, you didn't grow up so bad off yourself, Sherlock."

"At least I have half a brain to know where I don't belong…" Zeke checked his watch. "…at four A.M."

"Then what were *you* doing at that garage?" I challenged. "Getting a lube job?"

He blocked the main entrance. "Are you volunteering?"

"I meant for your truck, asshole." I fished around him for the door handle.

Zeke pressed his back against the thick glass door, folded his arms, and continued the stare down until he spoke in a more controlled tone.

"What were you doing in gang territory, Vic?"

"What were *you* doing in gang territory, Zeke Taylor?"

"My job."

"Which is?"

"A complete and utter shit-storm now, thanks to you."

"What'd I do?"

"What did you do?" he repeated.

Zeke stared up into the starry night as if seeking guidance from the great beyond in how to deal with a headstrong woman like me.

"How about unzipping our fly?" he continued. "How about exposing our undercover base of operation? How about setting back this investigation for God only knows how many months? Or years!?!"

I had the presence of mind to at least appear sheepish. "You were on a stakeout?"

"Something like that."

How could I have known I'd chosen the very spot where a Texas Ranger undercover operation was going down?

Okay, maybe I really was rather hapless. But don't you dare call me helpless, 'cause I'd have figured some way out of the mess I'd gotten myself into if Zeke and the Ranger posse hadn't ridden in to save the day.

Even with the sharp scent or ammonia following in my wake.

I sighed as if it killed me to have to admit something to the Ranger. "I was trying to get the lay of the area."

"Why?"

Another sigh to bide time and figure out how to approach this without giving Reggie away. "I needed some information."

"About?"

I shifted my purse to the other shoulder to garner even more time. When I'd mentioned Switch's name to Jimmy-the-Super, he'd reacted badly.

If I mentioned it to Zeke in his present state? Yeah, I might as well call the coroner to come clean up after the meltdown and resultant bloody explosion.

"I needed information on this old gang leader."

"Because?"

The leading questions were getting pretty tiring as the adrenaline rush from knives coming at me from the front and guns cocked at my rear coupled with a long night. All I wanted at that moment was a hot soak in the tub.

And a change of underwear.

"I'm trying to help a friend," I finally confessed.

That brought Zeke standing straight up to his lofty heights. "What's Bobby Vernet gotten himself into now?"

"Bobby?" Fists planted firmly on my hips. "I have other friends, you know."

"Yeah, but he's the only one who gets you into Nancy Drew mode."

"No, he's not."

"Yes, he is," Zeke shot back.

"For your information, this has nothing to do with Bobby."

He groaned and swiped a hand across his forehead. "For crying out...would you stop playing like you're some

PI and find a real career?"

Wait a minute. Here I was, being cooperative while receiving a tongue lashing from the Ranger, and now he was gonna denigrate my job? The job *he'd* recommended me for?

Oh, hell-to-the-no.

"For your information," I emphasized with a finger poke to his chest, stopped by a solid weave of Kevlar. "I have a real career."

"No you don't. You're only playing bartender babe to bide your time and tick off your parents."

I snorted. "Like you would know."

That got me glower, eyes red-rimmed with bags hanging beneath like he hadn't slept in days. The Ranger appeared more than beat in the ambient glow cast from the over-the-door security light.

"Actually, I would know."

"Well, knowing you is what made Grady even *consider* me for the position."

"I just never expected you'd make a long-term stint out of sloshing drinks, dancing on bar tops, and winning wet t-shirt nights," Zeke admitted.

"Employees can't participate in wet t-shirt contests."

"Doesn't stop you from winning them."

Score another one for the Ranger.

"Are you done yelling at me, 'cause I'd really like to get some sleep before sunrise."

"Wouldn't we all," he grumbled under his breath. "Just promise me you'll stop with whatever the hell it is you're doing and go back to being a bartender."

"But you just said I had no career tending bar."

When he sighed and rubbed his forehead this time, I succeeded in skirting around him into the apartment building. What I lacked in height next to the Ranger, I made up for in wiriness and speed.

As I jogged up the stairwell, I called over my shoulder. "Good night, Ranger Taylor."

"Leave this alone, Vic. I mean it."

"I know you do."

Knight-in-shining-armor or lack thereof, I had no intention of leaving Reggie to swing in the wind. But it'd behoove me to explore others on the blackmail culprit list before venturing out of my jurisdiction again.

Regardless of what Zeke thought, Momma didn't raise no fool.

You can stop laughing now.

CHAPTER THIRTEEN

The idiot behind me in the champagne Lexus honked his horn one too many times, thereby justifying opening the Vette's sunroof to the August oven and poking up my middle finger in a southern salute.

Four lanes of traffic had screeched to a standstill while news choppers circled what had to be a massive wreck up ahead. Wasn't like I could do anything other than inch along like every other Tom, Dickhead, and Harry. Like it or not, we were all in this together.

Snarled. Stuck. Pretty much screwed until Dallas's finest finished the task at hand.

So I did what any other capable Texas woman would do in this situation – turned up the music to drown out the honking horns.

Hey, it was either that or have a road rage incident captured on camera for the noon news.

It was better than the alternative, 'cause after the night I'd had – or lack thereof – Mr. Impatient did not want a visit from Miz Bitchy.

The headrest cradled my aching skull as I leaned back with a sigh. The questions I'd been dragging around and trying desperately to ignore bounded through my brain like a lioness pouncing on her prey. She just wouldn't be placated any longer with table scraps, and instead wanted a bite out of Reggie's hide.

What would we do if we caught the blackmailer? The only way to stop him or her was to turn the perpetrator over to the police.

But turning him or her into the police would create another paper trail. Which would then be part of the public record. Which would expose Reggie's past for public consumption. Which defeated the purpose of this clandestine clambake to keep Reggie's past a secret.

Besides, paying off the blackmailer still offered no guarantee he or she wouldn't release the records anyway. And if he paid the blackmail now, who's to say the blackmailer wouldn't later return for another taste?

See how trying to make sense of the insensible was screwing with my gray matter?

When I'd finally laid my head to rest, I'd had every intention of dropping the gang angle in favor of exploring others on the suspects list. But Zeke's mention of Bobby stirred up thoughts and memories.

And no, not the kind involving sexually charged dreams about Ford F-150s. I simply hadn't caught up with Bobby for a few weeks, and it was high time I touched base.

Since losing his wife and unborn son and being briefly imprisoned for their murders, Bobby had relinquished his position as the new children's pastor at Celebration Victory Church in favor of starting a prison ministry.

Not like prison ministries weren't common. But one run by a pastor who had been wrongly imprisoned like Jesus and His disciples made Bobby think he could relate to the prisoners better than most.

All of which played right into my ulterior motives for visiting.

Since Bobby was in touch with the local prison populace, he might be able to learn information about the local gangs, thereby helping with Reggie's situation without actual further contact on my part.

'Course, I'd have to tiptoe around the reasoning for asking to avoid setting off his reverend radar.

When I pulled into the driveway of Bobby's three-bedroom home, I was surprised to see a *For Sale* sign parked in the yard. And a familiar red Mercedes convertible.

Ol' Nosy Nana offered up a finger wave and a smirk from her front porch perch. That particular neighbor had had a front row seat to the chaos in June and likely thought the pastor was once again up to his elbows in salacious behavior worthy of the gossiping gaggle.

.I offered a five-fingered wave instead of my preferred one as I strode up to the front door and rang the bell, expecting one friend.

And getting another.

"Vicki?"

My best friend Janine answered Bobby's door, wearing a folded scarf on her head, a pastel yellow shorts jumper, and a smudge or two of dust on her nose and forehead.

None of the grime masked the blue, wide-eyed gaze of trepidation and the brows that shot toward her blond hairline faster than charges add up on Mom's credit card.

"Hey, Janine," I said trying to mask my confusion of seeing her here. At Bobby's. Without me. "Whatcha doing?"

"Well, I...um...you see..."

Bobby's six-foot-six frame loomed behind her as he reached his long arm around my immobile friend to open the screen door.

"Hey, Vic. Glad you could make it."

A zing of heat flashed through me like a woman in the throes of menopause every time I was within ten feet of my former squeeze. Just my body's residual memories of what had transpired between us eleven years ago.

All I had to do these days was simply remind myself that Bobby was a pastor. Poof! Immediate cool-down.

"What exactly am I making?"

I strolled through the doorway and did a three-sixty around the living room. Boxes were stacked and piled in every available corner, some in varying stages of undress – er, packing.

Bobby radiated mirth. Or maybe that was sweat. "Why the packing party, of course."

"Packing as in moving again?"

"Yup."

"After only a couple of months?"

He opened his arms wide. "Look at this place. All this space for one person?" The reminder of loss faltered his jovial mood for a sec before continuing. "Besides, I want to limit my personal needs from ministry donations, so I'm looking to rent a small apartment."

"Unlike the parents," I muttered.

"Moving in with them would save even more," Bobby said, completely misunderstanding the meaning behind my mutterings. "But it wouldn't be conducive to our relationship...or my sanity."

A knowing gleam twinkled in his eyes, revealing Bobby *had* understood the deeper gist of my words.

As his father's ministry had grown, so had the size of the Vernet asset holdings. Their current palatial estate was a visible reminder to the greater Dallas metroplex that Dennis and Mary Jo lived what they preached: give and you'll get.

Their demonstration of that tenet better illustrated the practice of *you* give so *we'll* get. Bobby's more frugal plans exhibited what I considered to be a more accurate interpretation of scripture.

Growing up together, I'd had a front row seat to what Bobby had experienced as the son of a larger-than-life, mega church minister. It didn't help tensions when my dad exerted purse string dominance as a way to get what he wanted from Pastor Dennis. Or just to prove how much control the sperm donor thought he had over the ministry's dictates.

As witnesses to the behind-the-pulpit machinations, Bobby and I had commiserated through the years over our fathers' shortcomings. And in the back of his brand new Ford F-150 the summer before he left for college.

The resultant police report offered ample proof of how far our commiseration had gone.

This past summer I'd gotten another first-hand view of Bobby's current struggle to live out the command to *honor thy father and mother*.

'Specially when they failed to bail him from jail.

It left the elder Vernets in a less than heavenly light and served only to solidify Bobby's wishes to *leave thy father and mother and cleave to thy wife*.

Amy's passing may have changed Bobby's marital status, but I wasn't aware of any command forcing a widower to return to the family fold.

But hey, what did a sinful succubus like me know, right?

A bright blush crept across Janine's face as if she had a front row seat to my mental musings. She thrust armfuls of books from the shelves into empty boxes scattered at her feet.

Can you say *guilty conscience*?

My dear friend had never learned the fine art of hiding her emotions, despite having this expert for a friend since before we'd learned to piddle in a potty. It was only a matter of time before the guilt – real or otherwise – built up and spilled over the dam.

"I'm so sorry," she sputtered within a ten second window. "I forgot to text or call you the other day to tell you Bobby needed help today."

"It's okay," I assured, handing over some books.

Janine continued in a rush like water over Niagara Falls. "My doctoral thesis is nearing a critical phase. Mother's been hounding me about finding a man and giving her grandchildren. There's the birthday trip to Louisiana this fall to see Grandmamma, and Mother won't shut up about how lovely it would be to share some good news with her, if you get my drift."

Janine's drift was rarely difficult to follow, even when she babbled incoherently.

"Then my advising professor is planning to dump so much work on me this coming semester I'll not see the light of day. And to top it all off, my dog died!"

"Bunny?" I cried as the waterworks tumbled down Janine's cheeks in earnest.

I wrapped my arms around my bestie as she dissolved into a tears and snot mess all over my black tee. Whoever said black doesn't show dirt has never surrendered the color to an emotional avalanche from one Janine De'Laruse.

Even though I'd never cared for her ankle biter, my best friend had loved that yipping Yorkshire terrorist – I mean, terrier. She'd treated it like her very own dress-up doll, painting its toenails, doing its fur up in bows and other bric-a-brac, even going so far as to dress it in themed clothes according to the nearest holiday.

Halloween and Christmas costumes were the worst. Figured that's why the tiny critter always seemed to be in a bad mood.

Or maybe it was just me.

I am more of a cat person, you know. They're somewhat indifferent and can pretty much take care of themselves as long as you remember to put out food every day, clean water, and scoop the litterbox cookies a couple of times a week.

And if I ever tried to put Slinky in a Halloween costume, I'd spend the following week nursing wounds that looked like Freddy Kruger had stopped by for a visit.

But knowing how much Janine loved her pet, I contorted my face into one of sadness and offered condolences to comfort her.

Or at least I tried.

"I'm so-o-o so-o-orry, Janine," I soothed in my best mothering voice. "Why didn't you call or come by?"

She sniffled and hiccupped between breaths. "You've had so much…going on too that…I didn't want to burden you with…my problems."

I held her out at arm's length to stare her down – and to protect my shirt from additional damage.

"Listen here, your problems are my problems. That's what friends are for."

"But you've been busy with the remodel," her voice shuddered, "…and moving…and then there's the hunk of burning Nick issue I still need an update about."

After working on the other side of the room, far away from the female emotive entanglement, Bobby perked up. "Who's Nick?"

Janine dabbed at her moist eyes with a tissue, careful not

to disturb the perfect eye makeup job any further. "Vicki's boyfriend."

"He's not my boyfriend," I said a little too quickly.

"I thought Zeke was your boyfriend," Bobby said with a brow furrow.

"I don't have a boyfriend."

"But weren't you staying at his place all this time?" Bobby continued in a full-court press.

"Yes, but..."

Janine interrupted, "She hooks up with him."

"Who? Zeke or Nick."

"Nick," Janine offered with a brow wiggle, tears for Bunny forgotten. "They recently spent the weekend down in San Antonio."

"While you were staying with Zeke," Bobby clarified.

"No." I finally got a word in. "I slept on Zeke's couch for five weeks, but I'm home now. We're friends. That's all."

"Then Nick is your boyfriend?" Bobby and Janine asked in unison.

"No boyfriends," I said firmly, shattering the hope my friends carried for me into microscopic pieces.

"But you're sleeping together," Bobby deadpanned.

"Yes," I blurted out before I could stop myself.

Lord, help me now! A conversation about the *current* guy I was sleeping with was so not a discussion I wanted to have with the *first* guy I'd slept with.

"Do you want to take my other confessions now, Father?" I finished.

"Actually, I'm a pastor, not a priest." Bobby smirked. "But I think we're good now."

I buried myself into heaving books into boxes, with mumbles and grumbles that would make most pastors and priests alike cross themselves with a blush. After the rush of back-and-forth conversation, accusations, and denials, I was gonna need a neck brace to recover from whiplash.

"I'm really sorry I forgot to tell you about today, though," Janine said, returning to her original soliloquy.

"We're good, Janine."

"Hey," Bobby began. "If Janine didn't tell you, then how did you know to come over today?"

"Actually, I didn't," I confessed. "I wanted to ask you a question."

"Oh. Well then, fire away."

Now that I had Bobby's *and* Janine's full attention, I had to focus on a way to ask without giving away any hint of Reggie's secret. After all, the De'Laruse clan was a design client too.

Janine wouldn't be able to keep her yap shut no matter how hard she tried. One whiff of fear, and Mrs. De'Laruse would draw a confession from her daughter better than any priest of the Inquisition.

"So," I started out strong. "There's this friend who once had gang ties a long time ago. That association has recently come back to haunt him."

Clean. Smooth. Straight forward. I'd successfully kept my disease-ridden mouth in check.

"Okay," Bobby said with confusion painted across his features. "What's the question then?"

The question. Right. Yeah, I really needed to stop hanging out with Nick. Ditzy was catching like a cold virus.

"In the confines of your prison ministry, I was sorta wondering if you connected with the prisoners individually or as a group."

"Both actually, but that's still not really a question."

"Well, then try this one on for size," I said with a huff.

"Do you work with local gang members?"

"Ah, good question." Bobby smiled, the little demon. "Yes, there are several gang members I've spoken with in the short course of the ministry."

"Another question then. Do you hear any details from these gang members? Things like why they're in jail, what gang they're involved with, rivalries...that kind of stuff?"

He nodded. "Some. But if you're looking for specific details, I probably can't help yet. It takes time to build trust, and I've only been doing this for a few weeks now. I don't want them thinking I'm fishing for information to share with authorities."

"Well, do you think you can find out something for me?"

"What are you asking about gangs for, Vicki?" Janine interrupted with a frown. "You're not in some kinda trouble again, are you?"

"Trouble? Me?" I countered. "I haven't been in any trouble."

"Yeah, that was me," Bobby offered. "What kind of information are you looking for, Vic?"

"A name...Switch. He's the original leader of a gang called the Switchblades."

Janine crossed her arms over her chest and shook her head. "I don't like this. Gangs? Knives? You're investigating for someone again, aren't you?"

What could I say without piquing her suspicions any worse than they already were? This was definitely material I didn't want to get back to her mom. Or mine.

"I plead the fifth?"

CHAPTER FOURTEEN

Everyone was on tap at the bar on Friday nights: Grady, Rochelle, Baby, Wanker, and of course little ol' me.

To keep drinks flowing at warp speed, Grady had Rochelle and Baby working the tables while me and Wanker managed the bar.

Wanker's what we call an old codger here in the south. He was about as true-blue a cowboy as modern times allowed.

Grizzled, long beard and matching hair straggled in a ponytail from beneath the weathered hat. I think at one time the hat had been light tan. Maybe even white. Now it sported stains so imbedded, the color leaned more toward grayish-brown.

But don't let Wanker's hat, age, or lanky frame fool you. If things ever got out of hand, he'd be the first in the fray, bashing heads together and dragging carcasses outside to sober up. There was a comfort in working side-by-side with him 'cause I always knew he'd have my back

Even if it was my antics that caused the commotion he had to clean up.

Or Baby's. That girl kept things barely legal and worked

the crowd like someone who had a hell of a lot more experience than her twenty-three years suggested.

Or maybe she was a lot like me, kept in a bubble until reality exploded that quasi-happy place like a twenty-two gauge shotgun, sending Baby on a spiraling course toward, well, my world.

My life's goals hadn't started out involving libation inebriation, lascivious lying down, and other assorted attributes. Yet, here I was. Or am. Or ended up – and I was dragging Baby along for the wild ride.

Watching her had me thinking on Zeke's comment from the other night. What were my career aspirations? Where was my life headed? Was I destined to be like Rochelle, in my thirties and stuck in a job just to make ends meet?

'Course unlike Rochelle there were no kids in my consideration. I wasn't the type to settle down and raise a herd of crumb-crunchers. Me a soccer mom?

Okay, you can stop laughing now.

Baby pranced over to the bar to the rhythm of the band, swishing her crinoline baby-doll skirt and settling the tray of empty glasses on the counter with a thud and clatter.

"Hey, Vicki. I need another round for table seven."

"From the tap?" I asked.

"Yep. That'll work."

Her too-bright blue eyes said she'd been enjoying plenty of sips and slurps like I usually did. 'Cept I got mine from behind the bar while she tickled it out of patrons playing drinking games.

A cry from the guys crowding the aforementioned table with several lifted hands, then Baby added to the order. "Oh yeah, and throw in a baker's dozen shots of Jack."

Whiskey mixed with beer. Yeah, her bottle-blond little head was gonna sport a headache like a jackhammer splitting concrete come morning.

"You sure about that, Baby?"

She grinned with a flip of her hair. "I'm gonna show these guys the meaning of the phrase *hold your liquor* before the night is through."

"Should I start a pot of coffee now instead of later?" I asked as I filled the order.

"Nah. I've already confiscated everyone's keys."

"I'm talking about you. If you keep this up, one of us will need to drive your passed-out carcass home and put you to bed."

"I'll be fine." She winked. "After all, I learned from the best."

"Sure ya did," I called after her as Baby balanced two trays brimming with alcohol and successfully made the return trip to the raucous table.

Rochelle came up with an empty tray and stood beside me, watching the swarm that swallowed Baby's diminutive frame.

"Every day that girl reminds me more and more of you."

"I'm not sure I want to take responsibility for this one."

"Someone had to pick up where you've left off."

"What's that supposed to mean?"

"Well," Rochelle started with hesitation. "Ever since this awkward phase...or whatever you want to call it...has developed between you and the boss, you've rather, how shall I put it, mellowed."

"Me? Mellow? Them thar's fighting words, little missy."

Rochelle laughed. "I'm not saying you've lost yourself completely, but you *have* mellowed."

"How's that?"

"You're not drinking as much as you used to for one."

A cry rose from the venue of the drinking game as Baby

launched up onto the tabletop, tossed back a shot of Jack, and started quivering her hips to the band's beat.

"You're not dancing on top of the bar," Rochelle continued. "Going home with a different guy every night..."

"Every night?" I interrupted. "It wasn't *every* night."

"Okay, every *week* then."

I gave her my best evil eye.

She just shook her head. "Point is, you've changed lately...and that's not necessarily a bad thing."

"Maybe it has something to do with almost standing at the pearly gates before my time."

"That's possible." She winked. "Or it might have more to do with a certain hot Aussie gentleman we've all come to know and..."

"Don't even say it." I shot her a scowl then glanced nervously around the room to make sure Nick wasn't walking through the door.

She shrugged. "Stranger things have happened when love gets involved."

"Lust, Rochelle," I said, tossing last dregs into the sink before loading glasses in the dishwasher. "There's a difference."

"And you know this how?" she asked, leaning forward to look me in the eye.

"That's it." I grabbed a shot glass and poured three fingers before adding another for good measure and tossed it down like a warm embrace. I shivered. "Sorry, Rochelle, but with talk like that, it's time for me to get shit-faced."

While filling orders, I proceeded to do just that for the remainder of the night. All this talk of change, coupled with my own contemplation of Zeke's words, had the avoidance radar tilting toward the end zone – er, red zone.

By the end of the evening, both Baby and I were on top

of the bar playing my favorite old game of *Guess the Color of that Thong*.

'Cept this time, the number of bets placed and hands groping my legs seemed less of a turn-on and more of a freak-show. What had at one time left me with a sense of euphoria – and an all-night squeeze – now left me feeling jaded and a bit hollow.

Rochelle was wrong about the connection I had with Nick. Our trip together proved that beyond all reasonable doubt. Even through my whiskey-sloshed brain, I knew what Nick and I had was lust, pure and simple.

Well, 'cept for the *pure* part.

And the fact I'd barely tolerated Nick's presence when we weren't doing the deed. Then there was also that feigning sleep thing most of the way home from San Antonio.

Me in love? With Nick?

That was an easy *hell no*.

But Rochelle was right about one thing. Something had changed, and it wasn't just my attitude toward the boss. Or Nick. I wasn't so sure how to feel about the realization, so I did what any psychosomatic gal would do.

Ignored it.

Or covered it up by swimming in alcohol. And this time, I didn't have someone to take me home and tuck me in. Or sex my brains out so I could avoid such thoughts.

Avoidance is my specialty, folks.

So time to find a new and willing victim.

The hangover headache was the first thing to stab my conscience – I mean, my consciousness – as morning broke the haze of last night's drunken spree.

Since it had been awhile since I'd picked up when Jack Daniel called, the aftereffects were magnified ten-fold.

My head felt as if Baby had done a tap dance number inside my skull instead of on top of the bar. Eyes were so gritty it felt like they'd spent the night playing in Mr. Sandman's sandbox.

Bad Vicki.

The second thing to register was the scent of brewing coffee and the clink of kitchen utensils.

I cracked an eyelid to discover I was safely ensconced in my own bedroom. The drapes were pulled to shut out the worst of the daytime sunlight. How thoughtful of...

I wracked my whacked brain, trying to remember if Nick had showed up at some point in the evening, but apparently all of my wires were a little crossed. Or a lot.

Had I taken Rochelle's challenge too far and ended up dragging some other poor schmuck home like a stray kitten? How had I even gotten home last night? Was my car intact?

Worry over the Vette rolled my sorry carcass from the mattress, and I staggered into the too-bright living room.

It took a moment for everything to come into focus, including the male figure stirring eggs over my brand new stove. Something about the backside seemed familiar.

As I stumbled into the couch and stubbed my toe, he turned around with a lopsided grin tilting the edge of his mustache.

"Mornin', Vic," my companion said in that familiar drawl.

My jaw practically bounced off the floor before my grating vocal chords grabbed hold.

"Grady?"

CHAPTER FIFTEEN

I'd had a dream about this once.

Or maybe twice.

I collapsed onto the couch and buried my pounding head into a pillow with a groan.

"No, no, no. This can't be happening."

The scent of scrambled eggs joined the coffee and sent my stomach into a swoon.

And I ain't talking the good kind.

I was so going to Hell for this one. After years of an all-out, avoid at all costs, no matter how tempting refusal to get involved, I'd failed.

Truth be told, I'd spent many an evening simply imaging what Grady was like between the sheets. And now I couldn't even remember the experience?

Not fair. Not fair at all.

Grady lifted my sprawled legs and sat on the couch beside me. "Relax, Vic. Before you let your imagination take you too far down the wrong path, you might want to open your eyes and see what you're wearing."

I decided to take his advice.

A quick peek between eye slits revealed the too-tight

blouse and skirt I'd worn the night before. Grady also had on the red chambray button-up and jeans from last night's shift.

A ray of hope stabbed me right between the eyes as I opened them wider. "You mean we didn't do it?"

"Nope," Grady said around a bite of eggs. "And try not to look so relieved either. You might offend my manhood."

"None intended," I muttered and accepted the offered steaming cup. A long sip ended on a sigh. "Ah, just what the doctor ordered. Irish coffee."

"Figured you could use it after last night's show. Just drink it slow."

The Texas-sized portion of eggs and salsa sitting on my coffee table made me shudder. I nibbled the piece of dry toast instead and forced it down with another stiff sip from my mug.

"Please tell me my Vette is okay."

"Safely locked in your garage," Grady responded. "You were in no condition to drive home last night."

As caffeine inched me toward this side of human, reality invaded. "What'd you do with your truck then?"

"It's at the bar."

"Was that safe?"

"Safer than leaving your little hotrod there all night. Besides, no one would dare touch my truck."

The image of Banker Boy with those rather nefarious-looking characters popped into my addled gray matter.

"You sure about that, boss?"

"Why do ya think I got all that security?"

"For fun?"

Both sides of his mustache tilted as Grady smirked. "If someone even succeeded in getting inside my vehicle, they wouldn't get far."

"But they could sure do some damage if they wanted."

"That's where my public persona comes in handy. If that didn't deter some idiot, then my buddies at the ATF would have a little to say about it. Then again, there's always Ranger Taylor to the rescue."

"Don't remind me," I murmured into my cup, trying to dislodge the memory of our recent encounter.

This was all Zeke's fault. Everything he'd said about my life – or lack of career aspirations – had set me up for last night's binge. He knew damn well that'd trigger my penchant for self-preservation.

Has to do with that avoidance thing, folks.

"You two on the outs again?" Grady took another bite of eggs swimming in salsa. "I thought things were looking up between you."

"Things will never be more than friends between me and Zeke again." And in my book, *friends* was still up for debate. "Once a cheater, always a cheater."

He washed his eggs down with a long sip of coffee then headed toward the kitchen for a refill. "Things aren't always what they seem, Vic."

I grunted around a tentative bite of greasy bacon. "Tell me about it. I never in a million years would've guessed you were an undercover Fed."

He paused in mid-pour. "You say that like it's a bad thing."

"Don't get me wrong, I'm grateful you were there to save me from a concrete kiss," I acknowledged. "But knowing you're a Fed and working with my ex-boyfriend sometimes feels…I don't know…weird?"

Grady sauntered over, taking a sample sip and watching over the rim before sitting down again. "So are we finally going to talk about the elephant in the room now?"

"Which one?" I groaned.

"Fair point," Grady offered. "How about we start with my being a Fed?"

"I haven't said a word to anyone, I swear," I said, crossing my heart and dotting my I's for emphasis.

Or was that crossing my T's and dotting my eyes? I really needed my brain at full capacity in order to have a cogent conversation.

'Specially about this topic.

"You've already demonstrated that you can keep your lips zipped. Still, everyone at the bar seems to have taken a peculiar interest in how you've been acting lately."

"Yeah, and Rochelle thinks we slept together."

"And Wanker," Grady mentioned. "I'm sure Baby does too."

I sat up a little straighter. "You do realize your taking me home last night only adds fuel to that fire."

"Maybe the fact I asked Wanker to escort Baby home will temper the talk."

"Fat chance," I muttered. "They're further apart in age than we are."

Grady winked with a chuckle chaser. "The age difference just gives people more to talk about."

"Ain't that the truth." I sighed and rubbed my forehead as if I could scrub away each and every thought, worry, and – well, headache. "I hate being the subject of rumor. Got enough of that from the Born-Again Brigade."

"Then tell everyone nothing happened," the boss offered with a shrug. "Rochelle will believe you, and if she believes you then the others will soon follow suit."

I shook my head. "She already suspected something was going on between us *before* last night."

"Tell her you're keeping a secret I told you."

I shot him a grimace – then regretted even that tiniest move. "Not like I already *am* keeping your secret or anything."

"True."

"And if she wants to know more?"

"Tell her I've got a case of crabs or something," the boss man said before popping the coffee mug up for a sip that did nothing to cover his chortle.

"Sure," I drawled. "That will keep the rumor mill from turning."

"She'll believe whatever you tell her 'cause it's coming from a friend, right? Case closed." Grady patted my leg. "You gotta trust people sometimes, Vic."

"I was cured of that years ago."

"You trusted me enough to get you home safe last night."

I leaned against the armrest and closed heavy eyelids. "I was drunk. I would've trusted a gang member to get me home safe last night."

Grady sobered. "Which leads to the other elephant in the room."

"Meaning?" I asked, testing my tummy with another nibble.

"Zeke told me about your little run-in the other night in gang territory."

I sat up too fast to a spinning world, the bacon clattering to my plate as I fought the urge to hurl.

From more than a hangover. "I already got the third degree from the Ranger. I'm not in the mood to hear it from you too, Boss."

"Not even gonna try." Grady raised his hands in surrender.

"Then why're you bringing it up?"

"Cause." Dark eyes deepened further into scary secret agent mode.

"You were followed home last night."

CHAPTER SIXTEEN

If Grady had hoped to scare me with his little revelation this morning – well, he succeeded.

The presence of a late night follower helped clarify better than any words spoken about why Grady had stuck around my place thru the morning. That was an elephant in the room I didn't need explained. Or even discussed.

'Specially if the follower was tied to Reggie's blackmail.

Time to get a handle on how to dig my friend out of this hole instead of merely spinning my wheels.

So after swigging down the rest of my Irish coffee, I switched to the regular stuff and took two aspirin for good measure. By the time I dropped Grady off at his truck, the roaring headache had reduced to a low growl.

Even though I typically spent Saturday afternoons recuperating from Friday night antics, I decided instead to drive into the countryside and turn up a long drive to enter the De'Laruse estate.

Just so we're clear, the country and I are not friends.

To put it mildly, I'd rather go to a piñata party and suffer through being the piñata. With the myriad bees, mosquitoes, spiders and other assorted insects that buzzed and crept in the heat, those Texas-sized critters always kept me busy smacking arms and legs until my skin looked like someone had taken a baseball bat to me.

But I'd suffer any indignities to help a friend.

I think.

The paper the blackmail notes were written on and the use of calligraphy spoke of quality. Money. And there was only one person I trusted to help me poke around the cash crop cliques without asking questions.

Or at least not too many.

The familiar face at the guard station waved me through the twenty-foot high, wrought iron gates even before I had a chance to roll to a complete stop. Since Janine's mom had grown up on a former Louisiana plantation, she insisted her children have that expansive acreage experience.

Their antebellum manor was built in true southern tradition, with first and second floor covered porches and porticoes wrapped around three sides.

This configuration allowed ample outdoor opportunities for Janine and her younger brother George to learn heat tolerance and how to comport oneself around assorted pests like properly bred ladies and gentlemen.

Around the bend, the trees opened to reveal the white columned mansion. The home was a gift from the elder De'Laruses when the business management end of the family's oil and gas enterprise moved to Dallas. It was a smaller yet modernized version of the antebellum homestead in Louisiana.

Charlotte's side of the family, that is.

When Janine's mom eloped with her dad, the one caveat for Charlotte's return to family grace was that her husband of questionable Creole background rescind his last name in favor of hers. Years of elocution lessons and a master's in business with a law degree on the side, Thomas was finally deemed ready to publicly accept the mantle of an empire.

The fact they were now the wealthiest family in all of Texas – and that's saying something in the oil capital of these here United States – spoke volumes about Thomas's commitment to the name of *De'Laruse*.

'Course, keeping Charlotte in the manner in which she was raised endeared him even more to those Louisiana elders. After all, they had a reputation to uphold too.

Kinda scary when considering the next generation sitting with his mother at one end of the porch.

Janine's younger brother typically spent his summers learning the ropes of the empire he'd take over someday. All day. Every day.

Well, 'cept for Sunday mornings. Had to put in the requisite appearance in the family pew and then lunch before heading into the office with his dad.

But knowing George's penchant for morning breaks, coffee breaks, lunch breaks, tea, afternoon breaks, and dinner meetings, he'd likely found new ways every day to disappear and do just enough to get by.

Or find someone else to do the work for him before taking all the credit. He was your quintessential next generation rich kid.

Okay, yes I was from a wealthy family too, but at least I actually paid my own bills. Most of the time.

'Cept when it came to the contents of my closet.

Well, and the recent renovation. But remember, that wasn't my fault. We'll just chalk that Momma Bear Syndrome.

But whereas Janine worked herself into a frenzy to earn a doctorate in music, her brother was a slacker, sleazebag, and overall slimebucket. Evidenced by his multiple and never-ending attempts over the years to cop a feel.

We're talking all the way from the cradle, folks.

I can't tell you all the times in church when he'd *accidentally* trip just to see up a woman's dress. Or brushed his hand against a certain part of a girl's budding anatomy.

It got so bad, Mrs. De'Laruse even took him to an ear, nose, and throat specialist because she was convinced he had an inner ear problem affecting his equilibrium.

Janine and I never could bring ourselves to explain the only problem George had was his overstimulated sexual curiosity. The guy had probably been looking at porn from the cradle.

Most times George reminded me more of *my* dad than his. With my dad's wanderlust – emphasis on the lust – it was always a distinct possibility. But I couldn't picture Mrs. De'Laruse stepping out on her husband or betraying my mother's friendship.

And with her penchant for sniffing out scandal, I also had trouble seeing Mrs. De'Laruse as someone who could hold her tongue and keep a secret of such magnitude for more than ten seconds.

Though Mr. De'Laruse *was* a certified workaholic. It was a miracle they'd found time to have one child, much less two.

George must've been dredged from the bottom of their combined gene pool.

"Victoria dawlin'," Mrs. De'Laruse drawled, calling me over to the wicker table and chairs where sweet tea and cookies signified the dessert portion of lunch.

I bent over her seated form to accept the air-peck to both cheeks. "Hello, Mrs. De'Laruse."

"How are you doin', dear?"

"Can't complain about anything but the heat."

"And how's your mother?"

"She's doing fine, but I imagine you've talked to her since I last saw her."

"You really should call her more often, Victoria," Mrs. De'Laruse admonished.

And with that guilt trip, I readied my escape. "Sorry to interrupt lunch, but is Janine home?"

A scowl pursed her lips. "That girl wolfed down her luncheon and hoofed it back to her room like an inbred ruffian. So disappointin'. So unladylike. It makes a mother wonder where she went wrong."

Her wide-eyed once over made it obvious where she thought she'd gone wrong when it came to her daughter.

The inbred comment, however, explained a lot where their son was concerned. Like most old southern family lines, there were likely generations of close-relational marriages buried within the De'Laruse DNA.

But I just smiled and did my best to bite my tongue.

"Say hello, Georgie," Mrs. De'Laruse commanded her twenty-three-year-old son before I could slink away.

"Hello, Victoria," George said as he stood, placed the linen napkin by his plate and ran his hands through unruly dark curls before coming around the table. "It's been a long time since you stopped by to visit."

"You're usually not here when I do."

The fake charm oozed to the forefront while the thinly veiled hunger gleamed in his blue eyes.

And I ain't talking from lack of lunch, folks.

The youngest of the De'Laruse brood was built more like his mother with a little more paunch than panache. Or a lot.

It didn't stop George from squeezing my chest to his though. Then placing his outside hand a little too low on my right haunch where his mother couldn't see.

What'd I tell you?

George was very adept at getting some T&A no matter the occasion. His mom's presence didn't deter me either. I gave him my own little reminder, finding that sensitive skin just inside the arm and giving him a little pinch in return. I felt rather than saw the wince as he quickly pulled away.

In the south, it isn't good manners to run off without spending at least a modicum of time in conversation. But we all know by now that *proper* isn't a word I've given much credence to these last few years.

At least I accepted a chocolate chip cookie before dashing into the sprawling foyer and up the grand staircase to Janine's room. The door was cracked open a smidge, which in my book is an invitation to let yourself in.

Janine sat at the desk near the floor-to-ceiling windows on the other side of her very pink canopy bed. Books lay open on her desk, across her bed, and scattered at her feet like a flock of birds come home to roost.

She scrawled on a yellow notepad like her life depended on it before turning to the line and staff pages set on an old-fashioned wooden stand, carefully crafting a musical score with a calligraphy pen like a woman straight out of the 1800s.

Ah, the life of a doctoral candidate.

Since my bestie had the misfortune of being born female, and therefore discouraged from pursuit of the family business, Janine had become a perpetual student. At present, Janine held not only a master's in accounting she'd never been allowed to use, but she was also nearing completion of a doctorate in music.

Other than teaching, I didn't know what she'd do with that piece of paper either. All Mrs. De'Laruse wanted was for Janine to find a successful man to marry and produce grandchildren.

Yet another family pressure I didn't have to deal with anymore.

Much.

"What's up, doc?"

At my greeting, tomes flew off the desk while the pen launched from her hand to leave a black blotch on the pale pink window sheers.

"Vicki!" Janine squeaked in her soprano pitch, eyes wide and brows heading toward the stratosphere. "You startled me."

"I'd have never guessed," I quipped. "Whatcha working on?"

"What I'm always working on these days." Janine sighed with a hand to her heaving chest.

"Learning how to relax?"

"How can I relax?" she wailed. "I've gotten so far behind on my thesis this summer. Then Dr. Husingkamp asked me to teach one of his freshmen classes, so he wants to see lesson plans on Monday before the start of the semester. And I haven't even finished scoring a single composition since June!"

"Really?" I scanned some of the books lying on the floor and picked one up. "Did you change topics recently from music to...*Setting up Your 501(c)3*?" I read aloud.

"Give me that." Janine swiped too slowly at the book I held just out of reach.

"What kind of a non-profit does a person with a doctorate in music set up?"

"A none-of-your-business kind."

Lips pursed just like her mother's as she held an open palm toward me. 'Course in her present state I'd never point out how much she reminded me of Mrs. De'Laruse when she did that.

You just don't say something like that to your best friend when she's already so obviously in an overwrought state of panic and distress.

I'd tell her later.

"This has something to do with Bobby, doesn't it?" I challenged as I placed the book in her outstretched hand.

The irritation in her bloodshot eyes dissolved into fear. "I...uh...it's..."

When Janine devolves into hesitation and stuttering, you know she's trying really hard to come up with something to say that isn't an outright lie.

It's how I knew before she admitted she had a crush on Steve Connors in the third grade. Before she told me about George's oral yeast infection being the *real* excuse for his week-long absence in ninth grade.

It was also why we got in trouble when her mom suspected us of sneaking out during a sleepover. My brilliant explanation had our sorry carcasses out of the noose before Janine put them right back in with one steely-eyed scowl from her mom.

But no amount of trouble would ever stop me from loving my Honest Abe of a best friend. It was rare to find a friend you could trust implicitly.

At least as long as you kept her away from her mother when she had something to hide.

"Well," I started, "I think Bobby can use all the help he can get. The Internal Revenue Service loves nothing more than to do everything they can to screw with non-profits."

Janine's shoulders relaxed. "My dad says the same thing. They audit his philanthropic entities practically every year, thinking they'll discover some illegal funneling of funds."

"Part of the joy of earning money and having the audacity to try and keep some of it, you know."

"He says that too."

"Three-quarters of Texans say that every April."

"Leave it to me, and I'd bet I could do something about it."

It was so obvious they were grooming the wrong De'Laruse. But sweet and trusting Janine running a multi-billion dollar empire?

Then again there was George.

I shuddered to think what her brother would do with that kind of money. At least under Janine's management there'd be plenty of philanthropic causes for legitimate tax shelters.

If history was any indicator, George would take the company the way of the porn industry.

"So, is that what you've been doing all summer instead of working on your thesis...helping set up Bobby's prison ministry?"

"Well...um...yeah," Janine admitted sheepishly. "It all started with a question he asked after services one Sunday. Bobby's a talented minister and so good with people, but he really doesn't have a head for business."

I also remember what Bobby had a head for at one time. I'd always carry fond memories of that F-150.

I cleared my mind of truck bed visions. "Being the wonderful person you are, you offered to help him set up everything."

Janine nodded. Was that a blush I saw coloring her cheeks? "I started researching some of the new tax laws governing non-profits. Then one of Dad's attorneys offered to do the legal work pro-bono."

"That was generous."

She smirked. "That was after I told him he'd gain some tax benefits for doing so."

"So that's why you were over at his place the other day. You've been spending extra time with him all summer."

"Well I...it's just that..." The blush came full on so fast, I thought Janine was going to have a heart attack. "There's nothing going on, I swear!"

I laughed. Then laughed some more. A full minute passed before I could breathe enough to speak.

"I'm just giving you a hard time, Janine. Gee."

"I'd never go after him or anything like that. I mean, it's only been a couple of months since Amy...and after you and him... It just wouldn't be right."

"That was a long time ago." Her shoulders were tight when I laid my hands on her. "But you're right...he's still grieving. I'm just glad you're the one helping him with all this non-profit crap."

I kneaded her muscles like an attentive coach to work out some of the kinks. Some coach I was, huh?

All summer I'd been focused on my own life and about when I could return to my apartment that I'd neglected my friend. It was obvious she needed to get out and have a little fun again.

Vicki style.

"Besides," I continued. "With you spending all this time working with Bobby, it leaves less opportunity for Lorraine Padget to get her claws into him."

Janine snorted. "You should visit church again just to see the spectacle Lorraine puts on around him, now that Bobby is considered *available*," she air quoted.

"I thought she was engaged to that old oilman. Mr. Summers wasn't it?"

"Still is, though you'd be hard pressed to believe it with

the way she fawns over Bobby."

My turn to snort. "I wouldn't be surprised if she dropped her fiancé any day now."

"Drop him by poisoning him, you mean," Janine offered with a grin. "That way she could get her mitts on the money *and* Bobby."

"How could she get the money if they're not married yet?" I asked.

"Daddy said Mr. Summers recently changed his will and added Lorraine as a beneficiary when they got engaged."

"Seriously?"

"Seriously. But it's only a specified amount until they get married. After that, percentages from the pre-nup will kick in."

Hmm. Lorraine might be onto something. Marry an old, rich guy who's bound to kick off in a couple of years, then enjoy the estate with a boy toy or two on the side.

But I wasn't as twisted and scheming as those of the Padget persuasion. I couldn't picture kissing a man older than my dad *during* the wedding ceremony, much less what comes *after* the wedding.

Consummation? Forget it. Someone like Lorraine would simply give the guy a sleeping draught then go to the hot, young guy waiting in the next room.

Me? I'll just keep enjoying the consummating without the complication of vows. No strings to tie me down.

And I ain't talking Pinocchio.

Janine exhaled deeply before I released her shoulders and plopped onto the bed among all of the Pepto-Bismol pink. Pink sheets. Pink pillows. Pink carpet. Pink walls.

I felt a little chalky just lying there.

It was time to sic Reggie on this room and bring Janine into adulthood – dragging, kicking, and screaming if we had to.

"So putting Lorraine aside," Janine said, swiveling the chair to face me. "Was there something other than Bobby you wanted to talk about?"

Speaking of Reggie – er, without speaking of Reggie. "As a matter of fact, there is."

"Okay, shoot."

"Are you sure you have time?"

"For my best friend?" Janine asked with a rapid bat of her unfairly long lashes. "You shouldn't even have to ask."

"Okay then, since I've been out of the debutante circles for a few years, I don't know what's happening among the uppity crowd."

"And with my doctoral work, and generally not caring about those silly gossips, I do?"

"Maybe not, but your mother does."

"Got me there," Janine admitted with a grin.

"I need you to show a smidge of interest in what's said among the socialites," I said, paging through a nearby textbook. "Nose jobs. Home remodel jobs. Things like that."

"Boob jobs?"

"Maybe even blow jobs."

"Vicki!"

"Hey, you never know what those girls will discuss at the Thursday afternoon ladies luncheons."

"That's at church," she scolded.

"Never stopped them when Mom dragged me to those things."

Janine tilted her head in contemplation. "Come to think of it, there were some rather saucy topics discussed when we leaned in to listen."

"Exactly."

Furrowed brows turned my way. "Does this have something to do with that gang talk at Bobby's?"

"Um...," I hedged.

"And don't you dare say you plead the fifth this time," she interrupted. "It sounds dangerous if it involves gangs, so I need to know what's going on before getting involved."

Like any good law-abiding Texan, I looked Janine right in the eye, opened my mouth and spoke in a way she could comprehend this time.

"I plead Beethoven's Fifth?"

CHAPTER SEVENTEEN

Now that I had Janine's interest piqued, I figured it was time to get down to business.

The consulting variety this time.

Consummation thoughts were put aside as we scurried past one seriously oversexed De'Laruse to avoid suffering another attempted pat-down. I'd never get over how close the genetic material was between my bestie and her baby brother.

Night and day, folks.

Since I had to get ready for work in a few hours, Janine followed in her red Mercedes as we made our way down the De'Laruse lane toward the highway. I chanced a call to Reggie's cell and got his drippy voicemail message instead.

You haff reached Reginald von Braun's messaging service. Vat a sad day, no? But all is not lost! Leave Reginald a vee, leetle note, mein liebchen, and he vill reach out and touch you soon. Ciao!

"Reggie, it's Vicki," I said over the roar of the Vette as I peeled out onto the highway. "You might want to change that outgoing message before you get hit with a sexual harassment charge. Anyway, when you have a chance to talk give me a call. Or swing by my place. Better yet, tell me where to meet you if it isn't too late. I've gotta be at the bar by six. Bye."

With a few hours to spare, I figured it wouldn't hurt to scope out the post office where Reggie had dropped the money. It wasn't too far across the river from my apartment, so after a quick swing through a nearby c-store for gas and cold cola, we hopped on the I-30 over to Dallas's main postal facility.

The huge building and multiple parking lots presented far too many opportunities for the blackmailer to get in and out unnoticed. Thus four eyes instead of two bettered the odds.

The front lot offered the best view, but I had to drive around several times trying to find an available parking spot. After getting cut off by idiots in big trucks and frazzled soccer moms a couple of times, I was tempted to pull a sneaky maneuver that involved using my car as a shovel.

'Cept I couldn't afford the higher insurance premiums that would inevitably come my way.

Sometimes being a good girl sucked.

Okay, so it was more out of protecting my baby from getting a boo-boo than any altruistic endeavors, but still. What had happened to chivalry? Respect for one's elders?

Well, that went out my window when the brat driving a green Smart car tried to zip around me into the next available slot.

If she'd so much as nudged my baby when I revved the engine and claimed the spot with a squeal of burning rubber, barely missing the guy in the Chevy who'd vacated it – let's just say, forget the Jaws of Life cause you'd have to use a can opener to rescue her sorry carcass when I was done.

Thank God for good ol' American-made horsepower and torque over some stupid sardine can. Someone should tell her the green looked more like what someone with a bad cold would blow out of their nose, not something to drive around where the whole world could see.

Smart car my ass.

Janine trotted across the pavement from the side lot then sank into my leather seat until her breathing grew closer to normal.

"Do you realize how close you were to clipping that ugly little car?"

"Hey, if anyone almost clipped someone, it was snot girl."

"Sometimes I forget how...um...powerful your driving can be."

I patted the dashboard. "It's not the driver so much as the car."

"No-o-o. I think in this case it's more like a bit of both."

I could take offense to that but left it alone to focus on more important matters.

My parking job offered a decent view of the post office front door area as well as the side lot, unless the guy cruising around in a monster truck decided to set up shop next to my Vette. Some guys will drive anything massive to overcompensate for what they lack.

And I ain't talking stature.

Trust me, ladies. Size *does* matter in certain departments.

"So what's the plan?" Janine asked.

I took another careful glance at our surroundings. "Since we've got a good angle on both lots from here, how about you stay with me and watch the side entrance while I keep an eye on the front?"

"Roger that."

I gave her the suspicious side eye. "Have you taken a break from romance movies and started watching cop shows again?"

"Like I have time to watch anything right now," she grumbled.

I shut off the engine and took a big swig of cold cola as we watched the endless parade tromping in and out of the building while vehicles continued jockeying for parking positions. Sweat immediately beaded on my forehead and my bare legs tried to repel the sticky leather seats with a layer of moisture.

When the tickle down my back started to turn into Niagara Falls, I realized what a bad idea I'd had. This was Texas. In August. A black car in hundred-plus degree weather with a thousand percent humidity.

What had I been thinking?

I had to be about one yard shy on fourth down to think this stunt would garner results. No one would risk taking a wad of cash from a post office box in broad daylight. They'd most likely come skittering around at night.

At night when it was dark. At night when most southern residents claimed it got cooler. Personally, I didn't think ninety-eight degrees at midnight was anything to write home about.

I needed a vacation. Somewhere north – say the Arctic Circle.

Janine flipped down the visor and blotted her makeup with a tissue. The girl had barely started glistening. Maybe there was something to her mom's acclimation insistence.

"So what are we watching for?" she asked before swiping on a fresh coat of lip gloss.

"Anything that seems odd."

"And who are we watching for?"

"Anyone who stands out."

"Like him?"

Janine giggled and pointed to a guy who looked like he was channeling Cruella De Vil. Or at least her hairdo. Maybe some people could pull off the black and white bouffant, but I imagine it was best left to the animators at Disney.

"Uh, no," I said. "Think someone more from the socialite syndicate. Someone who would normally send their lackey to run errands."

That got me an eye roll to rival a hormonally-ravaged teenager. "Lackey?"

"What does your family call the household helpers these days?"

"Their names."

"Really?"

"Well, Georgie calls one particular girl something entirely different, but I won't dare repeat it."

"Busty Brenda?"

"You're on the right track."

I just shook my head and swiped sweat from my eyes before a familiar figure hustled by with loaded bags in tow, wearing a crisp white linen suit jacket and matching pencil skirt tighter than permissible by Texas law. Looked like we had a former pageant princess who'd put on a little weight.

"Would you look at that?" I said, tilting my sunglasses down for a more accurate assessment. "Now that's definitely something unusual."

"Is that…?"

"That'd be a Texas-sized yup."

"Doesn't she realize linen is a loose weave?" Janine

observed.

"*That's* what you're worried about here?"

"But those seams are going to unravel if she's not careful."

"You mean explode at any minute...and we'll have a front row seat to it too. Come on," I urged, shoving open the car door and stepping out into the furnace.

Like a dynamic duo, we followed my arch enemy into the building, barely avoiding Little Miss Smart Car as she skidded around the corner again and sent a southern salute my direction.

Lorraine Padget got into a line while Janine and I watched from around the corner behind the glass wall. The pageanted Padget shuffled back and forth in her four inch cranberry-red platform peep-toes, periodically checking her watch and offering up an exaggerated sigh every ten seconds.

No, I couldn't hear it through the glass. Based on the reaction of every other person stuck in line with her, I was fairly certain the huffs were loud and overemphasized.

And that Lorraine could use a breath mint.

After about seven minutes, which in my experience was a very reasonable wait time when it came to government agencies, Lorraine reached the counter. Without preamble, she launched into a tirade – this time loud enough to hear through, if not *break*, the glass – and practically pelted the postal worker with a series of throw pillows.

"Wow," I muttered to Janine. "And I thought she only acted bitchy around me."

"She's made it an art form," Janine returned from peeking under my arm. "Especially when she thinks no one at church is watching, or when she has to deal with those she considers underlings."

"Ooo, good word. I like that one better than *lackey*."

All that got me was a poke in the ribs.

Janine stretched her back then leaned against the wall. "I thought you said something about a post office box."

"Yeah."

"So why aren't we checking that area out here," Janine said with a sweep of her arm, "instead of watching this week's episode of *Lorraine Loses It* in there?"

"I don't know," I admitted. "Curious, I guess."

What *was* I doing? I'd had a run-in with a bunch of thugs, gotten bawled out by Zeke, hauled home in a drunken haze by Grady, and dragged my bestie away from important work to play *Lucy and Ethel Go to the Post Office*.

Thus far, my attempts at identifying Reggie's blackmailer had yielded about as much as a hooker on dollar night. I was hot, tired, and sweaty with little to show for my efforts.

I pressed against the wall with Janine as determined heel clacking came closer until rushing around the corner. Lorraine's eyes widened right before narrowing in my direction.

"What the hell are *you* doing here?" she yelled, staring daggers through my skull.

"My my," Janine said in her best debutante voice. "Such strong language from a fellow member of the flock."

"And I'm just helping Janine hold up this wall," I returned, while Janine offered a fingertip wave. "And you?"

A quick glance down at the key in her hand before Lorraine closed her fingers around it. With a jut of her chin, the mask fell in place.

"I...uh...made the mistake of ordering some pillows for the breakfast room banquette from some fly-by-night company and had to return them. Tryin' to spruce up the place in time for our engagement party in January."

Next year? If she strung the engagement out too long her fiancé would die of old age before she dragged him down the aisle.

Hmm. Maybe that was her wicked plan. But if she didn't work fast enough, Lorraine would be left without the bulk of the Summers estate to spend.

Janine piped up. "Why didn't you call Reginald von Braun's firm? Mr. Summers has worked with him in the past. I'm sure he's still got an open budget there."

"I would've, but I wanted to show my dearest Derek that frugality isn't a curse word."

Which in Lorraine's case translated to more money left over for her when she did in the old geezer on their wedding night. Perhaps she was buying and returning things from other sources so she could pocket the cash.

Now *that* would be an inventive way to make a quick buck. Then again, there was always blackmail – which also might explain why she hadn't gone to Reggie for the banquette pillows.

"So what's the post office box for?" I asked.

"What post office box?" Lorraine returned.

"Uh, the one for the key in your hand."

Her grip tightened around it until I half expected blood to come gushing out from between her fingers like in one of my favorite horror flicks.

"That's none of your business," she huffed, spun on her heels without falling from her lofty heights, then marched outside into the fires of Hell where she belonged.

Janine leaned over my shoulder. "Was that odd? That seemed a little odd to me."

"Yeah, definitely odd," I confirmed.

We followed her outside and watched as Lorraine went

postal in the parking lot, leaving tracks leading straight toward Mexico. Or the nearest c-store for a hot dog to squeeze into that skirt.

Standing in the sun, I was beginning to feel like a broiled hot dog at Cowboys Stadium. Beginning to smell like one too.

So much for this barbeque.

Janine and I parted ways after she secured a promise from me to help with Bobby's upcoming fundraiser. Then I herded myself to the car, turned the A/C on max, and pulled out of the parking lot in time for Little Miss Smart Car to make another round of the lot and grab my spot.

Why she didn't head into the side lot was a mystery, but give that girl a sticker for determination. Better yet, get her a paint job in a less offensive color.

Like black.

The heat followed me all the way to work that night.

With bodies pressed in tight on the dance floor and the band sizzling in the spotlights, I wilted more each time the band took a break and everyone gathered around the bar for refueling.

The moment the crowd broke away to cozy up for the next set, I poured a glass of ice-cold beer and gulped it down. Then grabbed a couple of ice cubes and rubbed them across my nearly bare chest.

The tiny spaghetti-strap dress covered all my necessary kibbles and bits enough to call it publicly legal.

Unlike Lorraine's full-to-bursting linen skirt this afternoon. That woman now sat at the top of my suspect list – and not for public indecency.

As a news anchor with the local station, Lorraine had

investigative journalists at her beck and call. The network offered ties to the larger outlets in New York City, a perfect storm to access Reggie's records tying him to both cities.

Plus, as a network affiliate, she also had the mouthpiece to make a huge splash when revealing Reggie's past duplicity, thereby destroying his reputation on not just a local but national level as well.

The thought kept me burning even after the boss turned the air down a couple of notches. I despised summers like Garfield hated Mondays.

And duplicitous debutantes even more.

A hand tugged up my ponytail before Grady reached around my scantily-clad frame to grab some ice. The cool wetness across my back brought immediate comfort from the hell-raising heat.

Until the murmur in my ear ticked my heartrate up a notch – or two. Thoughts of Lorraine and Reggie whisked away on the boss's whispers.

"I love seeing you all sweaty, Vic. Only I'd prefer to get you that way somewhere a lot more private."

"Didn't you already squander that opportunity last night?" I asked.

"I'd rather you be sober when I take advantage of you," Grady returned. "And willing."

His chilled hands slid wet across my shoulders, dipping down my back as low as the sling-backed dress allowed. I closed my eyes and shivered.

Oh, I was willing alright. What did his federally-issued handcuffs look like?

That stopped my slutty thoughts in their skids. Oh. Right. Government agent.

"You better stop that," I murmured, "or there'll be little I can say to Rochelle to get her to believe there isn't anything going on between us."

"Hey there, Vicki."

My eyes snapped open as Radioman slid onto a barstool with a wide and knowing grin. The remaining ice chip slipped down my spine to puddle at the small of my back when Grady released me.

"Well if it ain't my favorite radio personality." I snapped the lid off a Sam Adams Summer Ale.

"In the flesh," he returned before taking a deep pull.

I shivered – and not just from the ice cube.

"Ah," Radioman said with a smack of his lips. "Just what the doctor ordered."

"I'll be your attending physician," I purred. "As long as you're not dying or anything."

"Of heat, that's for sure," Radioman quipped before taking another drink. "Eleven o'clock at night and it's *still* a hundred degrees out there."

"It's inching toward that in here." I grabbed another ice cube and rubbed it across my chest. "I think the A/C needs servicing."

The muscles in his jaw constricted as his gaze trailed my hand for a beat. "Something needs servicing alright."

I don't think he meant the air-conditioning.

The smile he offered when his cornflower-blue eyes met mine again spoke volumes and made my knees all noodley. Somewhere in the periphery of my naughty mind, I heard Grady's chuckle before he moved down the bar to help another customer.

"This helps though," Radioman continued before finishing off the bottle and glancing at the crowd. "Have you seen Seth yet?"

"Your lawyer friend?"

"Yeah."

"Not yet."

"He's supposed to meet me here."

"Big date?" I impishly implied.

"I was hoping." He leaned forward and took advantage of the momentary lull between the band's sets. "Whatcha doin' tomorrow night?"

I joined him in kind and rested my elbows on the bar. "You tell me."

"Dinner?"

The still image Grady had shown me of Banker Boy a couple of nights ago popped into my head. A date with Radioman offered an opportunity to learn a bit of background on his friend. Maybe even something that explained that parking lot interaction the other night.

I caught the downturn of Grady's mustache and the subtle shake of his head from the corner of my eye.

And promptly ignored it. "What time?"

"How does seven sound?"

"Sounds perfect."

He tapped my number into his phone while I prepared drinks for the band's upcoming break. Finally, after all the interruptions from Grady and Zeke and the recent hiccups with Nick, I'd get a chance to know the man behind the silky voice.

And yes, I meant that in the Biblical sense.

The thought buoyed me through the remainder of the evening and on the drive home. After entering my apartment, I tossed my keys toward the kitchen island and flicked the light switch out of habit.

'Cept this time the lights didn't even flicker.

My heart lodged in my throat. I'd completely forgotten about Grady's warning concerning last night's follower. Instincts heightened and my mind screamed that someone else was present in the dark.

And it wasn't just Slinky.

The drapes had been closed. Ambient light from the parking lot didn't cut through the inky blackness. The faint odor of cigars – Cuban – lingered in the air. The growing motorboat purr of my cat broke the silence.

Purring? That meant my critter was happy and content. Of all the...

The spit and flare of a striking match just about sent my heart into attack territory. The lighting of a single candle on the coffee table provided enough illumination to make out the uninvited company, my cat curled in his lap.

"We meet again, *Senorita* Bohanan."

CHAPTER EIGHTEEN

I fumbled my purse like a rushed quarterback on third down and nearly piddled in my panties when my phone and pepper spray tumbled out of reach.

The gentleman holding my kitty stood from the couch like the Godfather reborn. 'Cept this one was short, slender, and had a Hispanic flavor to his greeting.

He also wore one finely tailored Desmond Merrion suit.

Mr. Julio Benito Juarez was not only the Mexican Ambassador to the United States, but he was also father to Bobby's deceased wife, the secret love child spawned from a long-term affair with Amy's drug-addled mother.

I'd had the pleasure of meeting him at the governor's ball in June where he'd expressed his appreciation for my role in discovering his daughter's murderer.

Did I also mention the ambassador is a member of the Juarez family drug cartel? Actually he was more of a silent partner, working covertly with drug enforcement on this side of the border to bring his family down.

But you didn't hear that from me.

I only wanted to know three things as I glanced around my apartment at the tightly closed drapes. One, what was he doing in my apartment cuddling my traitorous tabby?

Two, how had he gotten by all the new-fangled security my mom had ordered and Reggie had installed?

And three, would he mind if I stepped away real quick to take care of nature's unexpected call?

On second thought, maybe I could hold it.

"Ambassador Juarez?" I finally sputtered out. "This is an unexpected…um…pleasure."

More like shock, startle, panic, and plain old *what the hell* in my dictionary. But it was no time to be rude.

"It is a pleasure to see you again also, *Senorita*," Juarez said, scritching behind Slinky's ears. Thus the loud purring.

No gun in his hands to use against me or my cat. Point in my favor.

Though on second thought, he could hold my baby hostage and just as easily wring Slinky's neck, something I honestly contemplated doing on occasion.

But only for a sec.

Still, point in his favor. He'd been kind and appreciative on our initial meeting. At the governor's ball. In a very public setting.

This time we were in my apartment. My closed off and very private apartment.

Which returned me to my original conundrum. How he had gotten by not only my security system, without all the forces in Dallas descending on him, but Jimmy-the-Super's surveillance emporium too?

In case something pungent was about to hit the proverbial fan, I needed to phrase my question carefully.

"What the hell are you doing here, Ambassador?"

Okay, not a great opening line, but a reasonable one – considering.

"Your Congress is still in its summer recess, so there's

very little happening in D.C. at present," Juarez said. "After returning from a visit with *mi familia*, I found I had business to attend to here before heading north."

It didn't require too much thought to determine what kind of business he stopped over in Texas to attend to. But I'd have no luck getting detailed information out of the tight-lipped Texas Ranger.

"No," I said. "What are you doing *here*? In my apartment? At three in the morning?"

So much for careful.

Hey, don't fault a girl for being distracted with thoughts of an upcoming date, startled by an intruder, and a little tipsy after a full night at the bar

Not to mention a building need to visit the bathroom.

The hint of a smile curled the edges of his thick mustache, reminding me a little of my boss. Juarez settled Slinky to the floor. I took advantage of his momentary movement and shoveled the contents back into my purse where they belonged then clutched it like a desperate housewife on Black Friday.

"It has come to my attention," Juarez started, "that you seek to help a friend."

"That Ranger has the nerve of…"

"*And*," he interrupted with a raised brow, "though I am usually hesitant to use names…in this case it seems you are seeking someone specific."

Yeah, right about now that would be a Texas Ranger known as Big Z – big as in Big Mouth in this case.

But I digress.

The ambassador didn't have to say another word to clarify his meaning about the specific name he inferred. I'd caught that Hail Mary on the first pass. Even when suffering the effects of full-blown inebriation, I'd never been *that* dense.

Oh, shut it.

"Why would you get involved in a penny-ante problem when you've got more important things going on?" I asked.

A momentary flicker of sorrow creased his brow. "To return the favor when you helped me."

Well, actually I'd been helping Bobby.

But apples and oranges.

I took a deep breath to calm my galloping heart and remind myself I was doing this for Reggie.

"I'm looking for a guy who used to be in charge of a gang called the Switchblades."

"Ah, yes. Nasty group."

"They're still around then?"

Even after facing the ones Zeke had rescued me from, I couldn't assume those guys had any affiliation with the Switchblades. I mean, there were tons of gangs around these days. What were the chances I'd actually run into members of that particular group?

"They are very active in certain circles."

With his fingers, the ambassador mimed holding a cigarette to his mouth, drawing in and blowing out.

"Drugs," I stated, sitting down on the couch.

Juarez nodded silently as he sat down beside me.

"Okay then, so the guy who started it would be somewhere in his sixties," I surmised aloud. "That is, unless he discovered the wrong end of a gun at some point. Or in his case, a switchblade."

"Always a high probability in such groups."

"He went by the name of…" I couldn't help the chuckle that escaped. Blame it on nerves. "Called himself Switch."

No surprise registered on the ambassador's face. After a lifetime involvement in politics, he'd probably become an expert at keeping true thoughts and feelings hidden behind the mustache.

Instead he slipped a card from his inside jacket pocket and wrote something before handing it to me.

"When you call that number, ask for Tomas Ricardo." Juarez stood and moved around the coffee table toward the front door. "And remember to tell him Benny gave it to you."

In the blink of an eye, Juarez blew out the candle then opened and closed my door in the accompanying darkness.

It took a few beats before my brain caught up to my body. Then I jumped up, wrenched open the door and stared down an empty hall. Then I looked over the railing to the vacant stairwell.

It was like he'd never even been there. If I didn't have the card in my buzzed little hands, I'd have thought I'd dreamed up the whole encounter.

Had I blacked out for a moment or two after he blew out the candle? Or three? Did the candle have a hallucinogenic effect released in the smoke?

I stared again into my darkened apartment. The lights weren't on, but this girl was home.

And I wasn't so sure that was an entirely safe place to be.

CHAPTER NINETEEN

A good night's sleep is next to...

Well, I guess my mom always said something more along the lines of *cleanliness is next to Godliness*. But in this case, a good night's sleep worked best for me.

After the strange encounter with the Godfather-like ambassador, I didn't get much until the lights flickered on about the time dawn peeked through the blinds.

The card was still in my hand when I finally woke up later that afternoon, a reminder that the events earlier were more than a dream.

I did a quick check to ensure I still possessed all ten fingers and toes for my date with Radioman. 'Cause I definitely didn't plan on getting much sleep tonight.

Hey, I needed something more than a tiptoe through the tulips to get my mind off of gangs, godfathers, and the goons that worked for them.

Don't judge.

My doorbell buzzed promptly at seven and sent a shot of adrenaline south.

I just love new relationships, don't you? Exploring attributes and what makes someone tick made for sparkling exchanges. Conversation could be good too.

Unless you were a male model named Nick.

Thoughts of Nick fell to the wayside when I finished clattering through the myriad door locks and dragged the thing open to greet Radioman.

Amber hair sported a softer but perpetual dent from headphones, but the leather jacket over a button-up was a new look for him. It all graduated to dark blue jeans that hung low on his hips and fit snug in all the right places.

His scent hit me between the thighs. Musky. Manly.

I grinned at the sweat glistening on his brow. "A jacket? In this heat?"

"I wasn't sure how dressed up you'd be."

His gaze traveled up and down my little cranberry-red halter dress. Adam's apple bobbed as his warmth penetrated my clingy number with a hug and his hand feathered the bare skin on my back.

"And I can always take the jacket off."

The breathy whisper so near my ear made me want to do just that – and more.

Bad Vicki. So very bad.

Did the waiting at least an hour after eating apply to any other activities besides swimming?

I barely had the presence of mind to grab my purse and lock the door before I further contemplated dragging him to my bed – er, mattress.

Like a gentleman, he escorted me to his black-patent Honda Accord and opened the passenger door for me before climbing into the driver's seat. Then with a grin and a squeal of tires, he showed me there was much more under the hood of his straight-off-the-showroom-floor car.

The scent of hot rubber had me wondering what other surprises he had waiting under the hood.

And yes, I meant that to sound dirty.

"Nice car," I said.

"Brand new," Radioman bragged with pride. "Got a sweet deal on her and couldn't resist."

"A *her*, huh?"

"Always," he said with a wink. "The curves of a car can't help but make me picture a voluptuous woman."

The interior suddenly warmed even with the air conditioner on max. "Uh…she had some pretty nice torque back there."

"It's nothing like what you're used to, I'm sure. She's only a V-6."

"Shhh," I cautioned, rubbing the silky dashboard. "You might hurt her feelings."

Even his throaty laugh was as smooth and sexy as his voice. "Two-hundred and fifty-two pounds of torque isn't shabby for a four-door sedan, I guess."

Now this was the kind of conversation I'd hoped to have with Nick on our San Antonio trip. The dichotomy between the two men was stark.

A solid reminder to make sure Nick understood things were over between us. I meant it this time too.

Girl Scout's honor.

"What's her horsepower?" I asked.

"Two-seventy-eight." A curious cornflower-blue glance slid my way as we stopped at a red light. "This is an interesting conversation I never expected to have tonight."

I shrugged. "I like cars."

"Obviously. Shoulda known with the one you have." Silence until the light changed to green and he took a right. "Do you like football?"

"Does a bear crap in the woods?" My crude humor didn't even faze him.

"Cowboys?"

"I bleed blue and silver."

That popped out a dimple. "Have you ever been to a game at the new stadium?"

The Bohanans and De'Laruses have shared a private box in both the old and new stadiums for longer than Janine and I have been alive. My formative years were spent in that luxurious suite, staring down through the big Plexiglas window at the action taking place on the turf while snarfing down five-star snacks.

When Zeke and I had dated, he loved watching football but hated the stadium crowds. Plus, he'd never known when he'd have to step out for an emergency on a case, so he'd just DVR'd the games instead.

The thoughts made me realize that Radioman knew virtually nothing about me. Knew nothing about the family name and enterprise.

All he knew was that I worked at a bar and liked cars and Dallas Cowboy football. If he was aware of anything more he didn't show it.

And I found comfort in the anonymity.

"I haven't been for a few years," I responded.

"Well, I've got tickets to the preseason opener...*if* you're interested."

"It's a date," I exclaimed as we pulled into the parking lot of my favorite restaurant.

La Buona Cibo Vino served the best Italian food this side of the Mississippi. What it lacked in ambience it made up for in spice and flavor to zing the palate.

Tonight I was definitely feeling – or smelling – a deep dish sausage pizza with fresh tomatoes and melting mozzarella all nestled in a yeasty yummy crust. My stomach seconded the vote the moment we sat down in what was once mine and Zeke's special hangout.

I quelled all thoughts of what the Ranger and I had once shared and determined to enjoy the night with someone new.

"So do you prefer I call you Bruce or keep addressing you as Radioman?" I asked, swirling red wine in my glass.

"I kinda like the moniker," he returned. "I even mentioned it to the producer at the station, and he wants to see about working it into my call sign."

"Really?"

"The station just has to make sure it doesn't violate any FCC regs or copyrights first."

"Well here's to helping further your career." I raised my glass and plinked it against his across the table. "So you talk about me at work, huh?"

"Maybe." The dimple peeked out again. "I haven't been exactly subtle about wanting to take you on a date."

"I'm glad you finally succeeded."

Salad and breadsticks arrived but didn't create more than a hiccup in our conversation. Yeah, this was definitely a far cry from being with Nick. Major improvement in the conversational compartment. I had high hopes for what lingered on the horizon.

Emphasis on the *linger*.

"So," Radioman started, "how did an intelligent woman like you end up tending bar?"

I batted mascaraed lashes like a world-class ditz. "Who says I'm smart?"

"Come on. I'll never forget that little guessing game you played when we first met. Guessing one of our careers correctly...fine. But all three? That was uncanny."

I remembered clearly that night two months ago when the three musketeers had strolled up to the bar and about fell off their stools when I pegged them within minutes. Since then I'd enjoyed the slow rise in temperature their presence at the bar brought.

'Cept for Banker Boy. His rare presence only made me itch to bathe in more than just alcohol.

"It's a gift," I responded with a smiling chaser.

"I'll say."

"Have to admit though, you were the hardest to determine."

Radioman leaned forward and traced his fingers across my hand with a whisper. "Hardest, huh?"

I released the salad fork and gulped the last vestiges of wine to cover the shiver creeping up my arm. Then had to work at it to quell the rush of naughty thoughts that word triggered.

"I couldn't decide between radio and television," I admitted a little breathily.

"What was the tie-breaker?" Radioman asked as his fingers trailed along my forearm like a promise of things to come. "Did it come to you like a fastball?"

Hard? Fast? Come? My nether regions quivered with all the metaphor promises.

My gray matter just rotted.

"I, um…," I stammered. "It was your hair."

"My hair?" he responded with surprise, running fingers along his temple like I wanted to do.

"And your voice."

Confusion furrowed his brow. "Oka-a-ay."

I pulled my hand away and picked up the empty glass. I was obviously getting a little tipsy, so I opted for water instead before trudging forward.

"Your hair had a deep indention in it…unnatural, as if you wore headphones all the time."

He acknowledged my observation with a head tilt.

"But your voice was smooth and sultry. Familiar. Rather made for television, if I might add. But television personalities don't wear headphones on the air. They wear earwigs."

Understanding dawned with a twinkle in his eyes and a growing grin. "Nice deductive reasoning."

"Like I said before," I conceded with a shrug. "It's a gift."

"Which brings me back to my original question. Why is an intelligent woman tending bar?"

Didn't I just have this conversation with someone recently?

Oh yeah – my *ex*-boyfriend. "I needed a job?"

"Don't we all," Radioman returned. "What else?"

"After graduating from college, I'd moved out of my parents place into my boyfr...uh, in with a guy I was seeing at the time."

The waiter arrived with mouth-watering pizza, which sent us tilting toward that particular windmill for a bite or two.

But Radioman's curiosity was far from quenched. "What's your degree in?"

"A general bachelor's in business management."

"Which opens a wide range of daytime possibilities."

"I'm kinda a night owl though."

"Me too."

A dribble of grease dabbled with his dimple, which I mopped up with a slow wipe of my napkin instead of what I wanted to use right then.

My tongue.

The deepening of his gaze and the catch of his breath made me realize he'd have liked use of that organ too.

What was the societal accepted number of dates before having sex? Three? Two? Maybe we could count all of the visits to the bar as dates.

Or foreplay.

'Cause if I had to wait another week for the Cowboys preseason opener for date number two, I'd rather consider myself socially unacceptable.

Yeah, yeah – don't remind me of the whole Nick debacle. What we'd had couldn't actually be called *dating*. I was trying to turn over a new leaf here.

And *not* in the style of Adam and Eve this time.

Think about it.

Radioman cleared his throat. "So a degree in business...doesn't that translate into several different types of corporate careers?"

Or slaving away for one's father. "It took all of two seconds for me to realize I wasn't cut out for the corporate world."

"What happened, if you don't mind my asking?"

I chewed pizza while weighing my words carefully. "Let's just say my dad had made plans for my career without asking for my input."

"Ah, didn't want to go into the family business?"

The pizza wedge almost stuck in my throat. "You know about my family's business?"

"Not per se, but isn't that usually the case when parents plan their children's lives? Expect them to run the family business someday?"

I calmed after guzzling half of the fresh glass of wine in one sip.

So much for sticking with water. "I suppose you're right. Is that how you ended up in radio? Daddy own the station?"

His laugh was rich. Deep like a shot of top shelf bourbon. "Hardly. My father had designs on me achieving his position on the ladder, not settling for something as *lowly* as a radio personality."

"Doctor?" I'd volunteer to let him examine me.

"Nah, lawyer," Radioman said before draining half his glass. "Wanted me to become the managing partner in his firm someday."

"A family legacy of lawyers, huh?"

Which meant he'd come from a smidge of money too. Which meant his dad might know my dad.

Or at least know *of* him.

"Now it's up to either my younger brother or sister."

"Oldest child breaks the cycle." I fluttered my lashes and raised my voice in my best southern ditzy debutante. "Why Mr. Radioman, you have successfully surprised me tonight."

He leaned forward, his eyelids at half-mast. "I'm full of surprises, Miss Bohanan."

Check please!

But somehow I restrained myself. "So I take it that's how you and Seth became friends."

Radioman nodded. "Roommates freshman year. We were both on the poly-sci undergrad track until I took a mass comm class just for fun my sophomore year. Required to spend at least one hour a week hosting the college's radio show. After that I was hooked, and took every available timeslot the remainder of the semester before changing my major."

"And the rest, as they say, is history," I interjected.

"Something like that. Created a few hard feelings with my dad for awhile, but things have settled these last few years."

"Wish I could say the same," I muttered.

No need to devolve into self-pity. Besides, I had another itch I wanted to scratch tonight – no matter how badly Grady would kill me.

"So then how did you and Seth bump into the third musketeer? Don't tell me Banker Boy was also pre-law."

For a sec I expected to get sprayed with a mouthful of wine. But unlike me, Radioman had some self-control. And manners.

He swallowed the drink with a cough. "Banker Boy? That's the best you could come up with for Doug?"

The guy's name was Doug? That brought on a whole slew of other moniker possibilities like Doofus Doug, Nickel-and-Dime Doug, Doughboy Doug…

Ding-ding-ding! We have a winner.

"Doug?" I prodded, leaving off the Doughboy part.

"It's a family name, I think," Radioman said. "Short for Douglas."

Or maybe Druggie Doug. The guy did sweat a lot – kinda like a certain detective I knew. But I think in Duncan's case, it was more due to a glandular condition.

Or too many donuts.

"So how then did you and Seth end up friends with Doug?"

"Fraternity drinking games. Doug and Seth were almost always the last two standing in the rivalry between our houses."

Reminded me of the alcohol X-games at Grady's, another continuation of the college party scene for adults.

"I never took you for a frat boy."

He waved off my concern. "Only my first two years, and only because of my father's wishes. I dropped the association when I changed majors."

"But you kept the friends."

Radioman contemplated my statement as he signaled the waiter for a refill. "Actually Seth's my friend in the triangle. He and Doug became friends after I left the Greek system. So I guess you could say Doug's the third wheel when it comes to my friendship with Seth."

"You're not close with Doug then," I said, poking at the subject a little more.

"Nope. Never have been." He took more than a sip. "And probably never will be."

Hmm. Me thinks there might be something a little more juicy in that pronouncement.

But I was done with prodding and poking around the periphery of friendships. Sounded like Grady could rest easy about my involvement with Radioman.

Undercover dating just wasn't my style. I was more the straightforward and out-in-the-open type when it came to relationships.

'Cept when it came to that special time of under-the-covers.

"So what kind of business does your family have?" Radioman asked, returning to more comfortable topics – for him, at least. "Real estate? Law firm? Evil oilman?" Eyes narrowed as he smirked.

"If you only knew," I mumbled.

"I know," he said, rattling the table with a slap. "Private detectives."

"Where'd you get that?"

"You know…after your little tryst with that guy earlier this summer?"

"Zeke?" I sputtered.

"I thought his name was Bud," Radioman returned with a frown.

"Bud?"

"The guy you worked with who killed that pregnant woman."

"Oh, right...Bud. Sure. I get it."

"So the family business...some PI firm?"

"Nah, nothing like that. My dad's just your average, everyday, small businessman."

I may be short on virtues, but at least I was honest.

Mostly.

With my vague businessman reference, the family background remained a nice, safe little secret. Chained and anchored to the dark depths of my life.

Now the PI firm quip? I saw no reason to muddy the waters with the new man in my life. It was best to conceal and carry the amateur investigator title alone.

Anyway, who needed a PI license when you were simply assisting a friend? This was Texas, after all.

Where a license to carry was anything *but* concealed.

A guy who used his lips all day on the radio sure could kiss.

You know, after all that mandible muscle movement to communicate to all of Dallas.

The nightcap had barely started when Radioman tugged full lips away and leaned his forehead against mine.

"If I don't leave now, I might never."

My nether regions kicked into full bloom with his declaration. "I don't mind if you don't."

I pressed my lips to his again and fumbled for the apartment doorknob. Warmth trailed down my neck and to my ear.

"I'm trying to be a gentleman."

"Chivalry is vastly overrated."

I finally succeeded in blindly popping open the door. But before I dragged him inside, Radioman pressed his hands against the doorframe with a groan.

"What about the game next Sunday?"

My sexually charged brain got stuck between a rock and a hard, hard, hard place. On the one hand, he was asking for a second date which meant he wanted to see me again.

On the other hand, he didn't want to see all of me. Right now. In my apartment.

In ways only passion could satisfy.

I traced his cheek with my finger. "I'm not sure if I should feel flattered or frustrated right about now."

"If you're feeling anything like I am," Radioman muttered, "I'd say we're both a bit frustrated."

"Then come inside," I said, grabbing a hand.

Eyes full of desire conflicted with his body's lack of movement. He didn't stir from the doorway, his arms remaining stiff – er, uh, immobile.

"I want more than just a roll in bed with you, Vicki."

"Well you're in luck, because I don't have a bed."

Confusion interrupted the heated gaze of desire. "No bed? You sleeping on the floor or something?"

"Just mattresses," I confirmed. "Until the bedroom set gets delivered."

Observation swept past me to take in my apartment. "Recent remodel?"

"Something like that."

"You must make good tips."

"It was sorta a gift from my mom," I admitted.

"Wow." He whistled in appreciation. Radioman apparently had an eye for details – and expensive taste. "Some gift."

"Yeah. Long story though."

He leaned over and kissed me on the forehead without letting go of the doorframe. "Tell me all about it next Sunday."

With that he was gone, taking the unrequited wind right out of my...

Aw, forget it.

CHAPTER TWENTY

Being awakened by an early morning phone call, after tossing and turning all night with fevered dreams of what *didn't* transpire with my date, never started the day off on my good side.

The moment I cleared the grit from my eyes, Slinky shoved his mug in my face with a caterwaul from Hell.

I wasn't sure which was worse. The constant drone of my phone or my demanding kitty.

"Hello," I barked into the phone.

Reggie's voice came through loud and clear. "Good morning, *mein liebchen*. A better day is on the horizon for you, no?"

Before I verbally abused my friend, Mom's little reminder flitted past my fogged brain: *a lady never loses her temper.*

Good thing I no longer considered myself a lady.

"You better have a good reason for calling me at..." I glanced at the glowing clock readout. "Eight AM? What the hell, Reggie?" I growled.

"Ah yes, the perpetual night owl. But Reggie always has good reasons for his calls," he quipped in that high pitched voice that made dogs howl.

Just call me Fido.

"Thirty seconds, Reggie, and then I pull the plug."

"Tsk, tsk, tsk. Did Reggie interrupt a morning rendezvous?"

I could just picture the wagging caterpillar eyebrows on his dark face. But now I was dreaming of a certain well-exercised mouth placed just about…

"You're down to twenty-five seconds."

"Remind me never to call you before ten."

"Twenty seconds."

"You'll never guess what this morning has wrought."

"Reggie!"

"A little birdie arrived to let me know your bedroom furniture has shipped," he practically squealed.

"Have we reverted back to carrier pigeons instead of texts now?"

"There's the Victoria I know and love."

I groaned and sat up, sleep drifting far into the lusty recesses of my mind.

Until I remembered that bedroom furniture meant a higher probability of breaking it in sooner rather than later with a certain radio personality.

"When will it arrive?" I asked, suddenly more fully awake.

"It's coming freight, so I'm anticipating seeing it no later than Thursday," Reggie promised. "If everything is in order, we could make final set-up for Friday or Saturday…if that works for you."

"Just in time for Sunday."

"What is Sunday?"

Did I say that out loud? "Uh…so I can watch preseason football in bed."

A low chuckle then Reggie reverted to his manly voice sans the false accent. "The Cowboys preseason home opener is next Sunday. Why aren't you *going*?"

"Hey, I'm impressed you know that."

"Another one of my many secrets."

"It just so happens I may be going, but that's not important right now."

I really didn't want to think about what might have been last night. There was also the fact that I had to wait a whole freaking week to try again.

His voice lost the playfulness. "Listen, I'm sorry about the early morning call, but I wanted to talk to you before any of the staff showed up. Have you discovered anything on your end?"

Besides virtually nothing? I dragged my sorry carcass from the mattress with a sigh and stumbled to the kitchen to start a pot of coffee.

Tracking down a blackmailer was proving to be a hell of a lot harder than what I'd gone through to discover a murderer. Well, 'cept for the whole almost-getting-killed thing.

"First off, I should probably tell you that I brought my best friend in on this to help me."

"Janine De'Laruse?" His voice returned to the rafters. "Are you crazy?"

"Hey," I retorted. "Janine wouldn't betray a flea to a can of Raid. Besides, I didn't exactly tell her *who* I was helping."

I sure as hell wasn't going to explain that I probably gave her just enough information for a woman of her intelligence to figure it out faster than she could choose a dress for Sunday services. But Janine could be discreet when she tried.

Sorta.

Maybe.

At least as long as her mother didn't get ahold of her.

"But that doesn't change the fact she's still a De'Laruse," Reggie argued.

"Exactly," I said, dumping two heaping spoonfuls of sugar into a mug. "She's involved in the elitist of the elite circles. All I asked her to do is listen in on the local chatter about anything to do with money and blackmail."

"That covers pretty much everyone in *that* particular class of the population."

Ouch!

But I had to give Reggie that one. 'Specially considering my own emotional blackmail of the sperm donor when it came to his phallic photographic portfolio.

Not something I wanted to contemplate at this too-early hour.

"Don't worry about Janine," I reassured, then took a sip of soothing and caffeinated nectar.

"If only."

"On another note, I had a run-in with Lorraine Padget down at the post office. Seems she was returning some pillows."

"Padget..." Reggie mused aloud. "Oh yes, the Summers account. She's his new buyer or something."

"Fiancé," I corrected.

I could almost make out the satisfying squeak of jaw hinges swinging loose in shock and surprise. "You're kidding."

"Nope. Now that they've set a date, it seems Mr. Summers has opened up his pocketbook."

Among other things.

"Curious pairing," Reggie said. "Isn't he like a hundred?"

"From what I've heard, he's younger than he appears. Probably somewhere closer to seventy when you factor in all those years of smoking."

"That's still a huge age gap."

"But not unheard of in today's meat market. And when you add money to the mix, you can attract all sorts of flies."

Like former beauty queens fluttering around a piece of sausage left out in the sun too long. Or in Lorraine's case it was the has-been beauty queen *looking* like an overstuffed sausage left out in the sun too long.

Okay, maybe that was a little mean.

Nah.

"Mr. Summers is an old-school oilman," Reggie continued. "Which means he's looking to cash in on something. If it's not love, what do you think he's getting in return for his investment?"

Did he really have to ask? And did he really expect me to say it aloud?

"Well, the coffers were opened probably shortly after she opened her legs."

There. I said it. Couldn't take it back. But now I felt like Slinky probably did after a thorough butt licking. I needed something to wash away the offensive and foul flavor.

Did someone say Oreos for breakfast?

"Getting back to *my* conundrum," Reggie returned like a true diva. "The money was in the post office box when I checked it last night."

That informational tidbit might've dropped Lorraine to second place on my short list – if I didn't know her better. Just because she hadn't picked up the cash yesterday didn't mean she hadn't intended to.

Which kept her firmly entrenched in the number one suspect category.

With Lorraine's devious personality and temperament – emphasis on the temper – it'd be like her to use blackmail to get what she wanted. Might go a long way in explaining her relationship with Mr. Summers too.

But since Janine and I had interrupted her gone-postal moment, she'd need another excuse to return to the post office for a little pick-me-up. In the meantime, there was still one person I'd yet to approach.

"There's still Switch," I said around cookie crumbs.

Reggie went all silent on me again. I could almost hear his knees knocking before he finally spoke up. "In all likelihood, he's dead."

"My sources say he's still alive."

The other end of the line quieted for a few beats. "Are these *sources* reliable?"

"This particular one is," I assured. "I even have a phone number."

Another hesitation. "Have you called it?"

"Not yet, but it's on my list of things to do today."

"On second thought, Victoria," Reggie whispered. "Don't."

Following commands, demands, and orders isn't one of my strong suits.

I'd have made one lousy excuse as a soldier in the military. With that incurable disease plaguing me, I'd have been court-martialed on the first day of boot camp after complaining about the uniform.

Olive drab does nothing for me.

Don't get me wrong. I'm a big supporter of the military and good ol' American might. I'd be first in line to welcome our boys home from overseas – pucker up boys and let me lay it on you.

It's just those early morning bugle calls, bad food, being told what to do, when to do it, and where to go would not only have my superiors constantly dishing it out but me shoveling it right back at 'em.

Knowing my luck, I'd be stationed somewhere I'd be certain to shrivel up and die from heat stroke.

Like the Sahara.

Did I also mention the uniform? Yeah, definitely not my style. I'm more the one to help some hunky Marine *out* of uniform instead of dressing *in* one.

Which returned thoughts to what I wanted to do to Radioman. Which made me think of my conversation with Reggie. Which brought me back to Switch.

Damnit.

Like Reggie, I was a bit nervous about contacting the aging head of a tough gang to question him about who might or might not be involved in some blackmail scheme.

Hey, it wasn't like calling up your best friend and asking for a lunch date.

It wasn't even close to calling an attorney to get you out of a jam. Or your accountant. Or an old bedtime gymnastics companion to make sure he knew it was over between you.

Okay, so I wasn't necessarily a *little* nervous about setting up the meeting with Switch. I was *a lot* nervous. Like I really wanted a root canal more than I didn't want to do this nervous.

But Ambassador Juarez had gone through the trouble of sneaking past Jimmy-the-Super and completely blowing by my brand spanking new security system to provide the phone number. The least I could do was make one simple phone call.

Right?

My tangled thoughts circled around to a certain Texas Ranger. Had the ambassador found out from Zeke about my late night jaunt into gang territory? I'd also mentioned Switch's name to Jimmy and Bobby, but they didn't have the connections that came with carrying a badge.

I hadn't told Grady, but then he talked to Zeke on a regular basis. Why would my antics be up for discussion when they had a drug war to covertly fight? And why would Juarez give a crap about helping me do something that would obviously tick off the Ranger?

'Cause Juarez hadn't told him.

I smiled. That meant Zeke had no idea about Juarez's visit to my apartment. Or the phone number he'd given me.

With all of the appreciation Juarez had graced me with for discovering his daughter's killer, the visit with Tomas Ricardo – AKA Switch, AKA a notorious drug dealer and gang leader – was probably sanctioned. Which meant I'd be safe.

Probably.

Sorta.

Maybe?

Turns out, maybe not.

CHAPTER TWENTY-ONE

On a typical Monday off from the bar, I spent my day cleaning house, running errands – you know, the typical routine most normal people did on weekends.

Since my schedule was anything *but* normal, Mondays allowed me to zip through stores with little to no lines and finish all my chores in a matter of hours. That left time for watching a movie, reading a good book, or visiting with friends.

Though I was hard-pressed to classify a notorious gangster as a friend.

After calling and making an appointment to see Mr. Ricardo, and receiving no response to several texts to Janine, my day slogged toward evening like the proverbial tortoise toward the finish line.

Not yet hearing from Radioman after our date might've had a little something to do with the drag too. I didn't want to be the first to break the silence and come off needy.

Time for a Dating 101 tip, ladies. Let the man make first contact after the initial date.

Makes 'em feel more in control of the relational flow. The worst thing you could do is flood a man with texts, phone calls, and messages. Sends a clear cut signal of desperation and clinginess that will send a guy packing ASAP.

And I ain't talking about *what* he's packing. You'll get to find that out for yourself later on, but only if you're smart in how you handle the opening pass.

Which apparently I'd fumbled with Radioman. His flat-out refusal to hitch a ride on the *Vickiwagon* had me wondering if I'd hear from him again at all. I just needed to figure out whether or not we were in a timeout or if a flag had been thrown on the play.

The conversation had flowed. As had the ample alcohol, which usually worked in my favor. Then the kissing had inflamed me faster than a firecracker fuse on the Fourth. But it was my next thought that punched me right in the kisser.

Sure *I'd* felt the fire, but had *he*?

Kissing was an art form. You either had the gift or you didn't. The response I'd earned from every guy I'd kissed since I was fourteen – and trust me, it wasn't *hard* to discern – kissing and I went hand-in-hand. Or mouth-on-mouth. Or mouth-to...

Vicki!

Point is, in all my years of plentiful practice I'd never considered the possibility that *my* kissing might be the problem.

Nah, that couldn't be it. 'Cause Radioman had already asked for another date.

The guy was obviously still into me. He had to be. But the fact I hadn't successfully lured him to my bed – er, mattress – sent my confidence tilting a little off-kilter.

For the first time in my dating life, I understood the desperate tic that plagued other women. My fingers itched to dance over the phone keypad. Countless time in the last twenty-four hours I'd dredged up Radioman's phone number and fought off the urge to click *call*.

How was I to solve this calling conundrum without falling prey to first contact condition? I did what any typical, red-blooded, American girl would do.

I grabbed a coke and a package of Oreos and cuddled up with the cat to watch a blood and gore slasher movie.

Okay, okay, so I'm not so typical. Most girls would watch some romance crap. In my case, I was trying to get my mind *off* of romance. Or at least the sex part.

Work with me, folks.

By six o'clock, I was ready to bounce off the walls like a caffeinated critter. For the life of me I couldn't focus, 'cause the horror movie only had me thinking of what I might be going through with Switch in a few short hours. I needed some calming conversation and lulling libations.

So I sucked it up and made a beeline for the bar.

The night at Grady's had barely begun, but the regular after work crowd had arrived and waved as I entered. Rochelle plopped a cold one in front of me before I even sat down.

"Now that's whatcha call service." I took a long and satisfying gulp. "Nothing calms the nerves better."

Rochelle offered a considering head tilt. "What could possibly have your nerves in a bunch on a day off?"

"Um...traffic?"

"Try again."

"The heat?"

"Close."

"Men?"

"Bingo," Rochelle said with a smile. "I've been dying to hear how your date went with...what do you call him? Radioman?"

"That's the one." I raised the bottle in salute to the made-up moniker. "The date was great…mostly."

Until he ran off and left my girlie bits in a bind.

"Stilted conversation?"

"Smooth as a baby's butt. Couldn't expect less from a guy who gets paid to yap all day."

"True," my co-worker acknowledged, then squinted. "Did you talk with your mouth full?"

"What? No!"

"Cause I know how sloppy you can get when you've had a few."

"The only drinking we did was wine with dinner, *Mother*."

"So it was the awkward goodnight kiss then."

"Great kisser." I sighed at the memory of curled toes – and unrequited passion. "Everything was going perfect until…"

"Awkward good morning?"

I shook my head and buried myself in my beer in shame.

No, I don't cry in my beer, folks. That'd mess up the taste.

Rochelle stopped wiping the counter in mid swipe. "Don't tell me he was bad in bed."

"Never even got there," I admitted.

Now I had the barkeep's full and undivided attention. She lowered her voice to where she could barely be heard over the piped-in music.

"Did he ask to do something…you know…kinky?"

"Didn't you hear me?" I asked raising my voice. "We. Never. Got. To. The. Bedroom!"

Snickers from the table behind indicated my timbre had overshot my intentions.

Everyone always said I possessed a voice that carried.

When I was young, the sperm donor had even claimed he could hear me all the way down in Houston and Mexico during business trips.

In the ensuing adult years, alcohol tended to amplify my vocal inflections. And my vocabulary.

Oh, hell. Maybe I had talked with my mouth full.

Rochelle leaned forward like she'd bought a ticket and taken a front row seat to the stage performance of my mental musings. She patted my hand and handed over another frosty one.

"Tell Momma 'Chelle what happened then."

"It's what didn't happen. He said he wanted to be a *gentleman*, whatever the hell that means."

"Mm-hmm."

"He wouldn't even cross the threshold into my apartment."

"Seriously?"

"As a heart attack."

"What a letdown."

"Among other things," I murmured. "Be honest with me, Rochelle. Are my thighs too fat? Butt too big? Boobs not big enough?"

"You're asking me?" Rochelle squawked. "I'm a thirty-*something* divorcée with two kids. If that's not enough to send a man running away in terror, I've got stretch marks to rival a roadmap, a butt that screams *mom-jeans* no matter what I wear, and boobs already headed into a permanent southerly migration."

She knocked back a shot of Jack. "At this rate, you might as well put me out to pasture or send me off to the glue factory. So trust me when I say that I'd kill to have just your thighs."

And Janine wondered why I wasn't ready to jump on

the kid caboose. She shoulda had a seat beside me for Rochelle's diatribe against the physical manifestations of motherhood.

Then again, she'd probably come back at me with something like *that's what keeps plastic surgeons at the top of the medical field food chain*.

I finished off my second beer. "Then what's wrong with me?"

"Nothing, hon."

"You've said it before. Grady's been treating me differently."

Yeah, that was because of other things, but the train was out of the yard and heading down the *Vicki's Feeling Sorry for Herself* tracks.

"I was at Zeke's place for more than a month, and he never so much as tried to touch me," I continued. "The only person who has given me the eyeball since the start of summer is a middle-aged detective with a glandular condition. And now Baby is entertaining the troops better than me."

"Maybe Radioman should've asked *her* out?"

I offered up my best narrow-eyed glare. Then belched. Rochelle laughed, grabbed a shot glass then poured in three fingers before sliding it toward me.

"Listen," she stated, "have you ever tried *not* rushing a relationship into the physical realm?"

"I don't follow."

"You know, taking things slow. Avoiding the bedroom until the relationship passes the viability stage."

I shrugged before tossing back the shot. "Guess I'm just a one trick pony."

"Isn't that streetwalker slang for a john?"

"I thought that was another word for a toilet?"

"Trick?"

"No, john."

Rochelle swiped the empty glass off the bar without replacing it. "Look, this could be a really good thing. It says Radioman's interested in more than just your body. It means he's interested in *you*."

"Hey, whether it's first, second, or third down, the defensive end is still gonna rush the quarterback when given the chance," I returned.

Rochelle just shook her head like a good mother. "Take it from a girl who's been around the block more than once, Vicki. Enjoy your time with this one. Pace yourself. He just might be a keeper."

"Then what do we do in the meantime?"

My mind drifted to last night. Lips on mine. Tongues doing the tonsil tango. Desire to drag him to my mattress and see what else he could do with that tongue.

Think about it – 'cause I sure was.

"Enjoy the conversation and the kissing."

Apparently my co-worker had scalped the tickets to those front row seats and gone elsewhere for the night's entertainment ventures.

"So what's a guy got to do to get in on this kissing?"

Speak of the devil – almost.

I spun the stool around to catch Radioman's lawyer friend sliding in next door in a tailored black suit minus the requisite tie.

"What'll you have?" Rochelle asked.

I interceded. "He'll take a scotch on the rocks."

Seth sent a thumb my way. "What she said."

While Rochelle poured his drink, Seth gave me the full-blown, head-to-toe, eyeball undressing.

With some people, such action got my catnip all riled up

like Slinky when the litterbox needed refreshed. But after the conversation with my co-worker, it was the stroke my ego needed.

Sorta.

"This is a nice view," he said with a smile. "Never seen you on this side of the bar."

"My night off," I returned.

"And yet here you are."

I offered up a toast with the vodka Rochelle had set before me – then realized with my first sip it was water. She tossed a smirk over her shoulder before scurrying off to wait on another patron.

"This is my home away from home."

"Kinda like me and my office some days," Seth said with a sigh and glanced around the room.

Nerves fluttered in my stomach. "Are the guys meeting you here tonight?"

"Doug was supposed to, but it looks like he got tied up late at the office too."

Good. No awkward moment with Radioman on the horizon. In my present, less-than-confident state, I really didn't want to run into him until I had a chance to buck up.

'Course that got me thinking about bucking broncos. Which then had me thinking about stallions. Which sent my gray matter to contemplating a certain set of lonely sheets.

"So speaking of Doug," I ventured into safer topic territory. "I asked Radiom…I mean Bruce, about him last night on our date."

Seth's mouth quirked. "That's a strange conversation for you two to have on a first date."

I shrugged. "I was curious about how the three of you met."

"Did he tell you about our fraternity rivalry?"

"Yeah. If I remember correctly, it had something to do with alcohol consumption then too."

Seth coughed away the sip he'd taken and laughed. "From frat rivals to friends. Pretty interesting, huh?"

"Interesting," I mused as Grady popped out of his office and eyed me from across the bar.

Instead of the typical mustache tilt this time he offered up a hard set of his jaw and a firm line of lips, as if he knew the conversational track I'd taken with Seth about Banker Boy.

The one he'd told me to leave alone.

With all of the cameras canvassing the area, I wouldn't put it past him to have planted a few microphone bugs like a scene from a spy movie. The realization sent a zing along my spine.

And this time it wasn't in the direction of my nether regions.

If there really were hidden microphones planted around here, that meant Grady had listened in on all of my interactions. All of my conversations at the bar. Even the ones Rochelle and I had concerning his fine...

Oh, hell no.

My co-worker chose that moment to return. "So Vicki here tells me you're a lawyer."

"Is that a positive or a negative in your book?" Seth asked with a wink.

"Aw, sugar." Rochelle smiled and gave him a placating pat to his cheek. "I don't do the cougar thing, but thanks for the consideration."

A wicked little grin oozed across Seth's lips. "Too bad."

I continued stewing about the extent of Grady's clandestine activities as he made rounds, his stare never really leaving mine. The possibility he'd listened in on conversations all these years threatened to stir up a hornets nest in my way of thinking.

Rochelle shoulda filled my glass with vodka instead of water. Might burn the boss's eyes a little when I threw it in his face – if he had the courage to head this way.

"Besides, I'm raising two kids on a bartender's salary," Rochelle continued.

Her favorite defense mechanism – throw two kids into the conversation and most guys ran toward the finish line faster than a sprinter in the hundred-yard dash.

But Seth stayed put – and put on his lawyer face. "Divorced?"

Rochelle's eyes widened. "Well, yeah."

"Was child support ordered as part of your decree?"

She rolled her eyes and snorted like a prized bull. "Just because a paper says he's supposed to pay doesn't make it magically appear in my bank account."

"Aren't they garnishing his wages?"

"That'd be easier if I knew where he'd disappeared to."

Seth tossed back the remainder of scotch and dropped forty bucks on the bar as he stood. Then he handed a card to Rochelle.

"I might be able to help with that. Call my office tomorrow."

She stared at the card. "Thanks, but I can't afford an attorney right now."

"Pro bono."

"For child support?"

Seth shrugged. "Sure. I can choose up to a certain number of pro bono cases I take on each year."

"I...I...," Rochelle stuttered.

I leaned into Seth's shoulder and got a whiff of the same musky cologne Radioman had worn on our date. The thoughts of what *should've* happened last night, if I'd had my way, flooded my naughty mind – until Grady popped into my peripheral vision and brought with it thoughts of lying, cheating men.

"She'll call you in the morning," I told Seth.

He nodded and checked his phone. "Well, since my friend has stood me up, I guess I'll mosey on elsewhere for an entertaining diversion."

Elsewhere called to me too when I checked the time on my phone an hour later. Though a meeting with a dangerous gang leader promised to be less than diverting.

Try more like panty piddling.

Piddling in panties – check.

'Cept it wasn't for the reason I'd originally imagined.

A clipped response to one of my earlier texts told me Janine was once again in full-fledged freak-out mode as she readied preparations for the semester's start. Which in my book said she was in dire need of a break.

Plus, with my heart threatening to pound right out of my chest, I could use some back-up to tame the cowardly lion courage coursing through my veins.

Whatever qualms I'd had about dragging Janine along as Watson to my Holmes whisked away as we drove through the elegant neighborhood. Homes were much larger than average. Beautiful, old-fashioned streetlamps dotted every corner like ones at the turn of the twentieth century.

I tapped my GPS a couple of times to make sure it hadn't taken us on a side trip to Neverland. I pulled to a stop beneath a streetlamp to double-check I'd correctly input the address into GPS. Then a quick check of what I'd written down when setting the appointment.

I had to have written it down wrong. Blame it on a case of overwrought nerves when I'd made the call earlier.

"Why are we stopping?" Janine whispered.

"This can't be right," I said, squinting at the paper in the ambient dash lights and comparing it to the GPS readout.

The details written were the same as the electronic input. Reality plowed right into the fantasy. I put the car into drive and continued up the hill.

Dozens of Victorian homes, their turreted spires rising three stories in most cases, sat on two and three acre lots surrounded by scrolling wrought iron fences.

Gingerbread dripped from wraparound porches that screamed for Hansel and Gretel to come over and enjoy a bite – 'cept in the one I was looking for waited a wicked warlock instead of a witch.

A couple more corners and then I stopped before a gate when the disembodied feminine voice explained I'd reached my destination.

The fence here was higher. Poured concrete with occasional wrought iron peek-a-boos for decoration and a scroll along the top like ornamental barbed wire to satisfy some sort of area building covenants. Looked more like an attempt to keep concentration camp prisoners from getting out.

Appropriate, considering most homeowners associations acted like Nazis when it came to enforcing their idea of an authentic neighborhood theme.

Janine spoke up, staring through the gates at the monstrosity. "Are you sure this is it?"

"No," was all I could think to say.

"Check the address again."

"I've triple checked it, Janine. Quadruple checked it."

"But that house looks like someplace a sweet, little, old grandmotherly lady would live."

"With a fence guaranteed to keep her from escaping."

Janine scrunched up her petite nose. "A gang leader lives *here*?"

"That's what my source told me."

She snickered. "Is that source the old woman in a shoe who had so many kids she didn't know what to do?"

"Ha-ha, no."

About the time I considered turning the Vette around and hightailing it out of there, the alarm I'd set on my phone buzzed, signaling the moment of truth had arrived. I was now officially late for this meeting.

Talk about your panty piddling.

Maybe I could call the number Ambassador Juarez had provided and explain the situation. But what would a notorious gang leader do to a girl if she missed a meeting entirely? The thought made me shudder.

The box at the gate squawked and brought a warmth to my nether regions.

And not the good kind.

"Name and purpose?" the gruff voice growled.

I rolled down the car window. "Vicki Bohanan to see Swi...*Mr.* Ricardo."

Silence. That didn't bode well.

"Should you give them my name too?" Janine asked.

"Yeah, that'd go over well. You might as well jump out of the car, wave your arms, and beg them to hold you for ransom."

Holy hell, what had I done?

Certified stupidity slapped me upside the head. I'd brought my best friend with me to the home of a known criminal. A blue-eyed, blond virgin. A De'Laruse no less.

Someone just point me toward the nearest volcano.

Before sacrificing Janine to the gods, I shifted the Vette into reverse and was about to blow this halftime show when a mechanical hum arrested my attention and the gates swung open.

"What are you waiting for?" Janine whispered.

"My bladder to stop barking."

Instead of running for the border like I wanted to, I crept inside the compound and parked along the elliptical drive near the front entrance, listening for barking dogs, snoring old ladies – and waiting for gunshots.

A man in a tailored black suit walked onto the porch and hustled down the steps toward us. I shot a glance at Janine and handed her the keys.

"Twenty minutes," I said.

Janine nodded.

"If I'm not back by then, or you see anything suspicious while I'm gone, you slam the car through that gate at warp speed and head straight to Zeke."

"What if the gate's closed?"

I took a deep breath and imagined my baby launching against the wrought iron at Mach 1. Tears came to my eyes as I pictured the crumpled accordion hood then reminded myself that friendship was more important than fenders.

I think.

I took another deep breath and let it out with a shudder. "Just hit it with both barrels and get out of here."

She winced then nodded again.

Maybe Zeke was right. Maybe I was a complete idiot with a death wish – and I'd gone and gotten Janine involved.

Black Suit beckoned me to exit the car by tugging the door open. I stood to allow Janine to maneuver into the driver's seat then closed the door and turned to my escort.

Someone get me some clean underwear stat.

CHAPTER TWENTY-TWO

"Seth?" I squeaked.

Hard dark eyes addressed me before the hiss of Radioman's lawyer friend broke through the shock. "Keep your voice down."

"This is the entertainment you left the bar to find?"

"This isn't what it looks like," he whispered. "Play along like we don't know each other, okay?"

"Not what it looks like?" My tongue stumbled over my lips.

"I'll explain later."

He held out his hand for my purse. But my gray matter had glazed over like one of Detective Duncan's day old donuts.

"Please," Seth continued as another tall, dark, and scary man followed the same path from the porch. "For both our sakes, act like we've never met."

Never met? Not what it looked like? And Grady had been worried about my association with Banker Boy.

Oh, we were so going to have a conversation later. One I'd be happy to include Grady in.

For now, I plastered on a mask to hide not only my

association with Seth but to cover up the questions of what I'd *really* stumbled onto here. The older *gentleman* patted me down and emptied my purse across the car hood, waving a metal wand across the contents before stuffing most of it back inside and handing it to me, sans the phone and pepper spray.

I handed the contraband items over to Janine and offered an encouraging smile that probably looked more like I wanted to hurl.

Satisfied, Mr. Tall Dark and Scary offered his arm like a proper escort. "Were you not instructed to come alone?"

My throat tightened and a single word came out more like the croak of a choking frog. "No."

"Your friend will stay in the car then, understood?"

I didn't trust my voice to tell him that was my plan too, so I nodded instead.

Tall Dark and Scary addressed Seth with a finger pointed toward Janine. "Watch her."

"Yes, sir," the young lawyer responded.

I shot Seth a scowl to wither his genitals and send home a message – something along the lines of *there's a castration in your future if something happens to my bestie.*

Mr. TD & S tugged me toward the house. "You will address my employer at all times as Mr. Ricardo."

I still didn't trust my voice so nodded compliance again.

"You are here as a guest and will only go where I escort you."

"K," I squawked.

The stairs were more stable than I was as I tripped onto the porch. Sometimes – like now – I wished I'd paid more attention during those cotillion classes growing up. I needed to project a confident assurance I didn't feel, not stumble around like I was on this side of a drunken stupor.

"As a guest, you will be under the full protection of my employer while on the premises, Miss Bohanan."

"Understood." My voice came out stronger this time. "My friend?"

"Will receive the same protection," he replied. "However, you will speak to no one about the contents of this meeting. Not even to your friend there."

"Got it."

A calculated look ricocheted over me before Tall Dark and Scary opened the front door. "Once you leave these premises, this agreement and all codicils are null and void."

Codicils? Null and void? I found my voice. "Who are you? Switch's lawyer?"

"Mr. Ricardo," he emphasized.

My knees started knocking all over again at the glint in Tall Dark and Scary's eyes. I prayed my mention of lawyers hadn't just given away my association with Seth. I needed to practice a little self-control as Rochelle and I had discussed mere hours ago.

This time over my disease-ridden mouth.

'Cause it wasn't just my life on the line here – no matter what the guy attached to my arm said. Lawyers were good at twisting words. Sometimes they could be downright slimy, evidence by the guy standing near my car.

I was starting to have second thoughts about another date with Radioman.

The door swung open to reveal a staircase straight out of one of Janine's romance movies. A winding mass of mahogany trailing up to the second floor was a sight even Scarlett O'Hara couldn't balk at.

"This way," Mr. TD & S directed up the stairs.

I heard every squeak of the wood. Felt every slight shift as I placed my feet upon each tread. If not for the live bodies standing guard nearby, I'd have sworn the house was haunted.

Or maybe it was all in my overwrought and scaredy cat psyche.

After the boneheaded traipse through gang territory the other night, I shuddered to think what Zeke would do to me if he found out where I was right at that moment.

I could almost hear him now – *What's the matter with you? What's with the death wish? Why'd you drag Janine into it this time? Are you dumb or just stupid?*

That last one really got my dander up. Me stupid? How dare he!

When I walked into the darkened study, I began to think Zeke might be on to something.

What name did Ambassador Juarez say to use? Bernard? Barry? No, Benny. Yeah, Benny was the one responsible for getting me into this.

Well technically Reggie, but I didn't want to take time right then to mince words – er, thoughts.

The scent of cigars and leather permeated the air and sent my thoughts on a quick memory lane jaunt with Janine and her Louisiana-based grandfather. That man had loved only two things in life – his wife and some of the most expensive cigars on the planet.

I still wasn't sure which killed him in the end.

A desk lamp provided the only light in the room and cast shadows as the hulking man rose from behind the gigantic carved block of wood. Even with the clipped crop of silver hair, I entertained no doubt he could pick up the desk and toss it at me with a spiral guaranteed to make a pro quarterback jealous.

When he brought his hand up, I expected I had less than five seconds to state my case before the report of a gunshot silenced me forever. Maybe that was why the carpet was red. Better to conceal blood residue.

Instead there was a snap of fingers and illumination of the room before Tall Dark and Scary left with a click of the door loud enough to make an elephant jump. Or a boneheaded barmaid barf.

Beady eyes stared from a face carved of stone. Deep pockmarks from a bad case of pubescent acne marred it.

Or at least that's what I told myself.

But the scar jagging from the corner of his eye across the cheek and to his jaw bespoke a life I'd once thought of when faced with Jimmy-the-Super.

'Cept in this case, I don't think a medical condition or military service would explain it.

"Miss Bohanan, welcome. Please be seated. Drink?"

Mr. Ricardo indicated a chair before stepping from behind the desk to a wet bar inset into the mahogany paneling. I was so ready to drink a little – or a lot – of everything I saw in the decanters to calm my nerves.

Instead I politely deferred. "N-no, thank you."

Noodley legs would've sat me down right where I stood, but I managed to wait until the wingback chair was behind me before I collapsed in a whoosh. In my life, I'd been in the presence of some pretty influential figures.

None more fear-inspiring than the massive man daintily pouring himself a drink.

With difficulty, I managed to dredge from the depths some of the manners Mom had tried to teach me when facing powerful heads of state.

"Th-thank you for seeing me, Sw...Mr. Ricardo," I stammered.

He sat in a matching chair opposite and reached into a humidor on the end table. "It's not every day the only daughter of one of Dallas's wealthiest oil men asks for a meeting with a lowly goods distributor."

Lowly? The man had given himself a promotion from gang leader to drug runner to *goods* distributor. From the look of his palatial home, the guy had worked his way up the food chain quite nicely.

He'd also done his homework – on me.

"We only share a name these days," I offered. "My father and I don't see eye-to-eye when it comes to money, marriage vows...pretty much everything."

"And that is why you live on your own and tend bar?"

I swallowed the acidic discomfort that erupted in my belly and put on a brave face. "I prefer to control my own destiny without shackles forced upon me."

Did the scar near his mouth just twitch? Was that amusement twinkling in his eyes? The flick of the lighter covered any noticeable reaction.

Wreathed in smoke, he settled into the tufted cushion. "So I'm given to understand we have a mutual acquaintance."

"Yes, sir," I responded, grateful to get the conversation on track as the minutes counted down toward my Vette's potential demise. "Benny thought you might be able to provide some information."

"Ah yes, Benny. I haven't had the pleasure of seeing him in many years. How is the old man?"

Talk about your pot calling the kettle black – or in this case gray. "He's good...considering."

"Considering?" The drug lord leaned forward.

"W-well," I stuttered again.

I never thought to ask Juarez what I should and shouldn't talk about with Ricardo. In all the hours I'd fussed and fretted about this meeting, never once did I imagine sharing a smoke and cocktails over polite conversation.

"You, uh, know he lost his daughter a few months ago."

A slow nod. "Yes, I remember hearing about that. To find out you have a daughter only *after* her death...unfortunate indeed."

Another languid draw on the cigar while he gauged my reaction. I harbored no doubt he was fishing for more information.

In this instance, my disease ridden mouth stayed shut. It took a proverbial hammer and nails and a good dose of superglue, but it stayed firmly closed. Mr. Ricardo wouldn't get anything else from me.

Finally he released a long and elegant exhale. "Now he repays your kindness for catching her killer."

"I didn't exactly catch him," I admitted.

"But you led authorities to the killer."

"You could say that."

I crossed and uncrossed my legs like a nervous teenager on her very first date. Ricardo already knew pretty much everything about the situation with Amy. About my involvement. For a man who hadn't seen his *friend* in many years, he stayed well informed about the ambassador.

Was it possible the Juarez cartel already suspected Benny of playing on the wrong side of the tracks? If so, was that the real reason I'd been granted this interview?

Twenty minutes ticked down quick, so I had to keep him talking. "I must say, Mr. Ricardo, you have a lovely home for a mere goods distributor."

Another tip for you ladies here. If you ever need to redirect conversation to a new topic, just stroke a man's - er, ego.

Ask him about his job. His accomplishments. Show appreciation for those material possessions like his house or his car.

Unless his name is Nick.

Once started, most men will brag about their prowess in spades. Until the evening wanes. Until you can't wait for him to drop you off at your place and leave.

Okay, sometimes it does backfire, especially if you're under a time crunch – and again, if your date is Nick. To speed things up, you can always go back to stroking something else if there's chemistry.

And yes, I meant that to sound dirty.

Ricardo acknowledged my comment with a wave of his cigar. "For someone from such humble beginnings, it is good to show others that hard work pays off."

"The beautiful mahogany paneling," I started as I rose and paced the study for something to do besides sit in fear. It also gave me a head start if I needed to make a quick escape. "The elaborate stairwell in the foyer. And if I'm not mistaken, the runner in the hallway is Persian, yes?"

A hint of a smile. "Your cultured upbringing serves you well."

"But I'm curious," I continued. "You strike me as more of a stone manor kind of man. Big. Strong. Why the delicate Victorian?"

The hard glint in his eyes tempered the smile. Crap – had I stepped in it already? How long did Mr. Tall Dark and Scary say those codicils lasted?

"This is only one of my homes," he said.

"I'm sorry, I didn't mean..."

"I built it for my *mamita*."

Throughout our conversation, he'd covered his accent well. But the mention of his mother dropped the façade faster than a cold front in January and chilled the room.

'Course that might have more to do with the vent grate

blowing cold air up my shorts.

"As I said, it is a lovely home." But no amount of sucking up could correct my off-course steering.

Mr. Ricardo rose. "Why did you wish to see me, Miss Bohanan?"

Direct and to the point. Might as well approach him in kind. Most businessmen preferred it in the long run anyway.

"A long-ago mutual acquaintance has rehabilitated his life," I said. "Much like you have yours."

The derisive snort indicated my veil of flattery was thin leaning toward obvious. "Reggie Brown. Or do you call him Reginald von Braun, too?"

The revelation silenced me for a moment as I struggled to drag my jaw off the floor. "You know?"

"Of course, I know. Known since the flaming tart returned from New York and opened his little decorating business. Did a respectable job on this place too, I might add."

The brakes in my brain screeched to a stop so fast, the smoke in the room wasn't just from cigars.

"Wait, wait, wait. He did the interior design here? For your mother?"

"He *is* the premier decorator in the region, and my *mamita* deserved the best," Ricardo said. "However, my attorney handled the details, because if he'd even seen my name, Reggie would've turned tail and returned to New York like the coward he is."

Okay, so at least he wasn't aware that Reggie only pretended to be gay. No need to bring that up and stir the kettle further.

"So if you've known all this time, why blackmail him now?"

"Blackmail?" he thundered before stubbing out the cigar in an ashtray. "Tomas Ricardo would never stoop to blackmail. I have no need for small change."

I guess the saying there's no honor among thieves was a misnomer – and I'd just offended one of the big ones.

"I'm sorry, Mr. Ricardo," I said in my most placating tone. "But I simply needed to make sure it wasn't you going after Reggie because of any prior connections."

A curt nod acknowledged my apology like a gentleman who'd learned the ropes of elite circles so as to better move among them. But too big to resort to blackmail?

I wasn't so sure.

Perhaps not monetary blackmail, but definitely one to hold information over someone's head to get them to dance to a new tune. I'd learned firsthand how that worked watching the sperm donor move in the corporate world. And in the religious realm. Why not in the criminal?

Shaking hands and greasing palms. Seemed there was little separating any enterprises these days.

"So little Reggie's in trouble, is he?" Mr. Ricardo mused aloud. "And asked you to help after your previous success."

"Well, I wouldn't exactly call it a success. More of…"

"Perhaps my network could discover the culprit for you, Miss Bohanan," Ricardo interrupted. "After all, a woman of your background and reputation should be more careful about being seen rubbing shoulders with the city's seedy underbelly."

No way was I gonna place myself in Ricardo's debt – no matter how innocent the *goods* he distributed these days.

A glance at the clock informed me I was mere moments away from seeing the Vette play the accordion. I just hoped my phone, Janine's phone, and the dashboard time display were synchronized so Janine didn't get confused and jump the gun.

Hey, the girl is smart, but there's something to be said for the impact of nerves on reaction time. One of the reasons why firearms training focused on targeting center mass instead of aiming for something smaller.

Like the heart.

"You've been gracious with your time, but you've told me all I needed to know," I said inching my way toward the door.

And escape.

In two strides, Ricardo stood before me with his hand on the doorknob. "It has been a pleasure to meet you, Miss Bohanan. I hope we have the opportunity to see one another again."

Meet again? Sure.

Like when the Cleveland Browns win the Super Bowl.

I didn't waste time switching seats and told Janine to just drive.

'Course after the compound gates opened. We were both in a rather silent state of shock to escape the goods distributer's property unscathed.

Seeing Seth there and then meeting an obviously successful gang leader, I had far too much to contemplate on the drive to the De'Laruse mansion to waste time on small talk. At least by the time I dropped off my best friend, my hands were no longer shaking.

'Cause I had the information Reggie needed.

On the one hand, I was pretty sure Switch hadn't sent the blackmail note. I mean, yes the guy had the money for the high quality paper stock and likely had someone on staff who was trained in calligraphy. But Switch could've made life miserable for my friend long before now.

Which brought me to the other hand. I wasn't so sure I should share the part about the former gang leader turned high-class goods distributor being aware of Reggie's ruse.

All of which left me once again with a shrinking short list of blackmailer candidates.

My money was still on Lorraine. With sketchy present actions combined with her career contacts – not to mention the right attitude – it only made sense.

My cell phone dinged with an incoming text just as I pulled into the garage. At this late hour, there were only a handful of people it might be.

Janine needing to vent? Grady with an emergency at the bar? Oh, I hoped not. After fishing the phone from my purse, the surprise sender made my heart tick up a notch and a smile tug at my lips.

Custom dictates 24 hrs B4 contact after first date. I waited 24.1 2 say looking 4ward 2 seeing U soon.

In the excitement as I focused on replying to Radioman, I failed to see the wall standing in the shadows until I plowed right into him.

The only sound I heard as a hand clamped over my mouth to stop my scream was my phone shattering across the asphalt.

CHAPTER TWENTY-THREE

I twisted in the vice-like grip and bit down hard on a misplaced finger before bringing my knee up to connect with that oh-so-delicate and usually flaccid spot between the legs of the male persuasion.

And trust me, I could be very persuasive with my life on the line.

Here's another tip, ladies. Being a single woman on her own in a big city, it's important to carry either a can of pepper spray or take self-defense classes.

There's also conceal carry, though some people have trouble pointing a gun at another human being, much less possessing the ovaries necessary to actually pull the trigger. Having dated a Texas Ranger, you can imagine which one of those choices I picked.

If your purse is like mine, pepper spray can be difficult to access at a moment's notice. Plus, its effectiveness isn't always guaranteed.

Unlike a bullet.

For some, the idea of taking a life even in self-defense, wasn't something they could live with. Me? When it came down to a mugging or attempted rape, it was either me or him – and I'll be damned if it was me.

You just needed the mental fortitude under pressure to remember to remove the safety.

Only problem with carrying a gun in your purse is the same as pepper spray – it gets lost in the muddle of wallet, checkbook, keys, lipstick, powder, emergency underwear for those unexpected sleepovers, condoms, etc.

Or you fail to put it inside your purse in the first place.

Since tonight's excursion involved visiting a person of questionable character, who probably wouldn't have let me within ten inches of his person without the requisite pat-down Mr. Tall Dark and Scary had provided, I'd wisely left it in my closet.

When my knee made the proper connection, the perpetrator released me and fell to his knees with a loud *umph*. Then I successfully fished the pepper spray from my purse and doused him good before sprinting into my building and up the stairs two at a time.

My hands shook so bad I could barely hold onto the keys to let myself in before slamming the door shut and throwing every bolt, chain and the proverbial kitchen sink at it.

Right about the time I planned to call the police, I remembered my one and only phone lay in pieces on the pavement.

Down the stairs.

Outside.

Oh, hell-to-the-huh-uh. No way was I going back out there.

The only other option was to run downstairs and knock on Jimmy-the-Super's door and ask to use his. Similar problem though – me leaving my nice, safe fortress of solitude.

Needless to say, I'd rather stay inside my fortress and scream my lungs inside out before venturing into the hallway again tonight.

Wait a sec. Jimmy had all of that surveillance crap in his apartment. Cameras all over the building. Scanning the parking lot.

Maybe he'd seen us and was calling the cops at this very moment. Perhaps he was even on the way upstairs to check on me to make sure I was okay.

Knocks pounded on the door as if we'd had a temporary telepathic connection. My savior had come to rescue me!

Or the attempted rapist had followed me. That thought sent all the blood draining from my head, and left me in a fear-filled daze before self-preservation kicked in.

I raced to the bedroom closet and grabbed my Sig Sauer P938 peashooter from the case, flicking off the safety and chambering a round with trembling hands before inching toward the door.

Now most people in the south would call out a friendly *who is it* before checking the window or peephole and opening the door when someone knocked or rang the doorbell.

But in these here such cases, calling out only lets the bad guy know you're home, are female, and approximately where you are located in the apartment.

Personally, I'd rather just shoot the bastard through the door and be done with it, though authorities might look down on that if I didn't at least check the peephole first.

Guess that's why God invented them in the first place.

I just never in my wildest imagination – or at least in my current scaredy cat state – expected to see that particular face at my door.

It took all of two seconds to release every bolt and chain

and open the door to a slightly stooped, watery red-eyed familiar mug. Anger and irritation rolled off him in waves as he eyed the gun in my hand.

Or maybe that was from the residual pepper spray scent chaser.

"Gonna shoot me now too?" he rasped before coughing overtook his speaking ability.

"I should after you scared me half to death, Zeke Taylor," I yelled. "What the hell are you doing sneaking around my parking lot at this late hour?"

He didn't, or more likely couldn't, answer and simply handed me the pieces of my dead phone. So I did what any self-respecting southern woman would do with her ex-boyfriend slash would-be attacker.

Invited him inside.

At least in this case it was warranted since I imagine Zeke hadn't meant any harm. And he's law enforcement.

Guess there was no need to call the cops now.

After setting the gun on the counter and steadying him on a barstool, I soaked several kitchen towels with cold water for eye compresses and gave Zeke a glass of water.

Slinky peered out from beneath the sofa, sniffed the air and sneezed from the fetching aroma of e*au de pepper spray* before scurrying away to the bedroom. My eyes watered a bit from the stench by that point too.

Do you think I may've overdone the self-protective hose down more than a little?

Don't answer that.

Once Zeke breathed a little more freely and his eyes grew a bit less rheumy, I laid into him with the full force of my freaked-out evening.

"You have ten seconds to explain what you're doing here, Ranger Taylor."

With his eyes still red and puffy, I couldn't tell if he was glaring or just staring. "Or what?"

"Or...or...," I hesitated before grabbing the Sig. "Or I just might start shooting and ask questions later."

The pepper spray had temporarily incapacitated his sight and breathing but had done nothing to stunt his reflexes. With a lightning-fast move, Zeke disarmed me, flicked the safety back on, then shoved my weapon into his waistband as he stood.

"I've had just about enough of your antics tonight," he grumbled. "You wanna have a question and answer bout? How about you tell me what the hell you were doing at the home of a known drug dealer?"

It took a moment for brain waves to trigger and stop the muscles in my lower jaw from swinging loose. "How did you...?"

"Know you were there?" Zeke finished for me. "Tomas Ricardo has been on the radar of every state and federal law enforcement agency this side of the Mexican border."

"But how did *you* know?" I clarified.

"Really? Did you not pay one iota of attention to my job while you were living with me?"

"Five weeks is hardly enough time to..."

"I'm talking before," Zeke thundered. "Back when we actually used to talk. When we dated. Before you..."

It was Zeke's turn to clam up as he shoved a hand through his hair, picked up the water glass and walked to the windows.

"Before I what?" I prompted.

"Forget it," he muttered, taking a drink and dabbing at his eyes with the paper towels before staring into the night. "Just something else you'll misinterpret."

Now the boy had my dander up. And after I'd helped

nurse him back to health even.

"Before I what?" I demanded. "Before I discovered who you really are? Before I found you with your arms around another woman?"

"See that's what I'm talking about," Zeke said, spinning around to face me. "You see one little thing and blow it completely out of proportion."

Oh huh-uh. He. Did. Not.

"Out of proportion? You were making out with another woman. That evil, back-stabbing, lowlife Lorraine Padget, no less."

"Hugging does not constitute making out."

"That's what I saw."

Zeke slammed the glass down and sloshed water across the island counter. "How can you be such a completely irrational female?"

Irrational? That was one toe shy of outright calling me stupid – just like I knew he would. I stomped over to the front door, undid all of the doohickeys, then opened it wide.

"Get out," I commanded.

Zeke stood his ground with a cock of an eyebrow.

"Get. Out," I reiterated.

We entered a staring contest – and I was in it to win it – until Zeke relented by placing my Sig in a drawer at the far end of the kitchen island. Where I couldn't get to it quick enough.

In three strides he stood beside me. He still reeked of pepper spray, but I wasn't about to allow my senses to react. I have *some* self-control, after all.

Stop laughing.

"Whatever you're doing, Vic…whoever you're doing it for…stay out of it," Zeke said, his voice softening. "Next time I might not be there to protect you…*or* your best friend."

I winced. Taking Janine for moral support had been just plain dumb, I admit. But I wasn't about to let the Ranger know that.

I slammed the door behind him in frustration then leaned against it with a sigh. The logical side of my brain told me Zeke was just looking out for me. And that he was probably right.

In more ways than one.

But you didn't hear that from me.

CHAPTER TWENTY-FOUR

"Aren't you hungry, sweetheart?"

Mom prodded me with the overused endearment as she sipped tea from the dainty china cup then nestled it on the saucer.

Out of desperation, I'd convinced her lunch would best be consumed and digested within the air-conditioned comfort inside her favorite bistro instead of our usual outside locale at the patio tables. That meant a confined crowd and noisier environment, two things she didn't relish.

But for me it offered a relatively glisten-free meal, considering the thermometer prediction topped out above a hundred. And that was before factoring in a thousand percent humidity with no breeze.

I really needed a stiff one. Breeze, that is. 'Course, I wouldn't toss aside one in the drink category either. Or of the male persuasion.

Think about it.

With a teetotaler mom in tow, I'd never get away with a real drink. Plus, talking about a man in my life threatened to give my mother apoplexy if the past was any indication. If it wasn't for the fact that I was anything but Godly, I'd swear my entry into the world was the second known virgin birth.

"I'm fine, Mom. See?"

I nibbled at the avocado sandwich if only to satisfy her. The heat had stolen my hunger. Or maybe it was something else.

First Grady and his extracurricular activities around the bar had our working relationship in a gut-wrenching bind.

Then Zeke and I were so far on the outs, it'd take more than a plasma weld to secure even a friendship at this stage.

Then there was Lorraine. The pageanted princess continued to haunt my thoughts and remained number one on my blackmail suspect list.

But without any hard evidence against her, I'd never free Reggie from her threats. If I ever actually succeeded in securing said evidence, I still had no idea how to avoid the coming public fallout because the police would have to get involved in order to stop her.

As if I didn't have enough scrambling my gray matter, now I had Seth to deal with.

Instead of focusing so much on Banker Boy's nefarious associations, Grady needed to take a hard look at Seth. And I'd rather liked that lawyer, too.

But discovering he hung out with the criminal element in his off time had me worrying like a quarterback reading blitz. On top of that, I had the additional concern that I'd introduced him to Rochelle.

Ho boy.

After Mr. Ricardo's recitation of my will – I mean history – I'd no doubt he now had every tidbit on Janine too. Any second now everything was gonna come back and bite me in the ass.

Yeah, Zeke was right. I'd made some stupid decisions lately.

But let's keep that between us, okay?

"You look tired," Mom said, breaking through my rambling thoughts. "Without that bedroom furniture, your sleep must be dreadful."

"The mattress isn't a problem, Mom," I assured. "Oh, Reggie did call to let me know the bedroom set has shipped and should be here before the weekend."

"That's wonderful. Then you'll be able to sleep on something besides that floor."

"Mattress, Mom. And it's been fine."

"Then why do you look so tired? Has your boss been working you too hard?"

"Work's fine. I'm fine. Mattress is still fine. Everything's *fine*."

Except my relationships.

But Mom wouldn't be able to stomach hearing about all of my extra-curricular activities of late. 'Specially while eating lunch.

The check was paid with a flourish of her signature before we moseyed across the street to one of her favorite boutiques. Air-conditioning never felt so sweet as I basked in the cool comfort, while Mom informed the personal shopper we wished to browse on our own.

We were left to piddle and poke through the racks as if it was the most fascinating thing in the world.

"I'm concerned about you, Victoria," Mom admitted. "That whole breaking into your apartment thing still has me on edge, not to mention that man trying to…"

"That was months ago, Mom."

I really didn't want to rehash the moment my life flashed before my eyes. And I definitely wasn't going to mention the run-in with a gang last week. Or about meeting a notorious gang leader turned *goods distributor* last night.

"But you just moved back in," she said, holding up a breezy, blue skirt I turned down with a vigorous shake of my head. "I can only imagine what living there all alone has done to you."

"I'm not alone," I said. "I've got Slinky to keep me company."

"A cat can't protect you like a man, dear."

"I don't need a man to make me feel safe."

I jerked from the rack the first thing I came to and held up the hideous mint green and brown monstrosity for her perusal as the two thousand dollar price tag dangled into view.

Reality check, ladies. Sometimes quality fashion and price don't coincide. Often you end up massively overpaying when you shop by brand only.

By then you're stuck in a dress that looks more like a garbage bag someone puked mint chocolate chips on in order to get your money's worth of wear.

Trust me, folks. Wearing vomit has a price.

Tears in Mom's eyes stopped the building frustration between us and deflated my anger. Okay, maybe the dress wouldn't look that bad on. Or maybe it wasn't the dress at all that caused her reaction.

For the first time in – well, too long – I really stopped to notice my mom. The tightness around her mouth. The fine lines tugging at the corners of her eyes. The dark circles that hadn't been there two weeks ago.

She was so worried about my sleep, or lack thereof, even though it appeared she hadn't slept well since the return to my apartment. A twinge of guilt pinched my heart.

She smiled behind the veil of unshed tears. "A mom never stops being a mom...no matter how old her child gets."

"I know." I placed my hand over hers. "I've just had a few things on my mind."

"I'm here if you want to talk about it."

"I appreciate that, but…"

She gripped my hand. "And it will go no farther."

Understanding flashed through me like menopausal heat. If anyone grasped the destructive effects of the gossip train, it was Mom. She'd stood firm beneath the constant barrage of whispers and backbiting stemming from her husband's many indiscretions, while I'd kicked the dust from my designer heels and escaped.

Leaving my mom behind to fend off the fighters by herself.

In the process I'd stopped trusting, and never realized until that moment how I'd lumped Mom into that category along with all of the other saintly sinners, ex-boyfriends, and other assorted lousy losers.

In the end, she'd been the one person in my corner all along.

We dropped hands, and I buried myself in a shoe rack to avoid looking at her before launching into my muddled mental musings.

Hey, avoidance tendencies don't disappear overnight, folks.

"Okay, so don't get to thinking anything," I started in. "But I talked to Zeke last night."

Green eyes brightened before she slogged through the dress rack I'd abandoned as if checking her excitement. "How is Zeke?"

"Frustrated with me," I admitted.

Only a slight hesitation in the hanger slither and slide. "Why is that?"

"Well, last night might've had something to do with it

when I…uh, hosed him down with pepper spray."

The hangers stopped clinking.

"And then sent him to the ground when my knee connected with his privates," I finished.

Mom sucked in her cheeks with a twinge of anguish.

I quickly continued. "It was late and dark, and I didn't know who it was when he surprised me outside my garage."

"An accident then?"

"Absolutely."

A smile spread across her face at that. "Well, at least there's some reassurance my daughter can take care of herself."

"Damn straight."

That got me *the look* before I went on.

"I cleaned him up as best I could, but then we landed into an old argument all over again."

"And that old argument was about?"

The only other person I'd mentioned the humiliating circumstances that led to the breakup breakdown was Janine. Mom had never asked, and I'd never volunteered the information.

At the time, the demise of my relationship with Zeke was more of an answered prayer for Mom, since she didn't take kindly to our cohabitation.

But opening up the old wound by talking about it made every sphincter in my body clench. Plus, with the sperm donor's penchant for panty piñata, this subject had potential to cause undue distress to more than just me.

I took a deep breath. "Before we broke up, I caught Lorraine Padget in Zeke's arms."

The boutique's canned music faded like the radio when driving through a tunnel. A slight tic in Mom's cheek was the only signal she'd heard me. She grabbed a pair of shoes off the rack near my head and slid them on with surprisingly steady hands.

"What did you do?" she finally asked.

I shook my head. "You don't want to know."

Silence.

"Let's just say that by the time Lorraine was fished from the lake, Zeke had my hand imprint across not one but both cheeks and had to buy not only a new shirt but a new Stetson, unless the old one floated to shore."

"He didn't strike you, did he?" Mom's voice nudged momma bear territory.

"No," I offered, holding up two different colors of the same blouse. "But he wasn't so lucky."

"Sounds like he deserved it."

"Maybe."

Mom pointed her approval to the turquoise-blue blouse on the right. "Listen, sweetheart, if you're struggling with feelings for Zeke, I'd advise you to set them aside. The last thing you want to do is attach yourself to a philanderer."

Mom knew best – unfortunately.

"But see, here's the thing. Every time we've argued since, Zeke mentions something about me misunderstanding or misconstruing everything...even when we're talking about something other than the circumstances of our breakup."

She passed off the shoes and the turquoise blouse to the personal shopper lurking in the background. "Is he trying to deflect responsibility?"

"I don't think so."

"That night..." Her voice dropped to a whisper to avoid prying ears. "Did you see him kiss that girl?"

I thought back to the rendezvous for dinner at the lakeside restaurant. We'd driven separate cars because Zeke had headed in from an offsite meeting and I'd spent the afternoon at Janine's helping her study for an upcoming mid-term.

I'd assumed I'd arrived first when his name wasn't on the waiting list. So after inserting us into the lineup, I'd strolled the deck along the lake's edge until rounding the corner on Zeke and Lorraine's little *tête-à-tête*.

Then proceeded to lose my mind.

In the ambient lighting from the restaurant, I'd seen them wrapped in an embrace. When I tried to picture it now, I couldn't remember seeing them kiss.

In fact, a black streak of mascara had marred Lorraine's usually picture-perfect appearance. After all, she was a television personality and loved nothing more than constantly reminding everyone of that fact.

"I...I don't think so," I finally admitted. "Now that I think of it, she might've been crying."

"Using the sympathy ploy for attention?"

"With Lorraine, that's a ninety-nine percent likelihood."

After picking up another dress and checking the size, Mom signaled the assistant to add it to her growing pile without trying it on. Seemed the subject of infidelity had my mom in mindless auto-shopping mode. At these prices, I could almost hear her credit card crying.

"Have you ever forgiven him?" she asked as we strolled into the rear salon to watch a handful of paper-thin girls strut and spin to show us the latest designer collection.

I sighed and plopped down at a table. A cup of steaming tea appeared at my elbow before I'd even blinked.

"Every time I think I have, it comes up again in an argument."

When Mom leaned forward and placed her elbows on the table, steepling her fingers beneath her chin, I almost choked. I couldn't remember a time when my mother put her elbows on the table. Quite the opposite, in fact. It was one of those cotillion lessons I'd promptly dismissed as soon as I left home.

"Perhaps it's time, Victoria."

We eyed the upcoming winter fashions and admired the return of cool jewel tones before the girls escaped to change. At least Mom put a little thought into the pieces she chose this time.

"Have you ever talked about it without fighting?" she asked. "Asked for his version of events?"

"No," I admitted. "Zeke's betrayal had seemed so obvious…then."

"And now?"

I shrugged. "What's the point in discussing long ago events?"

"Hearing his perspective can go a long way toward helping you truly forgive." Her eyes twinkled. "Were you not the one always championing the truth with your father?"

Truth – or some version of it.

Talking about that night over two years ago made me think too much of Lorraine. Which reminded me of Reggie. Which made me think of my bedroom set. That brought me around to Radioman. Then Seth.

Yeah, there were a lot of truths I was working on at the moment.

And none were panning out as I'd hoped.

Shopping with Mom usually left me on a high after filling my closet with new clothes, new shoes.

New headaches.

For some reason when I stared at the array of bags and

boxes littering my bedroom floor at the end of the day, I felt a twinge of something rather foreign. Something I couldn't quite put my finger on.

The building notice in the mail about the coming apartment remodeling project my mom had inspired might have contributed to that foreign feeling. Things were about to go haywire around the one place I felt comfortable again.

I tossed the letter aside then lifted out one of five new pairs of shoes and stared at the pearl gray platform pump.

Mom always said gray was an essential staple for a new fall wardrobe. They'd be killer with several of the dresses, skirts and blouses scattered across my bed. But how many pairs did a girl need?

Holy crap! Did I just think that?

Slinky tiptoed in between bags before attacking an imaginary culprit. The crinkling of plastic got him riled up until he streaked from the bedroom and tore down the hall like a hound was hot on his heels. I chuckled then sat amid the plastic clutter.

What was wrong with me? Call it dissatisfaction, guilt, or plain old buyer's remorse, but when I looked around at all of the new stuff, I realized I really didn't need any of it.

After the terrorizing my apartment had received from Bud, Mom had spent enough money to remodel then restock my closet ten times over. Enough to feed every man, woman, and child in two third world countries.

Okay, maybe that was an exaggeration.

Point is, I had more clothes and shoes post thrashing than I'd had prior – and that's saying a lot when my mom took me shopping every Tuesday.

Since I'd moved out of the family mansion, our weekly shopping excursions translated into the only time we spent together. At what point had I stepped over the line into taking advantage of my mom's generosity?

Between sharing with Mom about the issue with Zeke and now philosophizing over my relationship with her credit card, I approached a strange and unusual conflux of mental musings.

My hands trembled.

My throat felt tight.

Maybe I needed an antacid.

Better yet, a drink.

Before I could think too hard, I grabbed my cell and called the only other person who might understand my current dilemma and crisis of conscience.

"Hey, Bobby. You got a moment?"

CHAPTER TWENTY-FIVE

On the drive to Bobby's house, I sent a quick text to Reggie to let him know I had some good news for him about his situation.

A half hour later, I still hadn't gotten a response from him when I pulled into Bobby's driveway and parked beside a dark brown Ford Explorer. Temporary tag. Couple years old. Little more than the base model.

But it was the stretch limo parked on the other side of the street that had me reconsidering this visit.

The moment I stepped from the Vette, next door's Nosy Nana garnered my attention with a loud *psst* and a *come hither* signal that sent the skin under her arms flapping like an albatross readying for take-off.

The sharp screech of a familiar female voice coming from Bobby's stopped me halfway in Nosy's yard, my heels sinking in the soft earth.

She whispered loud enough for the residents the next street over to hear. "It's shaping up to be a kerfuffle the size of Texas in there."

"Sounds like it already is," I said as the voice from Bobby's house screeched up to crystal shattering proportions.

Any minute now I expected the windows along the upstairs dormers to bow out before bursting in a tinkle of glass. The high pitches would've impressed the hell out of Janine.

"Do you think he's in any danger?" Nosy asked with a deceptively concerned bat of overly mascaraed lashes.

"I think Bobby can handle his mother."

I considered running over and rescuing him from Mary Jo's wrath, until remembering how my presence affected the Vernet matriarch. I contemplated driving the next street over behind a row of boxwoods I'd once borrowed and hiding out until the place cleared.

Instead I returned to lean against my car in wait.

It wasn't long before yelling stopped and the screen door slammed against the house with a loud thwack. The rapid clip of heels tapped up the sidewalk before Mary Jo rounded the corner to the driveway.

Though her expression didn't change from the obvious recent Botox injections, the red flush inching up her face screamed her distress louder than overwrought vocal chords ever could.

"Hey, Mary Jo. How ya doin'?" I offered up a wide Cheshire Cat grin to prove I still had complete mastery over my facial muscles.

She pointed a bony dragon claw my way. "Stay away from my son, you…you…Jezebel!"

I resembled that remark.

"Stopping by after your clinic visitation today?"

She opened her mouth as if to rebut then reconsidered with a sniff of derision before stomping down the concrete drive hard enough to break a heel.

Now that'd be a sight I'd pay good money to see. Pass the popcorn, please!

"Good to see you too," I called loud enough for Nosy Nana to hear.

The limo driver – or rather the muscle-bound bodyguard – stepped out to open the door as Mary Jo faltered with a twist of her ankle before falling against him. That earned me a glare as if I were the cause of her stumble.

'Course I had just wished for her heel to break.

Sorta.

The look on Bobby's face when he answered the front door revealed he'd had more than his fair share of rough days lately. Figured I'd be safer asking about the Ford.

"Nice Explorer," I remarked. "Did you trade the BMW for it?"

That got me a growl before Bobby shut the door behind me a little too forcefully. "Why's everyone so interested in what I do with my own car?"

I held up both hands in surrender. "Sorry. Just making an observation. Didn't know it was Tuesday's touchy topic."

He sighed and ran a hand across his forehead. "No, no. Sorry, it isn't your fault."

"Brown's a good color for you. And if I remember correctly, you were always a little partial to Fords anyway."

His head popped up at the reminder of F-150s. I offered a smirk. Laughter cut the tension, and I plopped down on the sofa.

"Okay, you got me there," Bobby admitted as he sat in the chair opposite.

"So spill. What's eatin's at you, besides Cruella De Vil?"

"I thought you came over to talk to me?" he commented, ignoring the derogatory comparison to his mother.

Though on closer contemplation, I tended to give the Disney character an edge. *That* woman at least had a smidge of style. That is, when you discounted the whole hair thing.

And her fixation on puppy fur coats.

I waved my hand. "That can all wait. Seems something's on your mind about that SUV sitting in your driveway."

"You might say that."

"Did selling it make everything feel kinda final? You know, with Amy's death and all."

The Adam's apple bobbed with the reminder of his wife. Damn my diseased mouth.

"It isn't that. My mother stopped by on her way home from an...a meeting after you called."

Meeting my ass. Try an appointment with poison control.

"You mean she came down from her heavenly heights to grace the lowly masses with her presence?" I joked, trying to skirt the subject of his deceased wife and unborn son.

"Hey, she's still my mom," he argued with a smile stretched across his mug.

"Yeah, and I know how parents can be."

"She wasn't too happy when she saw I'd traded out the BMW for a *lesser quality* vehicle. Imagine I'll be hearing from Dad shortly."

"Wait, weren't they the ones who introduced you to the Ford Company when you turned eighteen?"

The smile dissolved into a chuckle. "Things have changed a bit in the years I was gone. Apparently Ford is considered a lower class of vehicle to today's *discerning* buyer."

"I could've told you that," I quipped. "I'm a Chevy girl myself."

Bobby shook his head. "When I told them I'd put the cash difference into my new ministry, Mom kinda went off."

"What's it her business what you do with the proceeds? It was *your* car."

"That *they'd* bought for us when Amy and I moved here to take over the children's ministry at *their* church."

The use of *their* instead of *our* church was either a rather glaring error in word choice or an indication of Bobby's change of heart where his parents' theological leanings resided. Dennis and Mary Jo's reactions to Bobby's stand against their closely held belief in the Santa Claus Savior would've been a sight guaranteed to carry me into eternity and beyond.

Talk about your popcorn moment.

"Whose name was on the title?" I asked.

"Mine," Bobby clarified. "We hadn't gotten around to adding Amy's name before...you know."

Wow. I knew the elder Vernets hadn't liked Amy, but leaving his wife's name off of the vehicle title? How blatantly obvious could you get?

Not to mention petty.

Wisely, I left those thoughts alone. "Then it was *your* car and therefore *your* money to do with as you saw fit. Case dismissed."

"Nice use of the legalese, Judge Vicki." A tilt of the head as if studying the situation, then Bobby took a turn toward the serious. "Have you ever thought about quitting the bar scene and *taking* the bar?"

I didn't even have to think about that one. "Uh, that would be no. I'm not into the monetary mooching and brown-nosing that usually comes with an attorney's job description."

"There's more to it than making money and aiming for partner at a big law firm by the time you're thirty."

I snorted. "With my luck, I'd be disbarred before I even

passed the bar."

Bobby shrugged. "Something to think about then."

"Hardly," I muttered.

He sat back in the chair and crossed his legs like a psychologist preparing for a therapy session. "So career aspirations aside, you said you wanted to talk about something. Was it the whole gang thing, because I've gotta be honest with you, I haven't had much luck so far with those currently in the prison system."

"That's okay, Sigmund Fraud. I've got what I needed on that front."

"Eloquent as always," Bobby said with another chuckle. "So what did you want to talk about?"

Let's see. There was Mom, Janine, Zeke, Reggie and the blackmail, Grady – oh, and now Seth and his nocturnal excursions, not to mention Radioman's rejection Sunday night. Where should I begin?

My mouth opened – and nothing came out.

I opened it again, then summarily closed it a second time. I probably looked like a fish trying to suck oxygen from dry land.

What was wrong with me? I was the expositor extraordinaire. The mouth off menace. The girl with a severe case of foot-in-mouth disease.

But with everything going on in my life, I didn't even know where to begin.

"Okay," I started. "There's Janine."

Bobby straightened. "What about Janine?"

The damn – er, dam – burst and my words came flowing out in a torrent. "I mean, she's my best friend, but sometimes I wonder why she puts up with me. We barely have anything in common anymore. I drag her around, getting her into all sorts of scrapes and into trouble with her mother.

"I'm always pulling her away from important things like working on her thesis. All summer, I've barely talked to her, much less seen her, except to ask her to watch Slinky for me while I traipsed down to San Antonio with some boy bimbo, who's only interests in life are sex and fashion."

"Vicki, I…"

"Speaking of fashion," I continued with nary a breath, "my relationship with Mom has devolved into nothing more than a once-a-week fashion show extravaganza. She spends all this money on me, buying this latest trend and that label, when there are starving children in India who would give anything for just a bite of a bacon cheeseburger.

"I've recently moved back into my apartment, which she also paid Reggie top dollar to remodel, and already my closet is full of this season and next season's clothes, with no room for a winter or spring wardrobe."

I was babbling at that point, but I'd lost complete control of my mouth. Bobby just sat back and let me continue.

"Then Reggie's asked me to help him with…" I actually caught myself. For a second. "…something life-altering, and I can't even seem to do that right. The only suspect I've been able to come up with is Lorraine Padget, but then I wonder if that's only because of our lifelong animosity toward each other and the fact that she muscled in between me and Zeke."

"Zeke? I thought…"

"And of course, anything where Zeke is concerned has me flashing so fast between hot and cold, I feel like a middle-aged woman in the throes of menopause." I proceeded to share about the whole Zeke and Lorraine fiasco of yesteryear.

Throughout my monologue, Bobby nodded and silently

encouraged me to continue until I spilled not only my guts but my pride as well. After all these years, I was reminded again of how easy Bobby and I had conversed and commiserated with one another.

Until the infamous incident had placed a wedge between us.

But somewhere along the way, the wedge had dissipated until all that was left was a friendship. A real friendship. Then I remembered that Bobby was now a minister, and all those old fears of what that institution had done to me came flying back.

But this was *Bobby*, after all – and the man I'd grown up with would never betray a secret.

'Course it didn't hurt that I knew a few of his too.

When I finally stopped babbling before the cows came home to roost – or is that crows? – Bobby got a word in.

"Tell me, Vicki. Are you still in love with Zeke?"

"No, but..." I stopped and gave the matter a little more thought before continuing. "No, I'm not in l...in l..." Damnit! "I don't care about Zeke like that anymore. But I'd hoped that after all these years and the time we spent together to help you that maybe we could be friends again. You know, like we have."

A soft and understanding smile tugged at the corners of his mouth. "But..."

"But every time we're around each other, conversation devolves into a fight, and I inevitably bring up the great Lorraine debacle."

"Have you ever asked Zeke his version of what transpired that night?"

I sighed. "Mom asked the same question. The short answer is no."

"And the long answer?"

"Involves name calling, hat tossing, a few fisticuffs..."

"Zeke hit you?"

"No," I admitted sheepishly for the second time that day. "That was me before Lorraine ended up taking a swim."

Bobby coughed. I gave him the evil eye to let him know this was not a laugh-out-loud moment.

Pretty sure he got the message.

"Do you think hearing his explanation might help you forgive him once and for all?" Bobby asked.

I shrugged. "It might."

"I think that'd be a good place to start."

But how in the world would I bring up such a topic next time I saw Zeke? The last couple of times we'd talked, things had ended up worse than before. I didn't take too kindly to being called stupid.

Directly or implied.

But we had to start somewhere. Maybe I could invite him over for dinner. But then he might get the wrong idea. And I was exploring a potential relationship with Radioman. But that vein didn't need additional complications – like how he did or didn't fit in with Seth's present antics.

Then I also had Nick floating around in my gray matter. I needed to make sure he knew things were over between us to avoid any other complications from that sector.

Damn. In trying to simplify my life where men were concerned I'd done nothing but add to the complications. My head pounded like a drumbeat in a call to arms at the Alamo.

Bobby leaned forward and patted my knee. "Can I tell you what I see in your relationship with Janine?"

I cringed. "Do I even want to know?"

"I see two women who've remain devoted to a

friendship that has spanned a lifetime and the changes that come with it. You've helped Janine learn to live a little, to let her hair down and release the pressures of a family situation where perfection is demanded. In turn, she offers you a constant, a stable rock to go to when your life gets a little, how shall we say…"

"Chaotic?"

"Challenging," he offered with a wink.

"That's putting it mildly."

"Now about your mom," Bobby said. "It's clear from your admission that your relationship with her now has a chance to mature."

"Mature?" I reiterated. "What's that supposed to mean? That we've had an immature relationship?"

"No, no. Wrong choice of words on my part. How about grow? Blossom into a more satisfying friendship."

"But she's my mom."

"And you're her daughter," he clarified. "At some point, every parent-child relationship hits a crossroads where the child severs the umbilical cord to make her own way in the world, and the parent-child dynamic changes."

An image of the old birthing videos we'd seen in school returned to haunt me. "Umbilical cords? Did you have to use such an icky analogy?"

Bobby laughed. "The message is essentially the same. And yes, it can get icky for awhile."

"But I moved away from my parents years ago," I countered. "I didn't just sever that umbilical cord, I chopped it up and fried it on the parental altar until it burnt to a crisp."

That got me a wrinkled nose in response. Hey, turnabout's fair play.

"But it sounds like your mom never really let go and

started using financial gifts as a means to stay connected."

"Financial blackmail is more my dad's department."

"Yeah, I remember," Bobby said. "But it sounds like you and your mom have gotten stuck in a familiar rut. Didn't she pay for a complete remodel of your place?"

"Sure, but..."

"Top of the line appliances?"

I nodded.

"And she buys you something new *every* week?"

"More than just something," I admitted.

"Even if you don't need anything?" Bobby prodded.

Acid churned a hole in my stomach. "I see what you're saying."

"She's been concerned for your safety lately, but it sounds to me like she's trying to compensate for something else in there somewhere."

"And I'm taking advantage of her guilt." I sighed.

Bobby's warm hand gripped mine. No zing at his touch. No trembling in my nether regions – and that made me about as happy as a placekicker after a three-point conversion.

The change in my relationship with Bobby offered hope that my relationships with others could change for the better as well.

Starting with my mom.

"Maybe it's time to find something new to do together," Bobby said. "Something that doesn't involve shopping."

"Like what?" I asked in baffled frustration.

"Your parents have many philanthropic causes they support, right? Didn't your mom once work as a nurse?"

"Briefly."

"Maybe you could spend your Tuesdays doing volunteer work at one of the hospitals."

My turn to wrinkle my nose, anticipating those antiseptic smells, sponge baths, and bedpans. Between that and umbilical cords, someone get me a barf bag stat.

"Or something else," he said quickly, sensing my revulsion. "There are lots of volunteer opportunities available out there."

And just like severed umbilical cords, they all sounded icky.

"Talk to your mom," Bobby continued. "I'm sure you'll figure out something. There's more to life than just money, Vic."

Yeah. Try telling that to the sperm donor.

And my mom's black AmEx.

CHAPTER TWENTY-SIX

With thoughts of umbilical cords, bedpans, and moms that shop 'til they drop running through my head, I'd almost forgotten about Reggie until he texted Wednesday afternoon while I was getting ready for work.

The bedroom furniture had arrived a day early, and he had the manpower available to deliver it late Thursday afternoon if I wanted. Set-up would take an hour or two and then he'd stay to discuss *circumstances*.

No matter how much Reggie dreamed of becoming the next James Bond, he'd never make a good spy if he couldn't be a little more discrete in his correspondence.

I mean really, *circumstances*? Even if no one else knew about the blackmail, that particular word in place of a more normal one would pique the average human's interest.

I replied with a thumbs up and wrote that I'd be at the bar tonight if he wanted to swing by. Then I tossed Rochelle a text to see if she wanted an extra night of bartending duty tomorrow evening in case Reggie and I went long.

Scratch that. A few extra *hours* before I'd make it into the bar tomorrow night.

I couldn't keep working willy-nilly with my schedule if I

hoped to break this slowly creeping dependence on my mom's credit card. The bedroom furniture would have to be Mom's final major purchase on my behalf.

For now.

Bobby was right. It was time for Mom and me to develop a more mature relationship, which meant I'd have to once again depend solely on my income.

Break the chains. Go cold turkey.

When I slung my purse over my shoulder and headed out the door, I could've sworn it moaned and whimpered a little. I half expected my wallet to be moist from tears when I tugged it out to check my cash stash before tearing away from the apartment building toward the gas station.

Instead of tears, maybe my wallet was sweating too.

Even though I didn't have that far to drive, traffic this time of the day was a real bear. It would never do to get stuck driving in Dallas with less than a half-tank of gas, so I pulled into the nearest station to pre-pay and pump in a few gallons.

My cell phone gave my butt a nice buzz as I finished filling the tank. Rochelle responded for tomorrow night with a big smiley face, which I took as a yes.

As I opened the car door, the hair on the back of my neck stood on end. Considering sweat had plastered it to my skin that was saying something.

Most of the gas pumps had patrons with attention focused on rising gasoline prices. The office complex across the street revealed continual movement of workers leaving the building, entering cars, or driving from the lot, which would make a stationary body stand out.

Nothing.

The quick scan of chaos gave me no clues as to the source of the sensation, but that didn't mean someone wasn't out there.

Watching.

Waiting.

With everything I'd been poking my nose into, I was once again on someone's radar. Might be Switch and Company. Perhaps Ambassador Juarez had someone keeping a close eye on my safety. Did Zeke have boots on the ground watching over me again?

Either way it creeped me out and left me feeling vulnerable and alone in a sea of humanity. An unusual sensation given my past penchant for being the center of attention.

Before I could think on it further, I peeled from the station and arrived at the bar in record time. Once I got inside and started my shift, the sense of personal space violation gradually abated. Regulars filtered in after a long day, and I relaxed into a comfortable rhythm.

With everything going smooth and tapping out a steady beat to the music, I 'bout piddled in my panties when a hand rested low on my hip. I spun around. Grady pulled back a bit at my reaction.

Or maybe it was the sling of rum across his shirt.

"Whoa there, Vic," he said, taking the bottle from my hands.

"Sorry, boss," I sputtered, dabbing at the splatter on his plaid button-up.

Grady grinned that slow quirk of his mustache. "If you'd wanted me to take it off, all's ya had to do was say the word."

"Not in the mood." I slapped him with the towel.

"Ya know, so you can wash it out before it gets stained."

"I'm a bartender, not your personal laundress."

"I'm takin' bids on a new position."

"How 'bout a shot of Jack instead?" I asked, popping the cold glass into my cleavage and giving it my standard three-fingered pour.

Grady slid the shot glass from between my boobs and knocked it back in one swallow like a tried-and-true Texan. The long-played game was usually a fun and flirty moment shared between us, but this time my boss set down the empty glass and gave me an ice-hard stare.

"You're tense," he observed aloud. "What's happened that has you all worked up?"

"Gee, I don't know. Family's on my case. Janine's busy preparing for a new semester. My boss has become a grade-A stitch in my side. Life is going nowhere. Haven't had sex in awhile…"

"Well, I'd be willin' to help you with that last part," Grady interrupted, loading dirty glasses into the dishwasher.

I scrunched up my lips to keep from smiling. "And I'm going to have to have a talk with Zeke."

That stopped his forward progress. "About?"

I mindlessly swiped the towel across the counter. "Nothing much. Just a little matter of forgiveness."

"You've been talkin' to that pastor friend of yours, haven't you?"

I sprayed down a particularly stubborn smear on the bar top and put a little elbow grease to it. "Both Bobby and my mom said that I need to get his side of what happened when we broke up."

"You thinkin' about gettin' back together with Big Z?"

"Hell no," I exclaimed a little too quickly, hitting the stain double-time. I gave up with a sigh. "I just want to be able to talk with him without the *incident* always coming up between us. Then maybe I can really forgive him this time, and we can become friends."

"That's a tough one," Grady said, crossing his arms and leaning against the counter. "I'm of the mindset that once a man and woman share more than spit and a little polish, it's pretty much impossible to be mere friends again."

"I second that," a familiar voice called.

Speaking of friends sharing spit, I whirled around to see Radioman's lawyer friend plop down on a barstool. Seth hadn't taken off the freshly tailored suit jacket yet. That was two new suits tailored to fit this week alone.

Gee, I wonder where he got the money for that bit of business?

"Nice suit," I sneered aloud as Grady excused himself and headed toward his surveillance stronghold. "New?"

"Just picked it up yesterday from the tailor," Seth said, flicking off a piece of imaginary lint from the dusky gray linen blend sleeve, his gaze following Grady. "Needed something that breathed better in this ungodly heat."

Yeah, linen breathed better. 'Cept when you rubbed shoulders with the no-good, slimy criminal element.

"So where's Radioman?" I asked, placing a scotch on the bar top.

The ice tinkled against the glass as Seth took a long drink before answering. "Still at work. Should join me in another hour or two."

The thought of seeing my man sent a zing to my nether regions. Wait. My man? When had Bruce become *my man*?

Second startling thought. When had I started referring to Radioman by his given name?

The moment Grady turned the corner and disappeared into the office, Seth spun around on the stool and hissed, "What in the hell were you doing the other night?"

"Me?" I leaned over the bar with a harsh whisper like

the shot heard round the bar. "You said you were Italian, but you left out the part where you're a lawyer for the *mob*."

"I'm not. Not really."

"Then what were *you* doing there?" I successfully turned the tables on him.

His lips thinned into a hard line, eyes unreadable as he hid behind his courtroom persona. "It's complicated."

I returned to scrubbing at the stubborn stain. "You said the other night it wasn't what it looked like. What did you mean by that?"

"Just what I said."

"Which doesn't really say anything."

He remained stoic. Silent.

"I have several friends in law enforcement, you know," I threw out in taunt. "Should I give them Doug and Bruce's names too?"

"No," Seth said a little too sharply. "And you can't mention a word about this to either of them."

And people said *I* had a loud mouth. "Give me a reason not to."

The cool customer, lawyerly persona had cracked wide open. "Ricardo is a client of the firm where I work."

"I kinda deduced that. Give me something else."

He threw back the rest of the drink then cleared his throat. "I came across something in the files that I shouldn't have and got caught. Now I'm doing penance."

"By working for a drug dealer?"

Seth winced and glanced around to see if anyone was paying attention to us. "The alternative would've left me either a few fingers short or more likely analyzing the composition of silt on the river bottom. At least this way, I can continue to collect information and eventually turn it over to the proper authorities."

That last bit stopped my tirade. I poured him another drink in consolation. "This sounds like a plot from a movie I've seen. Wouldn't you be disbarred?"

He grabbed the glass and downed half in one swallow. "Better disbarred than jailed…or dead."

In my peripheral vision, I caught Grady stepping out from the office, trying not to be obvious. Damn. Now I wasn't just suspicious but certain he'd hidden bugs somewhere behind the bar.

I joined Seth and threw back a shot of Jack before throwing a glare Grady's way. "Are you working with anyone specific in the police department?"

He shook his head and offered up a hopeful plea. "Maybe you could help me when I'm ready?"

He'd better get ready then. I had a feeling Grady, Zeke or someone outside of Detective Duncan's department would be beating down his door real soon.

As in tonight.

A gust of furnace-like proportions indicated the opening of the employee side door. Rochelle sauntered in about as wilted as a plucked daisy.

"Speaking of which," Seth said, switching to courtroom persona to cover our conversation, "when are you gonna denote a fun nickname on me?"

"I'm still working on it," I said, attempting to match his grin. "I didn't think you'd like Courtroom Harpy, so I wanted to give it a bit more thought."

That got me an outright laugh, but his eyes told me this conversation was far from over. I had to agree.

"Hey, Rochelle," I called over my shoulder. "Thanks again for tomorrow evening."

"You bet," my co-worker said. "I'll take all of the extra hours I can get if it means getting my own place sooner rather than later."

I handed her a mug from the tap as Seth slid the second empty glass toward me.

"That'll be all for me for now, Vicki," Seth said, then turned his attention on Rochelle. "Let's see if I can help you with that goal. Ready to sign some paperwork?"

"You bet," Rochelle responded.

I continued wiping the spot like a dog returning to its own vomit as I debated whether I'd gotten yet another friend in trouble by association. It'd be nice if Rochelle could finally get her due from that lousy excuse of an ex-husband. Those kids deserved a father who'd actually be a part of their lives, not just someone who offered up a casual sperm here and there only to renege on responsibilities.

Then again sometimes having a negligent father around was worse than a deadbeat dad. It took more than a proffer of sperm to make a loving and concerned parent. *That* I knew too well.

Grady meandered toward the bar and loosed a few dormant cogs in my brain. Dangerous, I know, but this time it wasn't thoughts or worries for myself.

Regardless of my on and off again frustrations with him lately, the boss was a man of honor. Responsible business owner. Had a sense of humor – most of the time.

Good secret keeper when necessary. Texan through-and-through. All the qualities for a good husband and father.

And they were closer in age.

"You're thinking hard there, Vic. Care to share?"

The only problem was whether or not Radioman could get a couple more tickets.

I tilted my face his way with the tug of a smile. "Hey, boss, what're you doing Sunday afternoon?"

CHAPTER TWENTY-SEVEN

I could hardly contain my excitement.

In mere hours my bedroom furniture would arrive and get set up just in time for Sunday's post-date festivities. 'Course I still had to finagle my way around getting both Grady and Rochelle on the same page before then.

After all, folks, it takes a lot of planning and mismanagement to work this hard at throwing two people together. And a little white lie.

Or two.

Hey, is it my fault when someone misunderstands my good intentions?

Don't answer that.

At just after four a knock clunked against my apartment door. But instead of Reggie standing there when I dragged the door open it was an unexpected surprise.

"Mom?"

Rubbing her knuckles, my mom swept inside dressed in a floral number with a matching fragrance undertone as if she'd just left the Thursday ladies luncheon at the church. After a quick peck on the cheek, she surveyed what I'd done with the place since the remodel.

"Reginald called to say they were delivering the bedroom suite today," Mom explained. "I had to come see it in person to make sure it meets my approval."

First complication of the day.

I'd planned to discuss the blackmail potential candidates with Reggie after everyone left. But with my mom thrown in the mix and if the past was any indication, she'd be around long after everyone else disappeared.

There wouldn't be opportunity to inconspicuously coordinate with him later either, as Mom tended to commandeer every moment of Reggie's attention.

Then again, she *had* paid for everything.

I'd send him a text to let him know when Mom left so he could return. Yeah, that might work.

"That's great, Mom, but it isn't here yet."

"Oh," she responded, disappointment in her tone.

"Matter of fact, I thought you were Reggie."

Mom sat on the sofa all prim and proper, with knees together and ankles crossed and tucked like a properly trained former beauty queen. I simply plopped down beside her.

"Do you have to work tonight?" Mom asked.

"Yeah," I responded. "But one of my co-workers is covering for me until I finish here."

"That's nice of her...or is it a him?"

"Her."

"Ah."

Silence. Mom fiddled with an imaginary wrinkle on her skirt. Then she pulled a tissue from her purse and swiped at the coffee table like a matador in a bullfight.

I remembered that trip to Spain with a shudder. As long as I lived, I'd never understand my dad's appeal for running with the bulls or the bloodlust of a bullfight. I'd much rather watch a more evenly matched and less gruesome brawl.

Namely two football players slugging it out on the fifty-yard line.

"You really need to dust more often, dear. I'd be happy to send Rebecca over once or twice a week. Or we could hire a service, but there's no guarantee you'll have the same person from week-to-week."

Before I allowed my catnip to get all bunched up, I reminded myself of the recent discussion with Bobby. Mom was only acting out of concern for me. But I still needed to take a stand and stop depending so much on her generosity.

Financially or otherwise.

"Thanks, Mom, but I usually clean on Mondays, so it isn't surprising there's a slight build-up by now."

"But it can't be good for your health, breathing all that residue."

"It's Texas in summer," I deadpanned. "You can't go outside without getting a face full of dust, so I doubt the little bit *inside* makes a dent by comparison."

Mom pursed her lips but didn't say anything more before folding the dainty linen square and tucking it away. Uncomfortable silence again stood between us like the collective breath before the opening coin toss.

I sighed. "I hate waiting, don't you?"

"Time seems to stop when you're anxious," Mom admitted as she checked her diamond encrusted watch, weighted with enough stones to give her carpel tunnel. "What time did Reginald say they would arrive?"

"He didn't. Just said they would be here sometime late afternoon."

"That's very unlike him not to set a specified time for delivery."

"It was kinda spur-of-the-moment, Mom. He figured I'd

want the furniture as soon as possible…considering."

A single tweezed brow arched my way. "Considering what, Victoria?"

"You know," I hedged. There was no way in hell I was going to share with my mother about my hopes for breaking it in Sunday night. "That I've been sleeping on the floor for the last few weeks."

"The floor? What about the mattress?"

"Well yeah, the mattress, but it isn't good on them long term. Plus, now he can close out this project ticket before fall decorating gets underway."

"I see," Mom muttered.

Don't think my little white lie was very convincing.

Having to talk around certain issues with my mom was about as fun as watching slugs in a race. Frustrating that we couldn't simply be two women having an adult conversation instead of me riding around the never-ending hamster wheel to nowhere.

The only time I relaxed around her was during our shopping excursions, which reminded me that it was time to grow-up the relationship I had with my mom.

"Hey, Mom?" I started. "I had an idea earlier this week."

"And what was that, dear?" she asked.

"About our Tuesdays."

Fear leapt in her eyes. Concern over the tenuous hold she clung to on having a relationship with me – *any* relationship with me – regardless of the cost.

"Oh, Victoria," Mom said, with a tinge of regret in her tone. "It's the only day we get to spend together."

I took a deep breath. "But how about we do something besides shop?"

"Something…else?"

I drew closer and placed my hand over hers. "It isn't that I don't appreciate everything you've done for me. If it weren't for you, I'd be homeless."

"Now dear, your father and I would never allow you to be homeless."

"Okay, scratch that," I said with a shudder, imagining life locked behind those prison doors again. "It's just I don't need anything else right now."

Mom blinked like waking up from a long nap. Then she patted her chest with long, manicured fingers. "I don't mean to be obtuse, dear, but what are you saying?"

Here goes nothing. "I have all the clothes and shoes my closet can handle."

A huff of frustration. "I knew we should've taken space from the bathroom and expanded the original closet footprint."

Leave it to my mother to misconstrue the obvious.

"No, Mom. The closet is big enough. It's the stuff inside it that I don't need any more of. Er, of which I don't need any more. Uh..."

"But we've barely made a dent in your fall wardrobe. Then winter arrivals begin next month, and before you know it we're placing spring orders."

I wasn't going to get anywhere unless I took drastic measures. I faced her straight on and grabbed her shoulders.

"Mom, I want to break up with your credit card."

Tears filled her eyes.

Oh, I was the world's worst daughter. I was so going to Hell for upsetting my mother. Or maybe there was a special purgatory for disappointing daughters.

"But I still want to spend Tuesdays together," I said. "Just not shopping. How about we do some volunteer work together instead?"

The hankie returned from its hiding place, and Mom dabbed at her eyes to avoid a makeup malfunction. If Reggie walked in on us now, I was going to get in so much trouble.

And not just for ruining my mom's makeup.

"Volunteer work?" she finally asked. "Such as?"

"I don't know," I admitted. "You used to work as a nurse." I gulped, imagining again those bedpans. "Or there's one of...Dad's...philanthropic causes."

Wash my mouth out with soap.

Or rum.

Better yet, where was a bottle of Jack?

Thankfully, we didn't have to continue this odd and uncomfortable train of conversation when a solid rap thunked against the door.

"I'll give it some thought, Victoria," Mom said as I stood and opened the front door.

"*Mein liebchen!*"

It was after seven before the furniture parade process finished.

Reggie was in full diva mode right up to the end, ordering the crew around and making Han out to be less assistant and more coat rack.

Once he finished styling the linens himself, Reggie proclaimed the room a masterpiece and finally gave his assistant something to do – take pictures of Mom and me standing beside him in front of the king-sized monstrosity.

The mattress sat so high I'd be practicing every night hereafter for a climb of Mount Everest. For once in my adult life I actually worried about what would break if I fell out of bed.

I sure hoped Radioman wasn't a bed hog. Or a thrasher. 'Cause pillow top mattress mountain could sure put a damper on rough-and-tumble foreplay.

Hmm. Maybe that's what my mom had in mind all along when she'd chosen it.

After wrap-up, Reggie sent Han to ride along with the crew back to the store. While I ponytailed my hair, freshened my makeup for evening activities, then changed for work, easy conversation flowed between Mom and Reggie. To make Mom happy, I slipped on my new pearl gray platforms.

Reggie fussed over me when I came out of the bedroom, while Mom glanced approvingly at my shoes – and little else.

Guess Bobby was right. You couldn't stop a mom from being a mother.

When Reggie saw she wasn't going to leave before me, he pecked my cheeks at the door and ended on a wide-eyed chaser. I wiggled my phone where Mom couldn't see, and he lifted his chin in acknowledgement of our clandestine plan before heading down the stairwell.

I turned around to Mom – and she was nowhere to be found.

A peek into the bedroom revealed her rearranging the enormous mound of pillows across the thick down comforter. She must've plotted with Han behind Reggie's back to have included so many.

"Hey, Mom? I hate to run you off, but I really need to get in a few hours of my shift tonight."

"Of course, dear. Give me five minutes to touch up a bit."

Fifteen minutes later, my patience had dissolved and the

foot tapping began. At this rate, I'd never get a chance to talk to Reggie, much less earn any money to start that life of living within my own means.

"Seriously, Mom. It's fine. I've got to get to work."

A final fluff and Mom surveyed her work with a critical eye before giving me a hug and strutting out the door in a cloud of Dior.

I sure hoped I hadn't hurt her feelings. Maybe after a night of sleeping on it, she'd understand and realize the need for our relationship to, as Bobby so eloquently put it, mature.

As Slinky launched onto the bed and tiptoed around Pillow Top Mountain, I tapped out a text to Reggie on my new phone, then dropped it in my purse sprawled across the sofa. Hopefully, Reggie hadn't gotten too impatient waiting for Mom to leave.

When the knock came a couple of minutes later, I could hardly wait to tell him about my visit with Switch and the lingering suspicions about Lorraine. If it wasn't her, I had nothing else to add to the equation, and would have to admit once and for all that I'd failed.

For the second time that night, I was surprised to see how mistaken my assumptions were when I opened the door to the wrong person. Like a lightning bolt from Heaven, everything coalesced together like the voices of a choir of angels.

But this time they weren't singing the Hallelujah Chorus.

CHAPTER TWENTY-EIGHT

"Han?" I flustered. "I uh...was just getting ready to...um...leave for work."

Reggie's assistant shoved his foot against the door and pushed his way into my apartment, closing the door behind him.

My Sig may as well have been twenty miles away instead of twenty steps to the bedroom closet. Once again I was caught with my proverbial panties around my ankles.

Han swiped a hand across his perspiring brow. Doubt it was strictly from the heat.

"I understand there was a problem with pillows," Han said.

The weighted bulge in his jacket pocket near where his hand hovered told me I'd better fudge my way out of there right quick.

"Pillows? Nope, no pillow problems. Everything's good with the pillows. Now I really have to get going. I'm already late for work."

Han glanced down at his phone. "Then what was this text you sent a few moments ago?"

"What text?"

"It said your mom was gone and it was safe to return."

"I didn't send that text to you," I murmured. "It was to Reggie."

The truth dawned on me further when Han's eyes narrowed and a smile tipped his lips.

"You cloned Reggie's phone."

The peashooter materialized from his pocket right before another knock thudded against the door.

"Back up," he whispered. "And don't even think about warning him off, or I'll shoot."

The way the gun in his hand wavered, I wondered if the coming shooting would be classified as purposeful or accidental.

The memory sensation of the pistol muzzle sizzling against my neck when Bud had tried to take me down two months ago was still sharp. I slowly walked backward until the kitchen island pressed against my spine.

Without taking his eyes off me, Han tugged open the door then leveled the gun at Reggie.

The designer's mouth formed around his standard greeting then died on his lips before he could get out anything more than mmm. Delight drooped into disorientation before falling all the way down into dread as Reggie's eyes widened and took in the gun pointed at him.

And who held it.

"Han? What is the…?"

"Get inside," Han commanded, missing the slight slip of his boss's accent before slamming the door shut and motioning Reggie to stand with me.

The weapon leveled again between us and shook in Han's grip until he clutched it with both hands.

"And don't get any ideas about rushing me," he continued. "I've been taking lessons for a month now and know perfectly well how to handle a gun."

Yeah, and the pope is – I really didn't know his nationality. Not Catholic, remember?

But let me fetch my gun and mark off fifty paces, and then we'd see which denomination bubbled to the surface when the best shooter won.

Fear churned into fury when Reggie clenched his fists. The accent not only slipped but disappeared entirely.

"It was you? You're the one who's been blackmailing me?"

Han's face scrunched up in frustration, and his eyes disappeared into slits. "Don't pretend you hadn't figured it out. Your little girlfriend here was about to reveal it to you."

I wisely kept my mouth shut and just shrugged when Reggie glanced my way. As my grandmother always said, well glory be, though there'd be plenty more impressed that I'd finally learned to control my tongue.

At least for a few seconds.

"I had someone else pegged," I admitted.

Reggie leaned my way. "Switch was involved?"

"Nah," I muttered.

The hand went to his hip and Reggie pivoted my direction so fast I felt the resultant breeze. "Then who?"

"My money was on Lorraine Padget."

"From the Summers account?"

"That's the one."

"But why would she...?"

"Apparently she didn't."

"Hey!" Han shouted.

Reggie's attention returned to his assistant. "Why, Han? If you were having financial problems, you could've come to me. I'd have helped you. Given you a raise. Something besides seeing you resort to blackmail. You've been my right hand for more than ten years."

"Exactly! For years I've been your whipping boy and done everything you asked while left in the shadows. And what have I gotten for my efforts? Lies and treachery."

"Lies and treachery? What on earth are you talking about?"

"I found out about your retirement plans. About your decision to sell the business to some big corporation instead of me."

"If you'd wanted to buy the business, why didn't you say so?"

"Because you never asked!"

While the two bickered it out, I cautiously glanced around the room for a weapon. Anything I could use to distract Bonnie from Clyde long enough to disarm the wayward sidekick.

"No contracts have been signed. It's all been talk and negotiation at this point," Reggie said, his voice oozing into the placating tone he used on clients. "If you've got the money, you'd be the perfect candidate to take over the business."

"That's the problem," Han whined. "I don't have the money."

Reggie gave me a desperate look that said *I'm out of ideas, what about you?*

Keep Han talking my eyes returned, but Reggie apparently didn't get that subliminal message. The silence stretched toward discomforting proportions. Some people just didn't respond well under pressure.

Thank God I wasn't one of them.

"So how did you find out about Reggie's plans? His past and all that?"

"Yes," Reggie said, picking up on my train of thought.

"I'd kept that information closely guarded from everyone."

I shook my head. "Not everyone."

Reggie's head jerked toward me so fast, I thought a concussive whiplash would take him down sooner than a gunshot wound.

"What do you mean, not everyone?"

"Well, I was gonna tell you tonight that Switch has known for years."

Reggie's voice pitched up about two octaves. "You talked directly to him?"

"Went to see him actually," I admitted. "He's got a great place, though it doesn't really fit the gangster image, but he mentioned he'd bought it for his mother."

"Really? Where's he living?"

"You know that old fashioned Victorian development on the edge of..."

"With the cute little streetlamps?"

"And all the gingerbread and..."

"Enough!" Han interrupted, shoving the gun out at arm's length.

Reggie and I both raised our hands in surrender at the same time.

Good thing we hadn't been at the Alamo, folks.

Reggie's blue-faced TAG Heuer rose directly into my line of sight. I'd never noticed the slight violet tinge in the color.

Then it dawned on me with a zing to my gray matter instead of my nether regions.

My rainbow-hued Sig Sauer. It wasn't tucked away in the closet. Zeke had slipped it into the kitchen island the other night.

Just around the corner from where I stood.

Now if only Reggie could gather his wits and keep Han

occupied. Not too hard when Han took up the spill-thy-guts mantle again as if we were the confessors of the Inquisition.

"All I ever really wanted was for us to be a team, Reginald. To be partners in every sense of the word."

"But you were. Are," Reggie coaxed and cooed. "You're like a partner to me."

Han sniffed. "Not in the way it mattered."

Were those tears in Han's eyes? Well, I didn't have time to worry about 'em.

My focus was on the gun's movement as I took a shuffled step to the side while Han remained focused on Reggie. Then another tiny slide and step.

"Han," Reggie continued in a soothing voice. "I've told you before. After the AIDS scare, I chose celibacy years ago."

"But that didn't mean we couldn't..."

"Mixing business with pleasure is never a good idea. It would've been unfair to you."

Where had I heard that one before? Oh yeah – the bar.

"But other couples have made it work," Han whined. "Why couldn't we?"

The gun in the assistant's quivering hands drooped a little more with each shuffle of my feet until the counter corner poked into my back. I slowly lowered my hands to the cold, smooth concrete countertop as I edged around the corner to give space to the love triangle confession.

Or maybe this was more a circle. Seems Han had spent his life spinning on the hamster wheel to nowhere.

Kinda like me and bartending. Maybe Zeke and Bobby were right and it was time to reconsider my career options – or lack thereof.

Reggie continued, "But now you can own the business outright."

"I can't. All my money went to that crooked private investigator."

So that's how Reggie's secret had been uncovered. Perhaps the PI was plugged into Switch and Company too.

"I know," Reggie said brightening. "I'll sell it to you on contract. You can make a payment from profits every month."

"What about the money in the PO box?" I piped up, then bit my tongue when Han's eyes narrowed and the gun targeted my way.

"I can't get it," Han admitted. "For some reason, my key doesn't work. The post office must've mixed up the keys somehow."

"Yeah." I snorted, channeling the sperm donor. "Government, right? Can't do anything without screwing it up."

Han nodded. "And I couldn't ask one of the workers to open it for me because they'd see what was in there. It's technically illegal for cash to go through the postal system."

And it was definitely illegal to blackmail someone too. And to hold them at gunpoint. But debating technicalities wouldn't help solve the current situation.

The brand new cell phone in my purse buzzed. The sharp and sudden report of Han's weapon silenced it.

His hands shook even more as we all stared at the smoking hole in the leather, bits of floating paper accompanying a spit, signaling a second death not only for the animal that gave its hide to Coach, but for my checkbook and cell phone as well.

Good thing I'd spent money on the phone warranty this time. It better the hell cover gunshot wounds.

My purse wasn't the only thing smoking. It appeared the bullet had made a through-and-through and come to rest inside a sofa pillow that smoldered.

Oh hell-to-the-no. I just got back into my apartment. It better the hell not burn down now because of some trigger-happy helper.

Han glanced at me sheepishly and broke the silence. "I can fix that."

I'd like to see him try. And before my complex became a five-alarm firepit.

"Hey," Reggie interrupted, pulling attention his way. "The key you sent me for the postal box worked."

"Do you have it with you?"

"It's at home. But we can go over to my house together and get it. That way we can discuss the terms of the sale on our way over and then pick up the cash for your down payment."

His assistant actually seemed to consider it.

That is until another knock reverberated against the door, sending Han into a pirouette rivaling a prima donna and blasting a second bullet through my thick door.

The resultant cry revealed Han's bullet had wounded something more than inanimate objects this time.

It was all the distraction I needed.

In the confusion after the first gun report, I'd successfully slid around the corner to open the applicable cabinet drawer. My Sig gleamed under the pendant lights.

With Han's second shot, I grabbed my weapon, flicked off the safety, and sighted the shooter in one smooth motion.

"Duck!" I yelled to Reggie as Han swung around toward me.

I didn't think about pillows, sofas, or what Mom would say about what we'd done to the new décor. My only concerns were for my friend, my feline, and my own sorry carcass as my finger flexed around metal.

I squeezed the trigger.

CHAPTER TWENTY-NINE

I'd gone and gotten someone shot.

Again.

Jimmy-the-Super lay sprawled and bleeding on the hallway floor, clutching his healing arm from the *previous* gunshot wound and cussing a streak so blue from the *new* gunshot wound it'd make a blue-stater blush.

The profanity-laced tirade continued for a full ten minutes until the police descended on my apartment like it was the last donut shop in Dallas.

At least this time Jimmy was conscious for the aftermath before he was whisked away in an ambulance.

Do you think it'll take more than a plate of barely edible cookies before Jimmy will forgive me again?

Yeah, that's what I thought.

But at least he was still alive and cussing.

Unlike Han.

Taking a life isn't something to laugh about or consider lightly. Matter of fact, I'd aimed for Han's shoulder – and instead got him right between the eyes.

Zeke's warning about firing under extreme duress echoed through my gray matter a little too late for Han.

Guess that meant it was time to start hitting the shooting range again.

Numbness settled in my brain, and unlike the rest of the body, I doubted it would send out little pinprick signals when feeling returned. Guess this was what they called being in a state of shock.

At the moment, I was too busy near the second ambulance to consider what I'd feel come morning. I couldn't even remember walking down from my apartment after they'd carted Jimmy away.

Or what had happened with my gun.

The blue and red strobe effect of the police lights didn't help my scrambled senses. Neither did contemplating the body count inflicted on my being – I mean, building. First Amy. Then Bud. Han made it three.

Can you say *strikeout*?

Like my mom always said, *Lord have mercy, I'm going to need therapy when I wake up from this nightmare.*

I didn't have much time to ponder the implications of what had happened when a familiar face rounded the ambulance's rear bumper.

"Aw shit. Is that you again, Nancy Drew?"

"Aw shit," I quipped in response. "Is that you, Sherlock?"

"Let's get this over with," Duncan said, sitting on the bumper beside me. "Who shot the vic?"

"Actually, I'm the vic here."

"Come again?"

"Han pushed his way into my apartment and started waving his gun around like a maniac," I said with a flutter of my hands. "He shot my purse, my phone, a perfectly good pillow, and somehow managed to puncture that ridiculous door to shoot Jimmy in the same arm as last time."

The detective flipped over a fresh page in his notebook and furiously jotted. "So you admit you shot the vic?"

"In self-defense after he shot Jimmy and the aforementioned accoutrements."

"I'm gonna need to swipe your hands for GSR."

"What's GSR?"

"It's a fancy acronym real investigators use for *gunshot residue*."

"Oh. I knew that."

He pulled out a vial and swiped my trembling hands with a moist Q-tip before dropping it into a bag, sealing and writing on it, then passing the bag off to another tech like a scene out of a crime show.

The reality of the situation leaked into my dulled brain like awakening from a bad dream. Or in this case a real-life nightmare.

"Where's Reggie?

I lurched up and threw off the blanket. A chill washed over me like it was twenty degrees instead of a hundred and twenty.

"Relax," Duncan said, pressing me to sit. "Mr. von Braun is in the building superintendent's apartment."

"Is he okay?"

"He's fine. Gave his statement. I just need to finish getting yours."

A statement. What all would Reggie have said happened leading up to this? If I mentioned the blackmail, that would open up a whole other can of worms and cause any number of headaches. But if our stories didn't match close enough, I could be implicated in a cover-up. Or worse.

'Cause I was the one who'd taken a life.

This mess had started because of those stupid blackmail letters. Letters that had come about because Reggie planned to sell the decorating business and retire.

Hmm. The gears in my brain started spinning again.

Bad sign, I know.

To protect my friend, I didn't mention the blackmail and instead kept my answers to Duncan's questions short and to the point. Focused on what had started this whole fiasco.

Reggie's plans to sell the business to someone else.

Then there was that whole unrequited love angle Han had confessed to. I knew firsthand how those pesky feelings could make one a little crazy.

Or a lot.

"Vicki!"

Speak of the devil.

"Don't say another word without a lawyer," Zeke instructed.

The Ranger wrapped his warm arms around me and shot Duncan a glare sure to burn a hole in his retinas. Couldn't blame him, after Duncan had played Zeke earlier that summer by trying to pin Amy's death on me.

"You sound like my parents," I grumbled into his broad chest.

"Take it easy, Ranger Taylor," Duncan said. "From the looks of things and the matching testimonies, it'll be classified as self-defense." Duncan checked his notes one more time before closing the pad and slipping it into his jacket pocket. "We'll be confiscating the Sig for ballistics."

"Tell me something I don't already know," I said.

"I'm serious, Vic," Zeke said. "No more talking."

"That's okay," Duncan replied. "I'm done here."

"Can I go back inside?" I asked.

Duncan gave me the once over. "If you need to grab something, Ranger Taylor here will escort you. But you'll have to stay somewhere else for the next few nights until we can clear the scene and close the case. And you might want to call in a cleaning crew."

Uh-oh. Bloodstain on the carpet where Han had fallen. I didn't think I could look.

Oh man, what was Mom gonna say after her extensive and very expensive renovations?

"Hey...um...Zeke?" I stammered.

"Yes, you can stay with me as long as you need," he said, leading me between police vehicles toward the front door of the building.

"Appreciate it, but that wasn't what I was gonna ask."

"You want me to go upstairs and get your stuff?"

I nodded. "And don't forget about Slinky. He's probably hiding on my bed under a mountain of pillows."

"Got it," Zeke reassured as he deposited me out of the way in front of Jimmy's apartment.

The medical examiner's team worked their way down the stairs right about then, a black bag with Han's body strapped to the gurney. I shuddered as they wheeled past and out the door.

"Hey Zeke? I need to ask one more favor...and this one's vitally important."

He gave me a look but refrained from making promises. "What?"

I knocked on Jimmy's door to check on Reggie.

"Don't tell my mom."

How had I ended up here again so soon?

Two weeks ago I'd left Zeke's place and returned to my apartment briefly before running off to San Antonio with Nick. Went on my first date with Radioman. Now I was right back where I'd started.

Slinky cuddled in my arms, all snoodled with me in the blanket as I stared out Zeke's floor-to-ceiling windows into the Dallas skyline, blazing against a veiled night.

Lightning flashed in the distance, a bolt snaking down like a giant hand swatting at a spire. Felt like more than Mother Nature had slapped me silly tonight too.

And then some.

I sensed rather than heard Zeke's approach, the deep grovel of sleep garbling his voice. "It's almost four in the morning, Vic."

"Mm-hmm," I acknowledged.

The warmth of his arms loosely encircled as he stood behind me. "Couldn't sleep?"

"Nope."

Numbness hadn't fully worn off, and I was tired beyond belief. But my brain still wouldn't shut down. Not after seeing Han's cold, dead eyes staring back at me.

"Hey, Zeke?"

"Hmm?"

"Have you ever killed anyone?"

His arms tightened ever so slightly and pressed my back deeper into his chest, resting his chin on top of my head.

"Yes. In the line of duty, it's sometimes an unfortunate necessity to save others."

The skyline blurred in the ensuing silence. Rain dotted then ran in rivulets down the glass like the tears I couldn't muster.

Until I realized the blur came from my eyes.

What fresh hell was this? I hadn't turned into some sappy, silly, emotional *girl*.

Had I?

"I didn't mean to kill Han."

"I know."

"The only person I ever in my life dreamed of killing was Lorraine Padget."

Zeke released a ragged sigh but didn't respond, as if he knew immediately where my train of thought took me.

"I never gave you a chance to explain the situation then," I continued, stepping from his arms to face him. "But I'd like to know now. What happened that night at the restaurant?"

"After all that's happened, do you really want to go there tonight?"

"I *need* to know, Zeke, in order to let go of it once and for all. To forgive."

Brown eyes swirled in doubt, calculating the risks. Knowing Zeke, he was also trying to read me to see what kind of angle I was playing. Strange and unusual emotions swirled my thoughts when I realized I didn't have any ulterior motive either.

When he reached a hand to brush the tear from the corner of my eye, his expression softened.

"Lorraine and I were friends in high school."

"If memory serves," I said, "you two were more than friends at one time."

"As were you and Bobby," he returned with a smirk.

The Ranger had me there. "Touché."

I focused on Zeke's silhouette in the ambient and intermittent light from outside as he spilled his side of the story. A story long overdue.

"That night it was really busy, so I waited for you out on the restaurant's deck overlooking the water."

Knowing Zeke's penchant for avoiding large crowds and his preference for the great muggy and buggy outdoors, that part rang true.

"Lorraine was there," he continued. "All huddled in a

corner, crying over some guy who'd left her to pay the check."

"She was crying over getting stuck with the bill?" I asked, incredulous. "The girl's on television. She's not hurting for money."

Zeke pressed his lips together as if deep in an internal debate. "There's more to that particular piece of the story, but it's not my place to share it."

Someone blackmailing Lorraine perhaps? Talk about your ironic twist.

"Fine. Go on."

"She told me what had happened with the check, and about how that affected something else in her life," he said, shooting me a look that said *don't ask*. "Then I hugged her."

"You hugged her."

"Yes, a hug. There was nothing to it but an offer of sympathy and encouragement for the hard times she was dealing with."

The image of that night flashed through my mind in concert with the window-reflected lightning. I focused – really focused – on exactly what I remembered.

"No kissing?" I asked, picturing Lorraine's mascara-streaked face resting against Zeke's shoulder.

"Nope."

"Not even the forehead thing?"

"None," Zeke returned, his eyes hardening as he faced me again. "I'd never have done that to you…to us."

The memory coalesced with Zeke's chin on top of Lorraine's head, just like he'd done with me moments ago. Just like he'd done countless times before tonight.

I sighed, feeling the fool for my rash reaction that night. An *emotional* reaction.

Sometimes it sucked being a girl.

"Why didn't you ever say anything?"

A gruff snort. "There was too much yelling and screaming and too many fists and claws flying. Besides, someone had to fish Lorraine and my hat from the lake."

"So you stayed behind to help her instead of following me," I accused. "Then you never came home."

"Stayed with one of my buddies. Figured you could use a night to cool off." Zeke ran his hand through his hair. "I didn't expect to come home to find you'd moved out."

I looked him square in the eyes, my voice low. "You never called either."

Silence. Regret passed like a shadow across the angular planes of his jaw.

"An error on my part."

An error I had an equal hand in.

With a sigh from the bottom of his toes, he headed off toward the bedroom. "I'm going to try and get a few more winks before work."

"Zeke?" I called.

He stopped but didn't look my way. "What?"

"Thanks," I muttered. "And for what it's worth…I'm sorry."

The import of those words passing my lips shocked me like a zap of lightning.

Huh. Maybe the relationship with my mom wasn't the only one that had matured this week.

"Maybe now you can see me as a friend," Zeke said, before closing the bedroom door.

Zeke and I friends? The thought sent warmth curling through me.

Or maybe that was heat from Slinky all nestled in my arms.

Yeah. Let's go with that.

CHAPTER THIRTY

With Han leaving an empty place in Reggie's business, by late Friday he'd made quick work of signing preliminary contracts with that corporate entity to purchase the Premier Interior Decorating Company of Dallas.

Wouldn't be long before Reggie made even more permanent decisions about his future, namely moving to San Antonio to be nearer a certain person of the female persuasion.

At least I was rooting for them.

Then he could retire the name of Reginald von Braun and become once again simply Reggie Brown. With the pile of money he'd have from the sale of the business, he'd be very comfortable whether he chose to start a family or not.

Speaking of money, since he wanted nothing to do with it, Reggie offered the blackmail cash to me in appreciation for saving his good name.

But I had a better idea.

Instead, I convinced him to make an anonymous donation to Bobby's prison ministry, thereby killing two birds – er, um – *helping* two friends instead of one.

By Sunday morning, I had my emotions in check and

sported *another* new cell phone and a different purse to protect a hot commodity sure to cause a little chaos. Janine offered a knowing look when I dropped the folded cashier's check into the donation box set up at the church.

"I knew there was another reason you agreed to come with me this morning," Janine accused. "You've been pumping people at the bar for money, haven't you?"

"Can't I help out a friend?"

"If memory serves, helping friends is what seems to have gotten you into trouble a lot this summer."

"You've got a point there," I agreed. "But you know I'd never miss the launch of Bobby's ministry."

Janine beamed her blue eyes sparkling. "It is pretty exciting, isn't it? Getting to be on the ground floor of a new enterprise?"

Spoken like a true entrepreneur. I mused again about the wrong De'Laruse being groomed for the takeover of the family corporate empire.

But that was a battle for another time.

My best friend skittered back and forth in front of the counter, while I tried to remain scarce behind it and keep a running tab on the total donations thus far to avoid falling asleep. Most of the saintly persuasion hustled by the donation station with hardly a glance.

Those few who gathered to hear Janine's pitch for Bobby's work dropped in a dollar bill here and a fiver there. Some were gracious enough to write a check and take the applicable tax deduction.

Bobby popped out of the sanctuary between each service and fielded questions from a gaggle of women both young and old.

Before the start of the third service, Lorraine Padget sliced through the crowd like a hot knife through butter and practically draped herself on him before making a grand show of placing a check in the donation box.

Me? I got a snarl directed my way like a pit bull staking its claim.

The poor guy. A widower only a few months and already the chase to claim his carcass was on. I thought to ask Lorraine about the status of her engagement, but given our present location, I figured it best to keep those comments to myself.

Maybe there was hope for my disease-ridden mouth yet.

After Bobby left to share the stage with his dad one more time, Janine and I finished tabulating the final trickle of donations for the grand announcement at the end of the service.

When she saw the amount of the anonymous cashier's check representing Reggie's blackmail payout, she gasped.

"Oh, we have to announce this one separately from the rest," Janine squealed. "Such generosity must be highlighted to encourage others."

I don't know how much it'd spur other people to give if they weren't already so inclined. Seemed more like guilting them into opening their pocketbooks.

But since it all went to help Bobby, who was I to question my bestie?

Shortly before the end of the service, a runner came by to collect the final tally and deliver it to Pastor Dennis for the big announcement.

Janine and I entered the darkened auditorium and stood along the back wall until our eyes adjusted. Then we made our way down the center aisle toward the front to the honorary seating designated for our families.

Usually the De'Laruse and Bohanan clans attended either the early or second service – minus myself since I'd ditched the double life years ago. However, with the big announcement slated for the third one, they'd chosen to be a part of the final service.

Pastor Dennis went on and on about his son. The catalyst behind Bobby's calling to this ministry. About his return to Dallas and the loss of his wife.

He carefully skirted Bobby's short stint in prison – and the fact they'd left him in there to rot – and merely referred to his being a suspect.

The whole time Bobby towered over his father, I couldn't help but notice the rising flush in Bobby's cheeks and the careful swipe at his eye as if to brush away a tear.

Meanwhile, the elder Vernet openly cried, mingling sweat with his tears as he played the sympathy card for the audience. I couldn't help but notice the dichotomy of the reactions between father and son.

Maybe Bobby was adopted.

The pastor made a big show as several older kids from the children's department pranced onstage holding an overlarge check image of five thousand dollars from the church.

I stewed. Reggie, who didn't even attend, had displayed a greater generosity than Bobby's own family.

When the runner from earlier appeared onstage and handed over the final donations tally Janine and I had collected, Pastor Dennis practically shouted the announcement of Reggie's anonymous donation.

The whole congregation stood in thunderous applause. All I wanted to do was run up on stage and highlight the hypocrisy.

But the sperm donor beat me to it.

My dad sidestepped into the center aisle, walked up onto the stage and presented his own check to Bobby – for a quarter million dollars.

Some people just had to hog the limelight.

Janine glanced my way while the crowd went wild, and Thomas De'Laruse dropped into his seat to furiously scribble out a check, most likely an amount to one-up my dad.

I dissolved into a fit of laughter. No matter who got credit for what, there was always someone else who had to overcompensate in one vein for what they lacked in another. In the end, Bobby won either way.

Talk about your dick measuring, folks.

And in church no less.

Since I wasn't real keen on hanging around a death scene, Slinky and I didn't get firmly settled again at my apartment until late Sunday afternoon shortly before leaving for the preseason opener at Cowboys Stadium.

Okay, okay. So the powers that be had sold the naming rights of the new stadium years ago. But to tried-and-true, die-hard Dallas Cowboys fans, it'd always be Cowboys Stadium to us.

Bite me.

The storm front had brought in more comfortable temperatures – for most people. With the dome retracted it meant no air-conditioning, which allowed the sun to call dibs on my sweltering carcass and promised an uneven tan of epic proportions.

Guess it was better than a blistering sunburn.

My evil plans to force Grady and Rochelle together somewhat misfired when Grady sat on the far side of Radioman, leaving Rochelle to sit on my right. 'Course I curled up right next to Radioman so he could experience all my glistening glory.

We were on a date, after all.

Aw, hell. I'd already sweat through my t-shirt and practically slid out of my daisy dukes soon after we'd sat. Despite the cool-down, it was still Texas.

Our seats, however, were nothing to complain about. Freaking awesome, as a matter of fact. We sat just off centerfield and halfway up the stadium to take in the full-spectrum view of play.

I glanced around at the near-capacity seating and eyed the luxury suites dotting various levels. The sperm donor, the De'Laruses, and assorted business associates were likely in one of the prime locales, drinking champagne and eating fresh lobster flown in from the coast that morning.

I personally loved sitting out among the masses, enveloped in the excitement. Swarmed by the raucous screams at kick-off. Enjoying the pungent scent of *eau de spilled beer* and vendors tossing dogs into the crowd with a tight spiral like a quarterback in a last-ditch Hail Mary.

The energy generated by the fans would light up the city for at least a week. I couldn't help the smile that stretched across my face until my cheeks ached as I sat amid the chaos.

And this was just a preseason showcase.

"Looking for someone in particular?" Radioman asked above the din.

"It's just I've never experienced this before," I yelled.

"I thought you said you were a huge fan."

Oops. My diseased mouth runneth off without my gray matter. If I was gonna keep my family connections a secret from this guy for long, I'd better come up with a satisfactory explanation right quick.

"You know, here near the fifty-yard line. These are great seats."

Yeah, that oughta do it.

"It's one of my guilty splurges," he admitted. "Season tickets to the Cowboys don't come up for sale often."

"How did you get two more on such short notice then?"

"Seth. We snatched these suckers up the moment they went on sale for the new stadium."

The mention of Seth caught Grady's attention through the crowd uproar over a bad call on the field.

Hey, it didn't matter if this game statistically counted or not. Cowboys fans were all about sportsmanship and fair play.

Well, and a great big 'W' in the win column, regardless of whether it came through second and third string players.

I had no clue what Grady planned to do about the information Seth had shared at the bar the other night. For all I knew, the boss had already made contact or was planning to arrest the attorney.

With the connection to Radioman, I suspected that was why he'd also readily accepted my invitation to the game

I was pretty sure Seth would play on the right side. By extension, Radioman remained in the clear – at least in my book.

Now Banker Boy? I'd leave that man in Grady's suspicious hands.

That left Radioman's hands all to me.

And this time, I planned to use all my feminine wiles to ensure they got a proper workout.

That evening, I got laughs all around as I reiterated events of donation Sunday before dropping Grady and Rochelle off at their cars parked at the bar.

However, I left out a few things in the retelling, namely

that Reggie's donation had come about because of blackmail. There was also the fact that I'd stayed a couple of nights with Zeke again.

But I didn't think it wise to share about a sleepover with my ex-boyfriend – as platonic as it'd been – with my new boy – er, friend. New friend.

Someone I hoped to see naked tonight. Maybe then I'd do a little measuring of my own.

Think about it.

Radioman escorted me to my apartment and glanced around when I popped the new door open. "Wow, you can't even tell where it happened."

I still couldn't remember exactly where Han's body had ended up and hoped that memory stayed buried forever. But I got a pretty good idea when Slinky sniffed around the general area where Reggie's guys had replaced the carpet.

After ballistics verified our stories and the police officially cleared me of any wrongdoing, Reggie sent his team in on Saturday to work round the clock to make it look like it had BHD – Before Han's Death. They even put new carpet down the length of the hall since Jimmy had bled all over the old.

The holy pillow – and no, I don't mean saintly – had simply disappeared into the ether.

Since pillows reminded me of Han, I'd stormed the apartment the moment I'd returned and bagged up every pillow in sight before stuffing them in the far reaches of my closet. Eventually I'd pull some out again, but for the foreseeable future the only pillows on display in my home would be the two I slept on in my bedroom.

And weren't those the only ones you really needed anyway?

"I still can't believe it," I said. "I mean, someone

actually died in here."

A shiver passed up my spine. Would Han's ghost return to haunt me? 'Course I don't believe in spooks and specters, but that didn't keep me from getting a little freaked out, thinking of someone dying in my apartment. On my living room floor.

Near where I stood.

The truth? I was a lot more than a little freaked out – hence the *real* reason I worked so hard to garner some nighttime company.

I didn't expect to sleep a wink anyway, listening to every bump and creak. I half expected to hear chains and moans instead of cat snores and was once again grateful for my kitty's presence. They say animals can sense the paranormal.

I said I don't believe in ghosts, didn't I?

Zeke had offered to let me stay another night, but I was determined not to let my fears get the better of me. I had to get over it sooner or later, so I chose sooner.

Yeah right, silly me.

Radioman must've sensed my shudder and curled his arms around in a firm embrace before planting a kiss on top of my head. I leaned into his warmth and savored the strength in his arms.

It was then I had a realization. I'd gotten my date to cross the threshold from the hall and into my personal abode. First success of the night.

I snuggled into Radioman's embrace where it was safe, and thoughts of ghosts and gunshots soon fled. I turned my face up to meet his lips. Heat plumed in my belly and lit a fire that reached all the way down to my toes.

Radioman spoke around kisses. "Aren't you afraid…of being here…all by yourself?"

"A little," I admitted breathlessly.

I pressed my advantage by sneaking hands beneath his untucked shirttail. Bare skin heated beneath my touch as I stroked up and down his spine.

His voice hitched. "How many dates...is this?"

"Two," I replied against hungry lips. "Officially."

"Unofficially?"

"We could always count..." My knees turned to chocolate pudding as he trailed kisses to my ear and sucked the lobe between his teeth. "...the times you asked."

"Mm-hmm."

"And when you've come to the bar."

"Hell yeah," Radioman murmured. "Up for some company then?"

Up? Oh now he was just playing naughty.

I let fevered kisses speak for me until his mouth trailed down my neck. He lifted me in his arms, and I wrapped my legs around his waist. Then with a free foot I shoved the door closed behind him with a satisfying thud before we stumbled to the bedroom.

Saddle up, boys. This cowgirl's goin' for a ride.

Yee-haw!

ABOUT THE AUTHOR

Sometimes life emulates fiction.

Life is filled with tragedy and Ms. Bale's writing reflects this reality. However, there is always a silver lining...even if one must spend their entire life searching for it.

In her previous career, Ms. Bale traveled the United States as a Government Relations Liaison, working closely with Congressional offices and various government agencies. This experience afforded her a glimpse into the sometimes "not so pretty" reality of the political sphere. Much of this reality and various locations throughout her travels make it into her writing.

She dreams of the day she can return to visit Alaska.

Connect with D. A. Bale online
Facebook: www.facebook/pages/D-A-Bale
Twitter: @DABale1
Blog: http://dabalepublishing.blogspot.com
Email: dabalepublishing@cox.net

Made in the USA
Monee, IL
02 July 2023